"The Real McCoy"
M/M Cowboy Western Gay Romance

Jerry Cole

@ 2018
Jerry Cole

This book is intended for Adults (ages 18+) only. The contents may be offensive to some readers. It may contain graphic language, explicit sexual content, and adult situations. May contain scenes of unprotected sex. Please do not read this book if you are offended by content as mentioned above or if you are under the age of 18.

Please educate yourself on safe sex practices before making potentially life-changing decisions about sex in real life. If you're not sure where to start, see here: http://www.jerrycoleauthor.com/safe-sex-resources/.

Edition v1.00 (2018.08.17)
http://www.jerrycoleauthor.com

Special thanks to the following volunteer readers who helped with proofreading: Penny T., Julian White, AliD, Ursula at Owl Pro Editing, Bailey H.S. and those who assisted but wished to be anonymous. Thank you so much for your support.

Chapter One

By the time he caught up with Connor, the state trooper was so mad he could barely put words together.

"I said, pull over!" he screamed, swerving dangerously close to Connor.

"Yes, sir, just a second," Connor said, balancing his weight on his saddle horn while he leaned down to the level of the squad car's window. "Finish line's just past the bar!"

The state trooper's next burst of profanity fell upon him with such force, he swerved back over the center line and hit the brakes.

As the patrol car fell behind him to his left, Connor gave Bonito a hearty squeeze of encouragement. There was hardly any need. His brother was three lengths behind him, and that distance had grown to five lengths by the time Bonito rattled across the finish line.

In the time it had taken Connor and Greg to circumnavigate the town of Knife Rock, a good-sized crowd had gathered on the porch of the Back Cinch Bar and Grill. The dozen or so of them let out a rowdy cheer as the line of table salt scattered across the street and Sheriff Nelson yelled out Connor's time.

The state trooper's siren had a less celebratory tone to it.

It took a couple seconds to get Bonito decelerated and turned around, and the state trooper was out of his car giving Greg an earful by the time Connor returned to the finish line.

"Well, officer," Connor said. "We pulled over."

The state trooper turned to Connor to continue the tongue lashing without skipping a beat.

"...strongly suspect the both of you are under the influence! And I will have you know that will increase the points on both your licenses!"

"Now, now, now!" Sheriff Nelson was a couple inches taller than the state trooper and about twice as wide. He had taken his sweet time getting over to the scene of the altercation, which had allowed the state trooper to scream himself completely out of breath.

"Excuse me?" The state trooper had spent so much energy screaming at Greg and Connor, his voice squeaked on the edges like he had a rock in his brakes.

"Officer, I think my department has this situation well under control." Sheriff Nelson flashed his badge out of his pocket, which was kind of unnecessary considering that he was presently in uniform. "This here was an officially sanctioned test of mounted patrol horses, and I will not tolerate big government interference in county business!"

At "officially sanctioned," Connor started examining the wrap on his saddle horn very closely. He was amazed that he managed to keep a straight face through "big government interference."

"I was not notified that you had secured a permit to conduct this test on a state highway," the state trooper said.

"Well, tell you what," Sheriff Nelson said. "If you wanna drop on by to our department's offices on Salt Lick Lane, I'm sure the gals there will be more than happy to help you out."

Connor took this opportunity to dismount his horse and head on back to the hitching post out front of the Back Cinch. It was none of his business if Sheriff Nelson wanted to send a state trooper out to get stuck in that godawful pit of mud. None of his business at all.

"You still glad you went and gelded that one?" Mike was perched in his customary spot, balanced on two legs of a tall wooden chair with a half-pint jar nearly emptied of whiskey clutched in one hand.

"Every time I have to stop him in a hurry," Connor replied.

"Hell, I bet you could still sell that trooper a breeding to him," Antonio said, a little quieter. "Look at them go."

The poor trooper had no idea how long it had been since Sheriff Nelson had gotten the opportunity to entertain himself like this. He was trying not to stumble backwards into the barrow ditch as the bigger man's chiding got wilder and louder.

"Have a julep, sweetie." Mama Jade came out of the bar with a mason jar of something that resembled a green salad on ice.

"Don't drink it," Antonio said. "I don't know what that is growing out back, but it ain't no mint I ever seen or smelled."

Connor frowned and poked gently at the ice.

"It is, too!" Mama Jade said. "Says right there in the field guide, you can look at it yourself. It's horse mint."

"Cause it ain't fit to eat for anything but the horses," Dalton said as he came out to the porch with three beers clutched in his meaty fingers. "Throw that shit on the ground, Dougherty."

Now, Connor was insanely curious. He raised the glass to his lips and took a cautious sip.

"Now you've done it, woman," Mike said. "If you poison that one, it's a hate crime."

There was no chance of being poisoned. The combination of plastic bottle whiskey, store brand sugar, and a random weed was so noxious on Connor's tongue, he nearly dropped the whole thing in disgust. "Jesus Christ!"

"No, Jesus had nothing to do with that there elixir," Dalton said. "That shit comes from...somewhere else."

"Here, let me try," Greg said as he approached with his little chestnut mare in tow.

"It's your funeral." Connor handed the glass over. He winced in disgust as his brother put the glass to his lips and slurped the contents down like it was fine wine at last call.

"Oh, what is that?" Greg said. "Some kinda bitters cocktail?"

"Told you it was good!" Mama Jade said.

"See this right here is why Linda's family won't let you marry her," Connor said. "You're a fuckin' animal."

Dalton handed Connor a beer and shook his head, horror writ plainly on his honest features. "He really will drink anything," he said.

"Which is why the cold beer in the cooler is getting reserved for people with taste." Connor clinked bottle necks with Dalton and took a second to appreciate having some potable alcohol.

Then a cellphone rang.

"Hello?" Mike's front stool feet clunked to the floor. "Speaking. Yep. Yep." The merriment had faded from his place. "On the east side of the hill or the west?"

Dalton offered him a bottle, which he waved away as he shook his head.

"Can you hold him there for a little bit, do you think?" Mike was eyeing Bonito and Lassie in an appraising kind of way that made Connor kind of nervous. "Okay. Well, thanks for letting us know. We'll be out there fast as we can. Thanks. Bye."

He ended the call and rubbed his face with his free hand. "Go get your sisters and hook up the half-top," he said. "Bull pasture hotwire must have another short in it."

"Oh, dammit," Dalton said.

"Dougherty..."

"They're out by the old fort, aren't they?" Connor was already tightening his cinch.

"Afraid so," Mike sighed, watching Dalton sprint for his truck. "Swear to God, can't turn my back for ten seconds on these kids." He got up slowly and put his phone back in its tooled holster. "Your mother doesn't know how lucky she is, Dougherty."

***

Truth be told, Connor's mother seemed to know less and less as the years wore on.

"No, Ma," Greg told her for the third time. "We had to help corral the Stoltz bulls, remember?"

8

"I never heard anything about that." Their mother's voice was sharp and deeply annoyed. "Sounds like another silly story from your brother to me."

"Ma..."

"I'm so sick of looking at those trees!" She was never a large woman, and these days, it took more effort and more people to keep her from dwindling to nothing. "Every day, I tell you boys about it, and neither of you care enough to do anything about it. I'm so sick of looking at them!" She was starting to cry now.

"Okay, Ma, the trees will be gone." Connor moved her heavy water glass out of her reach. "We'll get right out there today with the backhoe and pull them out."

"I'll believe that when I see it," his mother said. "I'm tired of your lying, too, boy. Makes me sick just looking at you!"

Connor met his brother's eyes and gave him a look. Greg halted his backwards retreat from the living room where their mother was holding court.

"Imagine your father...well. It's just as good he passed on when he did." She looked Connor up and down behind her glasses and shook her head. "I already have to live knowing you're going to burn in hell. I couldn't bear knowing he'd be burning too for what he'd have to..."

"Okay, Mom," Greg said. "I think it's time for your midday meds."

"Don't you go defending him!" Their mother reached for the glass, and its absence sent her into a moment of silent rage before the tears hit again.

9

"Jesus," Greg said under his breath.

"You all think I'm crazy, don't you?" she said, pounding on her lap with her thin fists. "You're all laughing at me! You're all against me, and you're all against God!"

"Mom..."

"Go ahead, boy," their mother said. "Give me my pills, give me all of them! Just give me the whole bottle so I can kill myself like you want me to do!"

"Oh, screw this," Connor said. "I'm calling Nancy."

"Nancy is a whore!" their mother said. "She's a whore and she's an illegal and I don't want her in my house!" Nancy had grown up two miles down the road from them, but that was beside the point. "She steals, and my sons don't care because they just want me dead!"

The wailing followed Connor out to the mud room. He had to plug his other ear so he could hear Nancy's line ringing.

"Santerelli Home Health, this is Nancy speaking."

"Hey, Nance, it's Connor Dougherty." As if he needed to clarify who it was with his mother's hateful screeching in the background. "Mom's having, uh, a moment."

"Oh, hi," Nancy said, her professional cheerfulness gone. "Did she shit herself again?"

"Where are you at?" Connor said. "If you drive fast enough you might be able to get here before it gets that far."

***

10

The stench of a weaponized laxative scrip, particularly in his mother's hands, could haunt a man for days. Connor shuddered and tried to put the thought from his mind as he hopped out of his truck.

Behind him, the graduate students hesitantly descended from their own vehicle. Their heavy work boots and long-sleeved shirts made kind of a funny combination with their smooth hands and tanless faces. Connor was kind of intrigued by the heavy-muscled one with the waxed moustache and expensive haircut. He tended to cling to the back, though, and let the ginger girl do most of the talking.

"Oh my God, this actually looks amazing!" The team leader held her hands in front of her as she approached the line of trees that was going absolutely fucking nowhere as long as Connor had any say in the matter. "I saw photos from last fall, but...wow!"

"Well, I actually got on the county a little bit about the drainage issues from the road," Connor said. "And eventually I harassed them until they got a surveyor out here, and what do you know, it was long due for re-grading."

"Did you let Dr. Garcia know about that?" the redhead was examining his windbreak on one knee, her eyes squinted.

"I dropped her an e-mail," Connor said. "The county has all the survey information. I can't make heads nor tails of it."

"Did you get the surveyor's info?" the redhead said.

"Yeah, I got it in my binder," Connor said. "And I kept notes like you asked me to." He smiled. "Actually, we got one of our hired hand's kids assigned

11

to keeping tabs on all you guys' environmental projects out here. She loves it."

"Aww, really?" The redhead grinned at him. "How old is she?"

"She's just turned twelve," Connor said. "We'll see if she outgrows the science ranger thing. For now she feels like she's saving the world."

"Well, she's at least helping us preserve this part of it." The redhead snapped a few photos of the road with her phone. "Ken, sweetie, did you get the auger?"

"I've got it right here." Even in his boxy research team duds, the big guy's physique radiated from him in the way he moved. He had a soft, genteel voice that made Connor chide himself for jumping to conclusions about people. But still. It had been a long week, and Connor couldn't help but indulge himself in a little wishful thinking where handsome young grad students were concerned.

The big damn drill he was assembling from the equipment box seemed to fit right in with his unrealistic little narrative.

***

"They gave you what?" Caleb choked on his potato salad, his eyes boggling wide.

"They ain't given me nothing yet," Connor said. "But, hell, if I've ever filled out that much paperwork that fast in my life."

"Ten thousand...." Caleb let out a long, low whistle. "Maybe I will go bug Dad with the granola shit."

"I already sent him all the information," Connor said. "I really can't tell you what kind of grant you guys qualify for until you let their team work on your land."

"Yeah, he won't be happy about that," Caleb said. "Last time we tried to work with the bunny lovers..."

"That was the Bureau," Connor said. "Bureau's just like that. These guys are different. They do their own work."

"But is it *good* work?" Caleb said.

"They managed not to fuck up planting trees and digging ditches," Connor said. "And they pay for their own engineers."

"I'll believe that when I see it," Caleb said.

"Just give it some thought," Connor said. "See, way I think of it, at the very least we have some real solid evidence we're trying to work with these people up here. Saving the planet, one windbreak at a time."

"You ain't been eating their brownies, have you?" Caleb said. "'Cause I swear I just..."

"Good afternoon, gentlemen!" Father Andrew beamed at them as he glided across the crackling lawn of Saint Mary's. "Enjoying Roberta's gardening talents, I see."

"Mostly her pickling talents," Connor said. "She could stick a prickly pear in a jar, spines and all, it'd disappear and nobody would complain."

"Hmm," Father Andrew said. "I think I've been a priest too long to believe that *nobody* would complain." He chuckled at his own joke before his face

13

grew serious. "I noticed a shortage of Doughertys in your pew today, young Connor."

Connor bowed his head and put his lips together. "Ma's been very unwell this week," he said.

"I'm truly sorry, my son," Father Andrew said.

Connor watched as Caleb booked it across the lawn for more potato salad. Yeah, he wouldn't want to deal with this either.

"It's a tough situation," Connor said.

"Losing a parent is difficult enough," Father Andrew said. "But to have to deal with that grief, and then also…" He looked above Connor's head as if the Lord needed to be a little faster with the divine teleprompter. "Well. I don't need to tell you how difficult forgiveness can be for human beings."

A bitter feeling scratched at the back of Connor's throat. He nodded.

"I'll pay her a visit tonight so she can receive the Eucharist," Father Andrew said. "The Lord forgives when we ask for his forgiveness. You, however." He chuckled a little. "You can take however long you need."

Chapter Two

"Come on, man, just relax…"

"You try fuckin' relaxing!" Ty Gibson's jaw was going to chop this length of rope right in two if Jake didn't figure it out.

"One, two,…"

The world went white with pain. Ty thought he heard a snap like a branch breaking, but that might have just been his imagination. He felt like it ought to make a noise when your shoulder gets forcefully popped back into its socket.

"Hey, hey!" Someone was shaking him. "You gotta stay with me, bud."

"Shit." Ty sucked in a warm, dusty breath of air. He was able to expand his lungs all the way this time, thank God. Or whatever was negligently watching over the Los Pinos County Fairgrounds this evening. Ty was in no position to be picky.

"You good?" Jake Simpson was standing over him with his hands on his knees. "They're running behind on the steer wrestling."

At the sound of his next event, Ty's strength returned to his body. He bolted up to his feet and almost fell right back down again. How hard had that bronc bashed his head against the arena fence?

"Jesus Christ!" Jake caught him before he could fall. "I'm not letting you enter the saddle broncs anymore if you gon' be like this, boy."

"Don't know how the hell we're supposed to get saddle bronc prize money if we don't enter," Ty said.

"Don't know how to get it if you don't win, either!" Jake crossed his arms. "Come on, bud, you suck! Breakin' a colt and ridin' a bronc is two different kinds of buckout and you know it damn good and well."

"Ain't nobody paying me to break colts," Ty said.

"Ain't nobody paying you if you miss your steer wrestling, either," Jake said. "Come on. Blue's tacked up already."

Rodeo was full of painful ironies. Currently on Ty's mind: falling off didn't hurt nearly as bad as getting back on again two hours later. There was pain shooting through parts of his body he didn't recollect damaging in his departure from that bronc, Mob Boss Mabel.

"You sure you're good for this?" Monty, Jake's not-boyfriend, asked. Monty was a nervous little Texan whose main talent was stealing from convenience stores. He'd been looking faintly ill ever since they'd brought Jake back to the trailer with his arm at a biologically inconvenient angle.

Ty opened his mouth to reply, but Jake cut in before he found any suitable words.

"He might be good and he might not be," Jake said. "Only one way to find out."

***

Ty had avoided puking while he was warming Blue up, but the temptation was stronger every time it arose. How hard had that bronc bashed his head?

The announcer spoke with a thick Cajun drawl that was hard for Ty to parse on a good day. Right now, he was only catching the little peaks and valleys of his cadence as he pushed his horse through the throng to get into the starting gate. *Just watch his*

16

shoulder, he told himself. *Just watch his shoulder and let the rest come without thinking.*

"You got this, bud!" Jake's not-boyfriend kept patting him hard on the knee like he was trying to slap him awake.

"Yeah." Ty couldn't make his eyes focus clearly on Jake's not-boyfriend's face. He didn't need to. He just needed to keep his eye on the little bastard's shoulder.

His horse knew, by this point in its brief and moderately successful career, what a starting gate was and what it meant when you put him inside one. He began jigging and dancing behind the bit, wiggling his ass to and fro in no particular rhythm, while Jake got in the starting box on the opposite side of the chute.

Ty felt his body phase in and out as he swayed side to side in the saddle.

"We got this, Ty," Jake was saying. The announcer's voice was rumbling close overhead now. Ty fought the urge to puke.

"Just keep your eye on his goddamn shoulder!"

What happened next was a matter of some debate among the onlookers. Some people swore that Ty's horse spooked at something and took off sideways out of the starting gate. Some people thought the run started normally, and still others figured it was Ty collapsing on his horse that triggered the spook.

Whichever way you described it, the next thing Ty was aware of was how dangerously close his head was to his horse's hooves. He felt like he took his time to process this before figuring out how to free himself from his saddle.

***

Ty Gibson woke up the next morning in the bed of his truck, a couple of saddle blankets under his back and a pillow beneath his head. He was back behind the gas station that had been letting them sleep there the past few nights so they didn't have to pay fees at the rodeo grounds. His head hurt.

It had long been his first instinct, upon waking, to check his pockets for the bare necessities of life he carried with him. Phone in his right front. Wallet in his left back. Knife in his left front. Ty sighed and relaxed on his makeshift bed for a second.

He kept his eyes shut against the desert sun as memories of last night came drifting in through the holes of his Swiss-cheese brain one at a time. The bronc, the wreck, the starting gate, the other wreck.

After a couple minutes, he squinted against the bright blue sky and got out of his truck. First thing to do was check on his horse.

Blue was still saddled, though someone had exchanged his bridle for his halter and tied him up with food and water. He was munching contentedly when Ty opened the trailer door, and he looked back at him with his usual good-natured indifference. Where was Blackie?

Ty's eyes came open a little bigger. If Blue was alone in the trailer...

He dashed around the rig and threw the tack room door open. The inside was devoid of both his rodeo buddies and his rodeo buddies' tack.

"What the fuck?" he said to the dark compartment. He hurried around to check the truck. The keys were in the ignition. Jake and Jake's Not-Boyfriend were nowhere to be seen.

As Ty hurried into the convenience store, it occurred to him what had probably transpired last night. He wasn't exactly a profitable rodeo buddy to have, was he? When your horse stopped making you money on the rodeo circuit, you sold it and got yourself something that could run.

What about when that happened to the guy you were travelling with?

The gas station was empty of his so-called friends, including the bathroom when Ty went to take a leak. Ty wandered around the vacant aisles for a few minutes, trying to wrap his head around what was going on. He was alone at a gas station with his horse and his trailer, two hundred and fifty miles from the next rodeo.

Shit. This was not good. And he hadn't won a dime last night.

Ty picked up a fruity pastry in a cellophane bag and poured himself a big styrofoam cup of caustic black coffee. He set them down on the register and kept his eyes on the ground as he fished his worn black wallet from his back pocket.

"Good morning," the girl behind the counter said.

"Morning." Ty smiled up briefly at her.

His heart froze in his chest when he opened it up to see not a single dollar bill in there. Instead, there was a note on a piece of paper torn from a fast food bag.

Emergency Room bill was $350. We covered the rest. See you around.

"Um." Ty looked down at the coffee he'd just poured. "Uhh..."

"Are you okay, hon?" Ty wasn't sure what look she had on her face. He was having difficulties focusing on the girl behind the counter.

"I'm gonna go look for change in my truck," Ty said. He hurried out the door, once again fighting the urge to puke.

***

The documentation in his truck told him that he had a concussion, and that he needed to take a few days to rest. The complete and utter lack of cash in his wallet told him he needed to get his happy ass back to the rodeo grounds as soon as humanly possible.

But as he started his truck and watched the needle on the gas gauge rise precariously toward the quarter-tank mark, a wave of tiredness overtook him that was more powerful than anything he'd ever felt. He just felt...dead, somehow, like all of his limbs had just up and quit on him.

A lump formed in his throat like he was fixing to cry, but somehow he just couldn't summon up the energy or the shamelessness to do that. Ty Gibson slumped in the driver's seat of his truck, wishing the bronc had just up and killed him instead of leaving him like this.

He wasn't sure how long he'd reclined in that posture before a gentle tapping came at his truck window. The girl from behind the counter was outside, holding his cup of coffee and not one but five little pastries in cellophane baggies.

At the sight of the pastries, Ty's body animated itself again. He rolled the window down.

Before he could say anything, the girl from the store thrust the coffee and pastries at him. "Here," she said. "I went and bought these for you. Looked like you were having a rough morning."

"Yeah," Ty said. He took the coffee and pastries with a vague attempt at a smile.

"Were you down at the rodeo?" She was a hefty, plain girl of about eighteen or nineteen with dirty blonde hair slicked back in a long ponytail.

"Yeah," Ty said.

"What event?" She leaned up against the bottom of the window, blue eyes squinting curiously and narrow mouth turned downward.

"Steer wrestling," Ty said. "Bronc riding."

"Oh." The girl gave him a nervous smile. It occurred to Ty that she was flirting with him.

Women did that. As thin as his hair was getting at the tender age of thirty-two, his body had never looked better beneath his worn jeans and his near-tattered undershirt. He hadn't had a chance to shave in a couple of days, but the dark stubble that grew on his cheeks tended to make him look haunted rather than homeless.

Even though, technically speaking, Ty was currently very much homeless.

"Do you win much?" the girl said.

"Not really." Ty wasn't sure how he had come to unwrap the soft, lard-sweet pastry the girl had

21

brought him, but there it was in his hands. "Thanks for breakfast, by the way."

"Are those guys coming back for you, do you think?" The girl from the gas station was looking past Ty now, at the inside of his truck which bore all the tell-tale signs of being somebody's full-time residence. Backpacks, coolers, toolboxes, a tiny soda can graveyard at the base of the passenger's seat. A milk crate full of old sci-fi books he'd picked up for a dollar at a thrift store in Abilene.

Ty shook his head. It wasn't worth spewing pastry all over the situation to say something they both knew. He wasn't gonna see Jake Tomlinson or his Not-Boyfriend ever again.

"I'm sorry, hun," the girl said. "If you want, I can give you my cousin's number. She lives on a ranch out east and I know they're looking for good hands right now."

"Yeah?" Ty sat up a little.

"Yeah," the girl said. "It's hard work, and my uncle's kind of eccentric, but you know." She smiled. "It probably beats sleeping here."

***

At the very least, Ty had gotten himself to a new gas station in a new part of the state where he could implore new people to lend him a little gas money. This one was actually a truck stop, which could potentially mean all kinds of fun and semi-profitable near-death experiences.

He found some quarters in the bottom of his center console and took a shower while his horse drank some water in the trailer. The hot water burned when it hit the road rash he'd given himself last night.

There was something refreshing about the sting, something that made Ty feel really awake for the first time since the rodeo at Los Pinos.

Freshly shaven and availed of the best plaid cotton shirt he had, Ty actually thought he looked a little respectable. He met the interviewer for the Triple V Ranch in the truck stop's cafe.

Though Ty came early, the short, wide man was already sitting there on one side of a red-upholstered booth. He had neat white hair combed over a broad and thick-jawed head, and he wore a thick white moustache that gave him the air of either the sheriff or the bartender in an old western.

Which one of those he was, Ty supposed, remained to be seen.

"So you're Mr. Tyler Gibson," the interviewer said. "I heard one of my cayuse mares just about killed you last night in the bronc riding."

"I..." Ty was halfway down into his chair when those words came out of the short guy's mouth. "I remember I made four seconds or so on Mob Boss Mabel..."

"Yes, son, that's right," the interviewer said. "Miss Mabel who you met at the fairgrounds is one of my best. You're not the first young man she's mauled, no, son, you are not."

Ty was still frozen halfway into his chair. It did not occur to him that he was supposed to say anything to the man currently in front of him.

"Sit down, son, sit down." The interviewer beckoned fiercely with one thick-fingered hand. "I went ahead and ordered chicken fried steak for the both of us. We're going to be here a while." He pulled a binder from somewhere under the table and set it down on the bench. "I have your federal paperwork, see, that we have to fill out, and then we need to go over the directions for your duties."

Ty sat down carefully, not sure if he was reading this correctly. "Uh, I'm here for the job interview, is that correct?"

"Linda said she already interviewed you." The white-haired man spoke as if daring Ty to contradict him.

Now, at this point, every red flag and alarm bell that Ty possessed in his head was telling him to get on up out of this booth and run like hell. He was young, handsome, and gay at a truck stop—there were options, greasy as they were, that were less sketchy than this one.

"Sir, I don't believe we've properly introduced ourselves?" Ty's voice squeaked a little.

"Why, I'm Mr. Stanley Briggs, of course," the man said, as if this should have been painfully obvious to Ty. "I'm your new boss."

As if on cue, a tired-looking waitress came over bearing two gigantic plates of chicken-fried steak, cole slaw, and home fries.

Once again, Ty's stomach acted of its own accord. This time, his mouth was its victim. "Oh, of course you are," he said. "I'm sorry. It's been a long day."

Even in his wearied state, Ty recognized the look on Mr. Briggs's face as the slack-eyed grin of a predator. "I reckon it has, son," he said. "I reckon it has."

Chapter Three

"So what happens then is that the meteor starts scraping against the little particles that make up the atmosphere, right?" Connor grunted as he thrust the posthole digger into the sandy soil. "Like when a chain or a ramp scrapes behind a truck on the road."

"Uh-huh." Antonio's son wasn't quite old enough to share his sister's love of science, but he was obsessed with space and always wanted to hear the meteor story. He was sitting on the tailgate of Antonio's truck, reading a picture book while his father helped Connor build a new fence across the north forty.

"So, they're pretty big, but they're pretty far off, you know? Like the burn off on the wells out on the Bureau land." He didn't mind digging the few holes that had to be dug by hand owing to awkward placement. As long as little Joey kept on dumping the milk jugs full of water down into the sandy soil, the posthole digger kept bringing up big, firm lumps of dirt without too much effort on Connor's part.

"What's that?" Joey said, pointing over Connor's head. "It's a horse!"

Connor turned around to see a rider hauling ass toward them, coming from the direction of the house, and he knew.

"Antonio!" Connor went running over to where their hired hand was working on the tractor. "Antonio!"

Maybe Antonio, too, had felt the chill that was seizing Connor's spine. Before he could even look over at Connor he had shut the tractor and the posthole digger off and jumped out of the seat.

They all three took off in the truck and met the rider halfway across the big, rocky field.

It was Greg. Greg's face was streaked with tears.

"She had a stroke!" Greg said, his voice a boozy wail. "She had a stroke, Connor! The EMS came and took her down to Kannady Regional."

Kannady Regional was a forty-five-minute drive. An hour, if you acknowledged the existence of any of the traffic signs between Poison Creek and Yergville.

Connor still felt cold to the bones.

"We'll meet you back at the house," he said. "She's gonna be all right."

***

One of the cruelties of cell phone communication is that nobody wants to leave devastating news by voicemail. They just say "call me, it's important" as if those four words are any less cheap or heartless than spelling it out after the message beep.

After two rings, a man picked up the phone. "This is Dr. Voss."

"Hi, Dr. Voss," Connor said. "This is Connor Dougherty. You called me while I was out of cell signal, regarding my mother."

"Mr. Dougherty," the doctor said. "Do you have a minute to talk somewhere private?"

The doctor hadn't mentioned it, but Connor sat down in the nearest available chair. "Yeah," he said. "Yeah, I'm ready."

There was a slow intake of breath on the other end. "Your mother was pronounced dead on arrival, Mr. Dougherty," he said. "I'm deeply sorry."

"God bless you, Doctor," Connor said. The room was shrinking around him. He felt his brother's hand on his shoulder, heard his whiskey sniffling behind him. He reached up to take Greg's hand in his and squeezed.

"We'll be expecting you at the hospital," the doctor continued. "We understand that you live some distance away…"

"I don't think there's a need to, uh, keep…" Connor swallowed. He didn't know what the doctor was implying. His mind was consumed by the image of his mother, her spirit gone, a mockery of a person sitting in a hospital bed for the sake of a damn pageant.

"Once again, I'm very sorry," the doctor said. "You have my number if you need anything else before you arrive."

***

The next three days were not a blur. They remained clear and crisp in Connor's memory as if they were expensive bulls paraded before him at auction. Doctors. Lawyers. Bankers. Priests. He was already familiar with the process of handing them the loose ends of Marjorie Dougherty's life; now he had only to watch as they all tied them together.

The ranch, too, needed running all this time. Cattle and horses were still eating; deliveries were still coming; fields were still being irrigated. Greg had taken little enough interest in running the ranch when their mother had still been alive. Asking him for any help now would have sent him into a spiral and only made things worse.

Connor was staying sober through all this, for the most part. He was never going to see his mother again, and he was never going to hear her voice. What that meant to him had begun to weigh heavy long before his mother had begun her final decline.

Connor knew he had not felt that full weight yet, and he knew he didn't want to be drunk when it hit him.

"You woulda forgiven me, right?" Greg said, leaning on the bar top for balance. "I just...I shoulda gone. I shoulda been there with her when she passed."

"Of course, I would've, brother," Connor said. He'd been nursing this beer for the better part of an hour, drifting in and out of the conversations that floated around him. "But don't be too hard on yourself."

"I just feel...I just feel like she got so scared, these last few months, you know?" He sniffled and took a gulp of beer.

"I don't think there was anything more you could have done," Connor said. His mind kept drifting back to the funeral, drifting back to the quiet condolences he'd gotten. You could tell who'd been there, who'd seen what Marjorie Dougherty had become in her last days.

He remembered Nancy hugging him, strong and silent, not a waver in her voice as she told him it was okay. He kept remembering that moment, kept replaying her voice in his head. It's okay.

"And I just can't help but think, you know?" Greg was staring off into the distance now, his eyes wet and unfocused. "What if I had Linda around? What if I could man up and convince her family to let her come up here?"

Connor nodded solemnly. "Linda's got a good head on her shoulders," he said. "We really could use a gal like that around..."

Maybe that was the wrong thing. Greg put his head in his hands and stifled a sob.

"Aww, man, it's gonna be okay," Connor said. He patted his brother on the back. "Her old man can't hold out...oh, hold on."

Connor's chest flooded with relief when he realized his phone was buzzing in his pocket. The law firm's name was on the caller ID.

"This is Connor Dougherty," he said, springing off the barstool and heading for the patio out back.

"Hi, Mr. Dougherty," Miss Trisha said. "This is Trisha Evans calling you from Carter Bobinski and Reeves. How are you doing this afternoon?"

"I'm doing well," Connor said. "Thanks for asking. How 'bout you?"

"I'm, uh, I'm okay," Miss Trisha said. Her voice had an awkward tinge to it. "Um. Mr. Bobinski has asked me to call you and inform you that he's gone over your mother's will, and, uh, we need to schedule a meeting." She swallowed. "She's, uh, arranged for the will to be, uh, read."

"Okay," Connor said. "Uh, how many people are we planning on gathering together here?" he said.

"That's all going to be arranged on our end, Mr. Dougherty," Miss Trisha said. "See, uh, why I'm calling you right now is, uh, okay." She took a breath. "So, I know it's common in the movies for a decedent to have a will read in front of family and friends, and a lot of people expect that to be standard practice in real life."

There it was again—that feeling like someone had left a window open in his vertebrae. "Yeah?" he said.

"Well, truth of the matter is, it's not standard practice," Miss Trisha said. "It's, uh...usually, a decedent arranges a reading for the purpose of causing a contentious situation," she said. "After their death."

It took a couple of seconds for Connor to decode that. "Oh," he said. "And you're calling me because you want to warn me about what's in the will."

"It's our firm's policy to advise family members, when possible, that they are about to be involved in a potentially difficult situation," Miss Trisha said. "These occasions can become very emotional for everyone involved."

"Well, thanks for the warning," Connor said. "Let me know when you're scheduling, and I'll have a guy stationed outside with a dart gun."

"Mr. Dougherty, I advise you..."

"Kidding, kidding," Connor said. "I got my temper from my dad's side of the family."

Since Miss Trisha seemed to find that genuinely funny, Connor assumed she had at one point met his mother.

* * *

The reading was held in Fort McGrath a week after that phone call, in a chilly office on the law firm's second floor. Connor and Greg were there, as well as their surviving maternal uncles and Father Andrew.

The proceedings started out well enough, with Mom leaving a substantial portion of her remaining

30

cash to her younger brother and making sure her elder brother got control of certain family heirlooms. To the church, she left all her gardening implements as well as about half her kitchenware, which Father Andrew appeared slightly confused about but took in good stride.

After that, Mr. Bobinski leaned back in his desk chair a little. He was an elderly, stoop-shouldered old man, and he preferred to have his paralegals do most of the interaction with human beings required by his practice.

The office, poorly lit by a small window in the south wall and an aging fluorescent bar above the desk, seemed to warn incoming clients of the lawyer's personality. The shelves were crammed with aging books, some collecting more dust than others. Near the window, the remains of a houseplant hung in a macramé holder, casting a weak shadow on the J.D. certificate hanging on one dark green wall.

"And... hmmm…" The lawyer's face darkened as he scanned the lines in front of him. He took a sip from the mug on his desk and licked his lips before continuing. "To my son Gregory," he said, "who walks in God's light, I leave sole possession of my house, my ranch, all assets connected to the ranch to be listed in Appendix A, and the care and keeping of any pets I may own at the time of my passing, as well as any remaining monetary funds from my estate, minus the sum of two dollars."

Before the people in the room could even process what was going on, Mr. Bobinski held up a silencing hand without looking up from the will. "The remaining two dollars," he said in a mournful rasp, "I leave behind to Connor Joseph Dougherty, as the sum total of the inheritance he shall receive from me."

Mr. Bobinski had to hold his hand up again to stem the tide of angry voices that rose from the assembled heirs. "As he refused to respect my wishes in life, so I refuse to support his lifestyle after my death."

Now, Mr. Bobinski drew back, with a little flourish of his hand as if he were a referee rather than a lawyer. Immediately, everybody had to get their piece out at the same time.

"She can't do that!"

"Well, I'll be damned..."

"Two dollars?"

All Connor could do was shake his head and shut his eyes. Out of everybody in the room, he seemed to be the least outraged. Of course, he'd been mentally preparing himself for this moment since he was fifteen years old.

"Well, it was her property." Uncle Richard, of course, was going to take her side on this. "The boy knew damn good and well how his family felt..."

"What the hell do you know about how this family felt?" Greg turned on his uncle with his face red and his fists clenched. "After all he did for her, after all those years he spent looking after her day and night!"

Richard's pompous frown turned to a sneer. "Marjorie deserved better than to have that kind of disgraceful behavior under her roof while she was too weak to..."

"You never lifted a finger to help her!" Greg's pudgy, awkward form was animated by rage. He towered over his uncle as he jabbed one finger in the air between them. "You know what she deserved, she deserved better than a couple of useless, bible thumping vultures for brothers!"

"What in the hell did you just..."

"Gentlemen, this is a time for honoring the memory of the woman we've lost!" Father Andrew inserted himself in the narrowing gap between Greg and Uncle Richard. "And... for cherishing the time we yet have with the loved ones who are still in this life."

"Some honor he's doing her," Uncle Richard said, glaring over the priest at Greg. "Defending that fruit loop while the rest of us..."

"Richard, Marjorie and I had many conversations about this subject." The gentleness was ebbing away from Father Andrew's voice. "This is not a time to pass judgment. This is a time to help your nephews mourn their loss and keep their family strong."

Uncle Richard got a little taller as he leaned back. For a second, it looked like he was going to punch the priest, or at least spit on him. But he thought better of it, and he turned to walk to the door.

"I don't have any faggots in my family," he said as he walked out.

"Oh, my." Mr. Bobinski adjusted his glasses and suddenly appeared very interested in a small notebook he'd picked up from his desk.

"Richard, come back here and apologize!" Uncle Tim stomped off after him. "That's no kind of language..."

Here it was. It was all closing in on Connor, while he sat hunched forward in the padded chair in the lawyer's dim office. The call from the doctor, the hug at the funeral, the look on the silage guy's face when Connor told him the news.

Never again. He was never going to see his mom again. Never going to hear her voice, never going to see her smile, never going to apologize for waking her with his bumbling around the house.

"Hey, man, are you okay?" Greg was stooping by his chair now, one hand on his shoulder. His breath smelled like whiskey and chewing tobacco, and he was less than steady on his feet. "Hey, man, we're gonna get through this, okay? You and me. Last thing, man, last thing I'm gonna do is…"

"Greg, I don't want to talk about this right now." Connor's voice was steadier than it had any right to be.

Greg, knowing Connor as well as he did, stood up and backed away. "All right," he said. "Just let me…"

"If you need me I'll be back in Knife Rock," Connor said. He was well aware of every ounce of effort needed to keep his composure as he stood up and walked toward the door of the lawyer's office. "If I make it back before five, I just might be able to spend my inheritance on a cold beer."

Chapter Four

The next strike of lightning hit so close, Ty didn't even have time to cover his ears. Every single loose object in the bunkhouse rattled along with the walls; Ty's heart might have skipped a beat or two.

The Briggs didn't see fit to run electricity out to the refurbished boxcars they'd turned into little cabins for their hired help. There was a generator out back if you wanted to run a computer or something, and there was a big white can of propane to run the hot water heater and stove pulled from an RV.

But the propane came out of your pay. And you had to take the can in to the gas station to refill it yourself. And it had to be the R and F Co-Op on Highway 22. Nowhere else.

At least the battery-operated lanterns were bright enough that he could sit at his kitchen table and read. Modern technology was really something else.

Another crash shook the roof - and another, and another, and dammit this was a hailstorm. There was no covered parking for him here, just a couple of twisted Russian olive trees shading a beat-up picnic table in the crook of the L shape formed by the boxcars. Ty just had to hope that he still had a windshield and a trailer roof when he went outside in the morning.

He picked up his bottle of whiskey and poured himself another glass. No electricity meant no freezer, but he still had most of a bag of ice pissing itself away in the sink. As the hailstone crashes grew louder on the tin roof, it occurred to Ty that he would currently be happy to drink this rotgut, ice or no ice.

"Dammit, Gibson, let me in!" a woman's shriek came from outside the door.

Ty jumped out of his skin and bolted across the kitchen in a single stride. "Sorry!" he said as he unlocked it and pulled it open. "Can't hear too good!"

"Jesus!" One hundred and eight pounds of soaking wet Linda Briggs catapulted herself into the bunkhouse kitchen, where she promptly shook herself like a dog. "I just about got my head busted in out there!"

"Do you need me to walk you back to the house?" Ty had to yell so he could hear his own voice over the din of the hail on the roof.

"Naw," Linda said. In her big, stiff oilskin slicker and her thick mechanic's gloves, she looked like she'd just come up from a hostile planet. Which, in a way, she had. "I gotta get back out and keep working on that feed truck while I have daylight."

"I think the daylight's gone," Ty said.

"We'll see." Linda's gaze settled on the plastic whiskey bottle by Ty's sink.

"You want a shot?" Ty said.

"I sure could use one." They had to lean close while they yelled at each other. Linda smelled like a wet horse. She'd already made a pretty good-sized puddle on the aging linoleum beneath her feet. "Thanks!"

"No problem!" Ty grabbed a plastic cup from the stack he'd bought at the Tasty Mart in town. As he poured, the battering overhead quieted to a sound that only shook most of his bones. He handed the cup to Linda.

"You don't happen to be a diesel mechanic, do you?" Linda tilted her head back and drained the whiskey in a single swallow. If the taste fazed her at all, it didn't show on her tiny, pointed face.

"No, ma'am," Ty said.

"Shit." For a second, Linda's mouth scrunched into a frown. She walked across the kitchen and helped herself to a second shot. As she poured, she turned to Ty and smiled. "Don't worry," she said. "I'll bring you a bottle when I go into town next."

Ty let out a weak laugh. "Awesome," he said.

Linda Briggs was a quick-footed brunette of about twenty-five who appeared, in her face and in her stature, to have been produced by one of the android factories in the book she was presently keeping him from. Her face was round and clear; her features were small and defined; her hair did exactly what she wanted it to and when.

No confirmation yes or no on the titty guns, of course, but she was strong as a bull and always seemed to be three steps ahead of you in a conversation. Ty wasn't sure he liked the idea of having her alone in his bunkhouse, drinking his whisky. Even if she wasn't a battle robot from the far future, she was still his boss's daughter. Even to a man of Ty's romantic tastes, one of those was at least as dangerous as an android super-soldier.

"So, what I think we ought to do," she was saying, "given the age of the truck and the fact that it's a feed truck, is just replace the bolt and keep an eye on the oil level while we start keeping an eye out for a newer model."

"Because the leak's not that bad now, right?"

"I mean, this leak isn't that bad, but there's more than one leak," Linda said. "Look, the damn engine's twenty-five years old. I don't know how leak-tight my dad's expecting this thing to get. But now he's wanting me to go take this somewhere and get the whole thing re-built instead of shopping for a new one."

"What's a rebuild going to cost on that thing?" Ty assumed Linda was talking about the massive, aging diesel semi-tractor they used to haul hay around at feeding time. It took about five minutes to start and lurched around in an ominous cloud of blue-black smoke the entire time you were running the engine; the less said about the tires, the better.

"On this engine?" Linda's delicate eyebrows shot up. "Low bid's sixty-five, and we'll be out of a feed truck for at least two months."

"Oh." Ty nodded. It wasn't really his place to say who amongst his bosses was right or wrong, but he could see why Linda was questioning her father's idea of money well spent.

"We'll make do somehow, I guess," Linda said. She sank another shot of Ty's whiskey and pulled her phone from her pocket. Watching her read something was almost as good as reading it yourself: her face went from annoyed to amused, from furious to giggly.

Ty took a sip of his own whisky. "Your dearly beloved?" he said as he watched her grin like a schoolkid at the phone's screen.

Reason number two he wasn't so sure about having Linda in his bunkhouse: she was extremely engaged. Every time she talked about the guy, her eyes got misty and her voice got soft.

Even now, she batted her eyes as she replied. "Yeah," she said. "He's going through a hard time."

"Oh yeah?" Ty said. He'd rather talk about anything else than his boss's daughter's love life, truth be told.

"Yeah, his mom just died." Linda frowned. "It's...it's been a difficult situation for everybody."

"Well, I'm sorry to hear that," Ty said. "Not much you can do to make that time in life any easier."

Linda shook her head. "Well, and I guess she went really downhill before she passed. I don't know." She took in a deep breath and set her jaw, studying Ty carefully for a few seconds. "I haven't...gotten much of a chance to get close to their family."

"Oh?" Ty took a nervous sip of his whisky.

"It's...I..." Linda paused with her head cocked and her mouth open. She looked at her cup and looked back at the whiskey bottle.

They both looked out the window. Outside, the hail had been mostly replaced by darkness and torrential rain. Thunderclaps came so close on each other's tail you couldn't tell one from the other.

"Well, my family versus Greg's family is a long story," Linda said, grabbing the whiskey bottle and walking over to the rickety card table where Ty took his meals. "But it's a story you should probably know if you're going to work for my family, so let's go ahead and sit down."

***

Even though there were two folding chairs accompanying the card table, there was really only room in the breakfast nook for one person. Ty let

Linda have that honor, and he perched his narrow ass on the edge of his kitchen sink while Linda drank his whiskey and regaled him on the years-long fight between her family and her boyfriend's folks.

"...so, I'm at this jackpot in Rock Springs, right?" She was gesticulating wildly with the red plastic cup. "And he drove out to see me, 'cause, you know, he loves me, and he wants to see me run in the biggest fucking jackpot of the year, right?"

"Yeah," Ty said. They were about halfway into the bottle. It remained to be seen how far they were into the story.

So far: Greg and Linda had met because Greg's family provided bucking bulls to certain rodeos up north. Now, Linda's family also provided bucking bulls to certain rodeos in various areas, including up north. Linda and Greg felt like this gave them a lot of common ground and nearly endless things to talk about.

Linda's family, on the other hand, felt like she was giving vital business information directly into enemy hands.

Now, from what Linda said, it wasn't anybody's fault that her family hated Greg Dougherty with a passion typically reserved for dairy farmers and the French. His mother was, as a matter of fact, French on her maternal side, but Linda had elected not to add any more fun Greg facts to the perfect storm of prenuptial animosity she was dealing with here.

He was already an Irish Catholic, which was a problem with her father for a long and academically dubious set of reasons. He drank on Sundays and chewed tobacco in the presence of women. He was a

40

staunch devotee and contented rider of Hancock-bred horses. And his hat was the wrong shape.

But back to the story: Linda's eyes were getting misty as she described her bone-shaking nerves, her embarrassing warm-up, her record-breaking barrel run that shocked her more than anybody watching, and finally the joy in her heart when she spotted Greg Dougherty standing on the rail cheering her on.

"I just...I just knew, looking at his face," she was saying. Her petite behind had migrated from the folding chair to the top of the card table, and she swung her legs in ever-increasing arcs as she progressed with the story. She was holding the whiskey bottle by the neck like it was a scepter, and the red plastic cup like it was her regal orb.

"Knew he was the one, huh?" Ty was still working on his second shot. He couldn't shake the feeling that this was some kind of test, one last question in a secret job interview he didn't know was happening.

"You know, I went my whole life never having anybody look happy to see me. I know...I know this is way TMI for you, and all, but..." She sniffled, and for a second her lip trembled before she took another swig of whisky. "I love my family, Ty. I would do anything, absolutely anything, to keep them happy."

"Sounds like, uh, that extends to, uh...yeah." Ty took a swig of whiskey and nodded as dutifully as he could. "Loyalty, man."

"And it's not just about me," Linda said. "My dad knows damn good and well that our families could work together. There's not a single reason..." She wrinkled her nose, as if she'd just realized what she'd been drinking, and then shook her head. "Good Lord.

He's never even met Greg's family. Won't even go with me when I visit their ranch."

"Well, a man's pride is a funny thing," Ty said. "I'm, uh, sure he's got his reasons."

"Tell me about it." Linda gazed out the window. She seemed to have realized that she'd just spent half an hour chugging rotgut and spilling the contents of her heart to a ranch hand she'd just barely hired.

"You know, my dad used to mine uranium for a living," Ty said. "The old-fashioned way."

"There's an old-fashioned way to mine uranium?" Linda's eyebrows shot up on her head.

"I mean, they discovered it in the 1780s," Ty said. "That's a science fact for you."

"Yeah?" A smile cracked Linda's face. "So, what's the old-fashioned way of mining it?"

"Well, you go down in the hole with a drill and a Geiger counter," Ty said. "And you start drilling in all these different directions, and you stick the sensor on your Geiger counter down into all these different holes."

Linda drew back a little bit; she was probably putting two and two together.

"And when the Geiger counter starts going nuts, you go, and you dig in that direction." Ty jabbed his thumb to the left. "Lather, rinse, repeat."

Linda nodded. "That's it?" she said. "Do, uh, do they wear, like, you know. A hazmat suit?"

Ty sighed and shook his head. "I said my dad used to mine Uranium," he said.

Linda looked at the floor; beneath her lips, you could see the outline of her tongue running along her teeth. "Oh," she said. "I'm sorry."

Ty shrugged. "He and my mom got divorced when I was real little," he said. "I'd go see him during the summers, sometimes, but my Mom just…" He shook his head. "I don't know. She had issues of her own."

"That's hard," Linda said. "Is she still around?"

"More or less," Ty said. She had yet to return his voicemail telling her about his new job.

Linda nodded and looked at her feet. Her tongue was running along the outside of her upper teeth again.

"I turned out alright though," Ty said. "And you will too." He smiled. "I mean, you can't be too bad now if you're puttin' off your one true love to help your folks out here on the ranch."

"Trust me," Linda said. "The moment my dad gives me a choice, I'm out of here. It's just…" She cut herself off, looked out the window. "Well," she said. "The storm's letting up."

It hadn't started hailing again. Other than that, "letting up" was a pretty stretchy description of what was going on outside that window.

"Yeah," Ty said.

"I'd better lope some horses and sober up before my dad gets home," Linda said, getting up and putting the hood of her slicker back up. "See you at evening feed."

As she hurried out of his bunkhouse, Ty had to wonder how much of this conversation had been in the territory of "saying too much." Every ranching family had its dirty laundry, of course. You just had to ignore it and be careful, lest they use that dirty laundry to wrap you in when they put you in a shallow grave.

Chapter Five

"Isn't there any way we could do this, uh, over the phone?" Greg's voice was heavy and tired. "Oh. Uh, okay. Right." He nodded as he paced across the living room. "I thought Connor had power of attorney, though." A pause, a gulp. "Right. Right. Okay. Thanks. Uh-huh."

With his reading glasses on, Connor couldn't see the particular emotions on his brother's face. He was watching him pace over the top of his laptop screen, waiting for words to come to him.

There it was! *The fact of the matter is,* he typed, *our watershed has a limited carrying capacity, and that carrying capacity is already taxed by existing agricultural and municipal use.* Perfect. Magnificent. Now he could pretty much copy and paste his notes from the meeting with the university people, and…

"Connor, do you remember who runs the new hotshot company?" Greg was walking toward him.

Connor took his reading glasses off. "Huh?"

"I'm on the phone with the insurance guy," Greg said. "Uhh, and I need to know who their insurance carrier is."

"It's all in the binder," Connor said.

"Uhh…"

"Do you have the binder?" Connor blinked as his eyes adjusted to the new perspective.

"It's in my truck…"

"The company's DBA is Circle R Hotshots, but its real name is Gutierrez Enterprises LLC. Lydia Gutierrez is the owner and operator," Connor said. "Stieffer and

Boss Insurance. That's Ess Tee Eye Ee Eff Ee Arr," Connor said.

Greg repeated the information into the phone receiver. "And is that liability or…"

"They have full coverage, but Shawn might need to review their certificate of insurance," Connor said. "Which, if they don't have it on file, is in the binder, which is why you shouldn't leave it in your truck."

"Sorry," Greg said. He shuffled off through the kitchen, explaining that he had the paperwork with him, if the guy on the phone could kindly give him just one second.

Mom had to have known that Greg would rather shit his pants in public than try his hand at running this ranch. Once all this paperwork transfer was done with, he'd probably resume his life of riding fence and drinking beer and chasing Linda Briggs around the rodeo circuit. Connor would keep on more or less running things, like he always had, and he supposed the two of them would continue to coexist more or less peacefully out here on the ranch.

But that left them a little distance from what they wanted, didn't it? Greg would be tied to land he didn't want to manage and a business he had no interest in running; Connor would be spending the rest of his life playing middleman between his uninterested family and the people who thought his family actually cared.

"Hey, Connor?" Greg's voice came from the entryway. "Uh, what part of the binder are the insurance certificates in?"

***

The afternoon sun was starting to make Connor sweat under his vest as he knelt in front of his little work area. The top of the windmill was coming back together piece by piece, with the busted bearing replaced. He couldn't figure out specifically what was wrong with the oil pump that was supposed to keep the bearings lubricated, but after three busted bearings in a year it couldn't hurt to replace that as well.

Anything to keep him from the top of the tower in the blistering sun.

Greg had still not arrived at the big tin water tank by the time Connor had screwed the windmill's motor back together. Without his help, there was no way to get it back up the tower again.

Bored, sweaty, and mightily tempted by the two-thousand-gallon stock tank full of cool water, Connor stripped down. The tank wasn't exactly deep enough to dive in, but it was always a good time climbing up the tower a few feet and launching yourself backwards into the water.

He paused as he climbed to regard his reflection in the goldfish-studded water below. His family had always assured him he'd fill out his lanky frame eventually, but he remained a bit of a beanpole nonetheless. Maybe it was just the distance and the water's distortion making him look so damn skinny. From up here, his broad face had kind of a boyish handsomeness to it; up close, you could see he hadn't shaved in a few days and could still barely grow a beard at thirty-five years old.

Movement on the horizon caught his eye. Greg's truck was cresting a hill to the southwest.

Connor turned around and dropped himself down into the stock tank. Goldfish scattered away from him as he landed with a splash that punched all the air out of his lungs.

"Jesus!" He came up for a gasp of air and shuddered in the sudden cold. It didn't take long for the heat of the sun to register on his skin, and after a few seconds, he was actually comfortable.

Slowly, Connor eased himself back into the tank. He rested his arms on the edge and floated with his eyes closed for a minute or two, savoring the cool water and the warm sun and the sound of his horse grazing by the stock tank. This, right here. This was worth putting up with all the bullshit that came with living on a ranch.

By the time Greg showed up, Connor was dressed again and mostly dry. His brother did not appear to share his good mood. In other circumstances, Connor might have asked him who died.

"Sorry I'm late," he said. "Linda's dad went on another bender and he won't come home."

"Won't, or can't?" Connor said.

"Probably both, if he's drunk again," Greg said. He stepped out of his truck with a heavy sigh.

"Well, if he can't come home, maybe she ought to take advantage of the lack of supervision." Connor walked over to the reassembled windmill head.

"She won't leave her mom," Greg said. "Not like this. They just had all their ranch hands quit on them these last few months, and she's working sixteen, eighteen-hour days just trying to keep the place running."

"Well, fancy that," Connor said. "He runs off the help, and now she has to stay at home wiping his ass and pouring drinks for her mom."

"Her mom's getting the worst of this shit," Greg said with a scowl.

"She's just as contemptible as her husband, if you ask me," Connor said. "How long have you two been together? Six, seven years?"

"Would you step a toe out of line if you were in her shoes?" Greg said. "It's not worth it cozying up to me."

"There's cozying up, and there's showing basic respect to your fellow human being." Connor shook his head. "Nobody in this family's so much as met a one of those assholes, and they have the nerve to talk about us like they've had the opportunity to pass judgment." He spat on the ground. "I don't know why you put up with it."

"I'm about tired of putting up with it, I tell you what," Greg said. "Someone needs to talk sense into her mother." He sidled up to the other side of the windmill head. "Jesus, that looks heavy."

"It is," Connor said. "That's why you're here."

Truth be told, getting the windmill head up the tower was not the hard part. The hard part was holding the first bolt hole in place while Connor got himself, the bolt, the washer and nut, and the wrench all at the right angle to get it screwed back together.

Naturally, this was accompanied by enough swearing and creative violent threats to be deeply concerning to anyone unfamiliar with the brothers.

Connor took the first chance he got to dunk his head in the trough when he came off the tower. The

49

water was a blessing on his face, though it carried a funky vegetable smell from the goldfish living in it.

"Man, I just can't help but think," Greg said as he climbed down. "On days like today, you know? She'd be so much happier here."

"She would," Connor said. "Just give her a choice, you know?"

"I can't give her shit," Greg said. "She has a choice, and she chooses her family every time."

"Then move on, amigo." Connor shot a sympathetic wince at his brother. "You can't rescue her from the situation she's in."

"But what if I could?" Greg said. "You know? What if I could figure out how to get her away from her dad, or talk some sense into her mom, or just, you know, help her get the situation fixed so she's not stuck out on their ranch?" Now it was his turn to plunge his head into the stock tank, and the upper half of his torso with it.

Connor shielded himself from the spray as Greg shook himself. "Jesus, you fuckin' Labrador…"

"You're already wet."

"Okay?" Connor rolled his eyes. "Anyway, how the hell do you think you're going to pull off a stunt like that?"

"I don't know," Greg said. "I don't...they won't talk to me, Connor. I know what I hear from Linda, but I never know if it's the full story, or if she's trying to make it, so I won't worry about her."

"And what do you mean by that?" Connor leaned back against the water tank, his eyes narrowed.

"I don't think she's telling me the real story about where her dad's going," Greg said. "I think she's hiding the real situation."

"That's a sign of a well-adjusted young lady," Connor said.

"No, I mean...I'm sure she has her reasons," Greg said. "She doesn't want me getting hurt, and she doesn't want to go running her mouth about all her dad's troubles."

"Well, I hate to break it to you, brother," Connor said, "but if you want to marry that girl, then her daddy's troubles are very much your problem."

"See, that's exactly my train of thought," Greg said.

"Mm." Connor's mouth turned downward. "You're smiling."

"See, I was thinking while we were up on that tower," Greg said.

"You weren't supposed to be thinking," Connor said. "You were supposed to be holding that damn windmill head in position."

"I was thinking about what might happen if I were to do a little information gathering about Linda's dad," Greg said.

"A little what?" Connor stood upright, a frown of deep suspicion etched on his face.

"You know, figure out what he's really up to. Because I'm thinking, maybe he's hiding things from Linda." Greg started pacing up and down in front of Connor. "And yeah, I've asked her if maybe he is, and she says she doesn't know."

"Look, buddy," Connor said. "I know how much you love Linda, but it sounds like she's not telling you the whole truth."

"Maybe she is, and maybe she isn't," Greg said. "But if she is, then she needs my help to get away from that father of hers."

"You didn't come up with this plan on top of the windmill tower, did you?" Connor said.

"No, I came up with it on the drive out," Greg said. "See, here's my idea."

"Oh, boy."

"No, listen." Greg paused in his little circle in front of Connor. "You're right when you talk about Linda's family being too good to get to know any of us. They barely know me from a hole in the ground. You, they wouldn't recognize at all."

"Uh-huh." Connor crossed his arms and tilted his head.

"And as hard up as they are for help, I bet they'd probably hire you on." Greg smiled. "Get yourself a couple of fake documents, come up with a little backstory, nobody there would know who you are."

"You been sticking your face in those diesel fumes again, Greg?" Connor said. "That's the dumbest idea I've ever—"

"Is it, though?" Greg said. "Nobody's gonna get hurt. Your job would just be to, you know, hang out and do some grunt work and see what it is that's keeping Mr. Briggs away from the ranch for so long."

"That's insane!" Connor said. "And what happens when I get found out?"

"Hopefully you won't be," Greg said. "I don't know. We have to try something."

"This idea is a little beyond 'something,' buddy." Connor shook his head.

"But think about how happy Linda would be if we could just get her away from those people," Greg said. "Or at least, you know, maybe figure out how to get them warmed up to us a little." There was more than a little of the pleading kid brother in his face and in his voice.

Connor could swear he felt his heart crack a little. "Come on, Greg," he said. "We have to be realistic, here."

"I'll give you the ranch, man," Greg said. "I don't care if our uncles sue me, or if I go to hell for violating Mom's last wishes, or whatever. I'll give it to you, free and clear."

"Wait, what?" Connor said.

"I don't care if you find out what's going on, or if you get found out and Linda hates me for it." Greg's jaw had that set it took on whenever he had made his mind up. "We have to at least try something, Connor. I already lost Mom. I don't know if I can stomach losing Linda, too."

"This plan might make you lose Linda," Connor said. "Don't you understand that?"

"Yeah, but...but at least I'll know why." Greg nodded. "I'm serious, Connor. Swear on my life. Swear on Mom's grave. If you help me, the ranch is yours and everything on it. Every cow, every horse, every rusty nail, piece of baling twine, and an unlabeled O-ring."

"You're fucking crazy," Connor said.

"Yeah, well." Greg looked at the ground, then back to Connor. "Someone has to pick up Mom's slack around here."

Chapter Six

Once he got into the swing of it, it was easy enough for Ty to sink a nail through a couple of one-by-eight pine boards in under a few blows. For some reason, half the buildings around here were done with battened siding instead of sheet metal.

On the other side of the shed, Linda and Luanne were hard at work doing much the same thing he was. They still had yet to find another able young man to work with him on the ranch, and the master of the house was in poor health following his return from an undisclosed location, so mother and daughter were both out here hammering nails with Ty.

The thing with untreated pine boards like these, you see, is that they absorb water when it gets wet. Conversely, they dry out again when it gets hot and dry. This tends to make a thin, untreated pine board twist and warp like a piece of cardboard or thick leather. Slowly, surely, over a couple of seasons, these boards will pull their own nails out of each other and need to be replaced.

Linda and Luanne seemed to be aware of this. Linda and Luanne were out here hammering away anyhow, so Ty felt like it was best for him to just shut up and pound some nails.

This was just one of eight batten-sided sheds that occupied the front ninety acres of the ranch, where horses and cow/calf pairs grew fat all summer long on the lush grasses of the Chipeta River Valley. The Triple V ranch occupied the head and bosom of that illustrious hub of agriculture, looking out from a corner of the foothills to the broad plains below.

The ranch did a little bit of everything, which was to say it excelled in nothing Mr. Briggs attempted to do with it. There was plenty of lush grass for cow/calf pairs, but the pastures were only full to a quarter of their capacity if you counted Linda's horses. They had a decent working relationship with the Bureau and a useful lease on several thousand acres, but Ty had yet to learn of any major herds that were actually grazing out there. They had enough rough stock and running stock to host their own rodeo, but those animals all sat on dry lots eating hay.

So, you might understand why Ty was a little surprised when, at one point in his musings on the incompetence of his new employer, he looked up to see a couple of scraggy-maned young horses with the ranch's brand on their hips strolling on by the shed.

He was starting to develop that uncertainty about whether or not he ought to point it out when something was wrong here. Linda immediately relieved him of that uncertainty.

"Dammit, Dad!" she said. "If I get up there and that damn fence charger is shorted out again..."

"Should we go get a lead rope?" Mrs. Briggs came over with that tippy-toe gait of hers, looking around with her eyes big. "Do you think we can chase 'em back in, sweetie?"

"No, Ma, we cannot," Linda said. She was running for the truck. Ty followed. "Come with me. We're gonna have to round 'em up."

All three of them piled into the aging red farm truck without a word. Linda got the engine started, and they took off after the broncs at a speed that made bumps into a real experience for everyone. There were about a dozen of the escaped horses, all of them now running hell bent for leather as the truck pursued them.

"Ditch!" Linda yelled, slamming on the brakes as Ty saw the lead horse take a flying leap over something in the grass. The pickup slid a little bit as it came to a halt, broncs galloping into the distance away from it. "Shit, shit, shit..."

There was no need to add to that. Ty and Luanne clung to each other in the backseat.

"Linda..."

"We gotta keep them from getting out to the highway!" Linda was booking it back toward the house. The little quarter-ton pickup had long ago worn its shocks out, and every bump and over adjustment threatened to send them all to their final judgment before the horses made it as far as the creek.

The truck roared up to the ranch compound and swung around east to survey the lots where the rough stock sat around and ate up money that could theoretically be going into getting metal siding for the cowsheds. But back on track: the bank of fence chargers was smoking faintly, and now and then a stray arc of electricity would shoot from one busted metal component to another. Over in the silage bays across the north valley, Ty could see some bucking bulls having the time of their lives.

"What in God's name happened here?" Ty said without thinking.

"Dammit!" Linda's voice had never been so loud, nor half so warlike. Ty opened his truck door and fled as fast as he could, as Linda's frustration vented in a tear-filled streak of profanity it was best not to remember if anybody asked.

＊＊＊

Herding horses, for those of us just now tuning in, is nothing like herding cattle. Cattle are, well, able to be herded. Herdability, in fact, is part of what makes a cow a cow. See, regardless of their horn length or their temperament or their size or the status of their testicles, cattle were ultimately bred by design to be a slow-moving means of keeping fresh protein available for human consumption.

Horses were basically designed with the opposite idea in mind. They're not particularly tasty or wooly or affectionate or good for pest control, and the reviews of their milk are pretty varied in most parts of the world.

But horses are fast. By God, they are fast. They are fast in a way that no other creature can match up with. And when there are a lot of them in a group, "fast" takes on a whole new dimension.

Ty had been fortunate enough to sneak up on the broncs while they guzzled water out of the creek. They were upwind of him, and the willows along the creek bed gave him good enough cover that he could more or less approach them unnoticed from the southeast.

Trouble was, Ty and the ranch were on the wrong side of the river. There was no way to get on the highway side of the scruffy semi-feral horses without alerting them to his presence.

"Well, shit," he said under his breath to Blue, leaning back in his saddle and assessing the situation. The whole point of broncs was that they were jittery, ill-tempered, and athletic. If he approached them dead-on with a tired horse, he'd be playing a game of catch-up he couldn't win. He started moseying back to the east, trying to pretend that he wasn't paying keen attention to the horses grazing by the wide, lazy water.

Out on the highway, a familiar red truck slowed down and came in through the open gate. It stopped, and a tiny figure jumped out to close the gate as fast as she could manage.

"We got the bulls in!" Linda's voice came from behind Ty. She was running for him hell-bent for leather, looking not unlike a jockey on her big disagreeable buckskin.

"They're just past those..."

"I see that!" Linda said. She zoomed past Ty and cut upstream, and Ty followed. "Crossing's down here!"

"Your mom got the gate closed," Ty said.

"Yeah, but that fencing's not gonna hold these broncs," Linda said. "We been using it for hay pasture these past two years!" She slowed to a big lope as she pointed her horse across the creek. "We gotta keep 'em off the highway or we're screwed!"

Ty bit his tongue on his immediate response to that. No doubt, Linda knew damn good and well how important it was to spend money on fencing.

About eighty yards upstream, the little herd of broncs noticed their presence.

"Oh, dammit," Linda said. She cocked her seat back for a second, and her horse put the hammer down and started sprinting like his ass was on fire.

Ty followed suit, though Blue couldn't really keep up with any of Linda's good horses. The little herd of broncs wheeled and crossed back over the river. For a second, Ty's hope's rose as he watched

59

the little mass of brown and sorrel flow back toward the ranch.

But then, they encountered one of the same ditches they'd already crossed; this time, it proved to be an impassible obstacle, and the broncs shot east again with a good fifty yards distance on their pursuers.

Nothing, absolutely nothing, like herding cattle.

***

The heavy-duty rubber hose had been black originally. It was now striped with silver from one end to the other by duct tape repairs, and it left big dark spots of sprayed-off moisture in the dust behind it.

Ty kinked it off as he took it out of the big pasture's tank. Every joint in his body complained as he dragged the hose across the dirt alley to a pen of well-behaved Corrientes steers who hadn't contributed to the rodeo stock breakout festival.

"Gibson, I'd better have a word with you." A stern male voice came from behind Ty, making him jump halfway out of his skin.

He turned around. "Yes, sir?" he said, unable to hide his terror at the wide, white-haired gentleman who was approaching him at much the same gait a pissed-off bull approaches a fallen bull rider.

"It is my understanding," Mr. Briggs said, "that you spent two hours today running my finest saddle broncs around the front pasture. Is that correct?"

"Sir, I…"

"I asked you a direct question, son!" Mr. Briggs said. "Did you, or did you not, spend two hours of my time, running my finest saddle broncs all around my front pasture, in the plain and day lit view of the Lord God, the neighborhood, and everybody?" He said it like that. Everybody, not everybody.

Ty's lungs inflated, and he focused his wide eyes on the ground in front of him. "I did, sir," he said in the calmest voice he could manage.

"And did I hire your sorry ass to terrorize my rough stock and potentially cause injuries to my animals that could cost me a whole lot of money?" Mr. Briggs said. He had a vein showing on his forehead, and his clenched fists were white at the knuckles.

"Uhm..." Ty blinked.

"I asked you a..."

"No, sir!" Ty said. "You did not."

"Do not interrupt me when I am speaking to you, son!" Mr. Briggs's shoulders wobbled a little bit as he shouted at Ty. "When I hire a man, I assume that I have a level of trust in him that he is not going to damage my operation!"

Ty blinked. Was he...was he not supposed to herd the escaped stock back into their pens?

"I tell you what, I have gotten nothing but attitude from you, from day one!" Mr. Briggs said. "You are arrogant! You are disrespectful! And if you are going to be incompetent on top of..."

"Dad!" Linda was riding up to them on a sorrel. "What the hell is going on here?"

"Don't you take that language with me, young lady," Mr. Briggs said. He turned on Linda, allowing Ty to slink over to the Corrientes' water trough and stick the nozzle of the hose in there.

"My language is not our problem today," Linda said. "I've been begging and begging for that electric fence to get fixed, and nothing has happened."

"Well, when I can't find good help..."

"Ty is good help, Dad!" Linda's grip tightened on her reins. "And he did exactly as I asked him to. If you have a problem with my plan, you ought to come to me about it instead of griping at him."

"Don't take that tone with me!" Mr. Briggs advanced on Linda.

Linda's horse dutifully backed away from him, keeping one ear on Mr. Briggs and one ear on its mistress. "This is not about my tone," she said. "This is about how are we supposed to run this place without any help?" Her voice was low and level, but it shook with the weight of the rage dammed up behind it. "Don't act like this is the first incident you've blamed on the help when it is your own damned fault..."

"This is not the time nor the place for this discussion!" Mr. Briggs said.

"Then talk to me in the truck shed!" Linda said. "I need to show you what's going on with that damned hay baler before the whole truck explodes on me!" She wheeled her horse and trotted away.

For a second, Mr. Briggs wavered back and forth, looking from Ty to his daughter with furious confusion on his face. After a couple seconds he deflated slightly and turned away with a dismissive wave of his hand.

"I'll deal with you later," he said. "And get that damned hose repaired!"

***

The previous occupant of the bunkhouse had left behind a bug zapper shaped like a tennis racket. Ty used it to put an end to a large and particularly lantern-obsessed beetle, then set it back down on the rusted patio table.

In the wake of this evening's thunderstorm, the night was warm and damp. The moisture had awakened a dank, swampy smell in Ty's bunkhouse that he didn't want to deal with after a long day of work. Out here in the lamplight, he could sit back and enjoy his book and a moderately cool 3.2 beer from the gas station down the highway.

"Is that any good?" Linda's voice came out of the darkness before she did, still dressed in her work clothes and clutching a glass bottle of whiskey that cost substantially more than the one they'd shared last week.

"I'm not sure," Ty said. "We'll see how this, uh, space circus turns out."

"Why would you need a circus in space?" Linda set the bottle down in front of Ty and peered at the cover of his book. "You've already got, uh, monkeys in space suits."

"That's a Yukira and he has a family," Ty said, looking over the cover at Linda. "What's up?"

"Just bringing back what I borrowed," Linda said, gesturing to the whisky. "Unlike some people around here, I like to see to it that our ranch hands want to stick around."

"Oh, thanks." Ty nodded at her. "Appreciate you sticking up for me today."

"Not a problem," Linda said. "You do good work around here."

"Well, I appreciate that," Ty said. "Thanks for the job."

Linda looked him over, then chuckled as if at some private joke.

Ty raised an eyebrow. "What?"

"Do you mind if I ask you a kind of, um, personal question?" Linda's eyes narrowed to mascara-lined slits in her face.

"I do mind, actually," Ty said.

Linda startled back a little bit. "Oh! I didn't, uh, mean any offense by it."

Ty let his book fall and rest its spine against the patio table. He studied Linda's face carefully. "I know you don't mean no offense," Ty said. "But I keep my private life more or less private."

Linda nodded slowly. "I get you," she said. "What I meant was more or less of a warning, in that regard," she said. "I know plenty of fine young men with all kinds of private lives, and I think you ought to have whatever private life you feel like having, if you catch my drift."

"I catch it," Ty said without smiling.

"My dad has gotten...well, sensitive, as of late, about other people's private lives," Linda was saying. "And I expect the reason for that, well." She smiled bitterly. "I guess that's part of his private life, isn't it?"

"I suppose it is." Ty put his book back up to his face, trying to act like his heart wasn't pounding in his chest.

"I'm watching your back, Ty Gibson," Linda said as she turned and walked away from the patio table. "Just be sure that you're watching it too, you hear?"

"Loud and clear, Miss Linda."

Chapter Seven

"Come here, little buddy." Connor advanced quietly through the sagebrush, trying not to further spook the calf.

Up above them on the bank of the gully, he heard Bonito snort as he chased the momma away. Her panic was understandable, as was her desire to turn Connor into Irish stew but acting on those understandable urges wasn't going to help anybody in this situation.

The calf bawled in terror as Connor approached.

"Hush, now," Connor said, placing one hand on his head and turning it gently aside. With his free hand, he freed his fencing pliers from his belt and started cutting away at the ancient roll of discarded square wire that he'd gotten tangled in.

Despite the calf's thrashing and kicking, Connor managed to get him free before he hurt himself any further. He seemed sound enough on his feet as he bounded away from Connor and back to his irate mother.

Connor sighed as he surveyed the gully. That roll of square wire wasn't the only garbage that had accumulated down here over the years. He could see some bent T-posts, a ruptured water tank, several tires, and a windmill that had gotten mangled in a storm when he was just a kid.

He pulled his phone from his pocket and snapped a couple pictures of the debris. When he got home, he could put an ad up and have some enterprising kid come out and take all this scrap to the recycler in Fort McGrath. Underneath the grass and sagebrush, there were probably a couple of heavy and/or rare engine parts lying around. A smart scrapper could get a nice chunk of money cleaning out a dump like this.

Bonito walked up to meet Connor as he came up the old game trail that led down into the gully. He snorted and held his head out to Connor, plainly indicating the ear that needed scratching.

"Oh, was I gone too long?" Connor said, obliging his heavyset black gelding. For all the mischief he had caused in previous years, there was no better horse than Bonito for a long day of riding fence. He could go all day, doing just about anything that needed doing without a single complaint.

Truth be told, that put him ahead of most people in Connor's book.

They were about a mile from the house, headed homeward at a big walk that just sucked up the ground beneath Bonito's feet. It was a good gait for thinking and would encourage Connor's mind to wander whether it had anywhere to go or not.

Today, as had been the case for the last several days, he found himself wondering what it would be like if he actually did wind up getting the title to this ranch. It would be all his call, everything. What stock they raised, what vendors they used, how they went about managing and stewarding their land.

Of course, the way things were shaping up, he was going to be running the show anyway. Greg didn't want to run the ranch. Greg wanted to play trucker and make goo-goo eyes at Linda Briggs, and he was more than happy to leave the running of the ranch to Connor.

But was it always going to be that way? What happened if, for example, Greg moved on from Linda and married a woman who didn't take kindly to the university people and their studies? What happened if Linda's father decided he was going to start maneuvering for the ranch?

Now, that was a sobering thought. Connor felt a chill in his blood as he started putting two and two together with this situation. If Linda's father was in money trouble, and if he realized that Greg was currently the only one with a claim to the ranch...

"Jesus," Connor said. "I do have to at least try, don't I?"

***

Mama Jade listened to Connor's explanation with a twisted smile on her face. She had always been somewhat given to lighthearted criminal activity, and this kind of thing was prime entertainment for her and her cronies at the Back Cinch Bar and Grill.

"Now, I assume there's a reason," she said, "for you to be going and doing all this, uh...espionage." She lowered her voice to a whisper for the last word and covered her mouth with a menu.

"I'm just trying to plan a nice surprise for Miss Linda," Connor said. "Nothing harmful, I promise." He flashed a winning smile at her.

Connor hadn't given her the full details, of course, and he wasn't planning on telling her the entire story. Just what she needed to know in order to help him.

"Well, if it's not going to hurt anybody." Mama Jade giggled and looked at Caleb. "I think we should do it."

"Now, you can't tell anybody." Connor made sure that Caleb, Antonio, and Mama Jade were all looking right at him as he spoke. "This is technically a fraudulent employment situation I'm getting myself into, and even though I aim to work hard for these people, the law isn't on my side."

"The law's never on the side of an honest man," Caleb said.

"Shows what you know about honest men," Antonio said.

"I know as little as I do because it keeps me honest," Caleb said. "You know I'm not a liar because I'm dumb as shit."

"Gentlemen!" Connor said. "And lady. I trust you all because I've trusted you before. Okay?"

"Okay," Antonio said. "So, what do you need from us?"

"I need references," Connor said. "Because I'm going to go and be this whole new guy."

"What's your name gonna be?" Caleb said.

"I'm thinking something like...Buck," Connor said.

"Sweetie, you are gayer than a three-dollar bill," Mama Jade said. "You walk around with a name like Buck, people are going to think you are a porn star."

"That's not even how the saying goes..."

"Buck is a dumb name, I'm sorry," Antonio said. "What about Jake?"

"I don't like Jake," Connor said.

"What's wrong with Jake?" Mama Jade frowned. "Oh, you could go by Skip. Skip's a good name for a puncher."

"And that way you might get off a little easier if you get busted for the fraudulent name," Caleb said. "Obviously, your real name's not Skip..."

"Skip it is," Connor said.

"Skip McCoy," Antonio said. "All-American Cowhand Extraordinaire."

"I like it!" Connor grinned and picked up his beer glass. "Where is Skip from?"

"Does it matter?" Caleb said.

"Of course, it matters," Antonio said. "Some places are gonna check all your papers and make sure you have references and everything."

"Say you're from Omaha," Mama Jade said. "It's big enough, nobody would expect folk there to know you."

"And you did rodeo for a long time," Caleb added. "I'll be your old team roping buddy."

"I was a header, of course," Connor said.

"With an ego like yours? Obviously." Mama Jade rolled her eyes. "I'll be the manager at the feedlot you worked at previous."

"And I worked there with you," Antonio said. "I drove the feed truck, and you were one of the punchers."

"Okay," Connor said. "What was the feedlot called?"

"Who's asking?" Mama Jade's voice had the tone of sudden thunder. "You with the government? Huh? You got ID?" She put her hands on her hips and advanced on Connor. "I have my rights as a landowner and my rights as..."

70

"Okay, okay," Connor said, backing up with his hands in the air. "Seriously, though, we should, uh, make sure we have all our stories straight first."

***

Connor could remember the afternoons spent with Dalton, Caleb, and Antonio, watching Antonio's father carefully scrape away at the red oak boards that would become the confessional's new screen. He used to pray when he worked on projects for the church. You'd never hear him, just see his mouth tracing the familiar Spanish syllables as rough lumber chipped away into the forms of saints and symbols.

Every time Connor went to confession, the smell of the varnish took him back to the shop as it was before Luis died. He could feel the bare warmth of the December sun, the thrill of waiting for the right distracted moment to pull off a high school beer heist.

"What sins have you come to confess today, my son?" Father Andrew's voice was just above a whisper, kind and inviting as it always was during the Saturday sacrament. That, too, was a balm on Connor's heart.

"Well, let's see," Connor said. "For starters, I guess, I've let my job become the number one priority in my life. Again." He sighed. "Uhh, I've taken the Lord's name in vain and I've used foul language." He liked to go commandment by commandment to keep it all straight. Usually, this next part was as routine as confessing to impure thoughts.

"Uhm." Connor cleared his throat.

"Take your time, my son," Father Andrew said. He'd been listening to Connor unload his sins in this order for the better part of thirty years. He had to know what was coming next.

"Well, Father," he said. "Uhh...well." He cleared his throat, or maybe he was trying to unstick it. "My mom died recently, you see."

"I'm sorry to hear that, my son," Father Andrew said. "The loss of our parents is one of life's greatest challenges."

Was it? Connor screwed his eyes shut and rubbed his forehead. "Yeah," he said. "Uhh...I just. I don't." He swallowed, like that was going to keep him from breaking up here in a few seconds. "I'm not...honoring her memory, in a respectful way, Father," he said. "I don't know how."

His voice had started to crack on "memory." By the time he got to "I don't know how," he sounded like a scared little kid trying desperately not to cry.

"Ah, I see." Father Andrew's voice was soft and drawn out; it was easy to picture him nodding slowly on the other side of the red-oak screen.

"It was just...our relationship was so painful to both of us," Connor said. "Ever since I was little, it was just..." He had to take a couple of deep breaths. "All we knew how to do was hurt each other. It was like it was part of who we were, as people."

"Mmm." Father Andrew was nodding again. "It always seemed to me that complex people have difficulties understanding each other," he said. "And when there is a lack of understanding, things that seem helpful to you are in fact harmful to the other person."

"She was," Connor said, not bothering to hide the soggy grief in his voice. "She was...complicated. I just...I know she loved me, Father. She loved us boys so much."

"Marjorie was a good woman." If he regretted dropping the pretense of anonymity, Father Andrew gave no indication of it. "But even the best among us is still human, my son. We succeed at some things. We succeed very well at other things. And at still others…"

Connor was covering his face now. His grief was spilling out of him in muted barks, stinging his sunburnt cheeks as his chest shook. "I was just so angry, Father," he said. "She just didn't know…I don't know…she was so afraid, Father," he said. "And we were all so damn…oh, sorry…"

"It's quite alright, my son," Father Andrew said. "I haven't absolved you yet."

"Thanks, Father." Connor couldn't help but smile despite his sniveling. "I just don't know how to…how to balance the ledger, I guess," he said. "You know? I mean, what she wrote in her will." He grimaced, shut his eyes. "Is that really the last memory I'm gonna have of my mom, Father?"

Another long, contemplative sigh came from the other side of the screen. "You know, my son, when I was first assigned to this parish, the finality of death seemed to me to be the most obvious and unbreakable part of God's law. The living live. The dead die. There is neither point nor purpose to arguing against it."

"Yeah?" Connor nodded.

"But when I was first assigned to this parish, I knew nothing of ranch life. I knew nothing of ranchers." He chuckled softly. "Had Mary Magdalene been a ranch wife, I do not believe that Christ would have made it to his tomb. The angel would have had to wrestle him personally out of her care in the guest bathroom."

Again, Connor had to grin despite himself. The image of his mom, her Savior's head in one hand and a tub of DMSO in the other, barking for their dad to make more coffee at three in the morning...if that wasn't blasphemy, he didn't know what qualified anymore.

"What I mean to say, my son," Father Andrew said, "is that we seldom find ourselves prepared for the death of a loved one. Especially in a family like yours, where death must approach...in secret."

Connor thought back to that waiting room, to the expression of shock on the doctor's face. His mother, enraged, offended to her core by the very notion of a heart attack in someone that young.

"She really did think she was gonna live forever," Connor said. His own voice had calmed substantially; it was hard to stay upset for too long when Father Andrew was holding your spiritual hand. "And we all kind of went with it, huh?"

"Mmm." Father Andrew cleared his throat. "Faith runs strong in your family, my son," he said. "Do you believe you will see her again one day?"

"I..." Connor blinked. "I mean, I hope," he said. "She doesn't seem to agree..."

"But it was not her place to decide what will become of your immortal soul," Father Andrew said. "Just as it is not mine, nor is it the place of any human being."

Connor nodded. "I...I do my best to live the kind of life God wants me to live," he said. "I mean, yeah.

Yeah, I think...I hope, I hope I'll see her again one day."

"But do you *believe*?" Father Andrew said.

Connor took a deep breath. "Yeah," he said. "Yeah, I do believe I'll get to see my mom again one day."

"And in holding that faith, my son," Father Andrew said, "I believe you do honor your mother's memory."

Connor didn't really have much of a reply to that. He smiled. "Thanks, Father," he said.

"Let us both be thankful for our faith," Father Andrew said. "Now, is there anything else you wish to confess?"

"Umm, let's see." Connor swallowed, thinking of a few things he'd have to leave out of this confession. Father Andrew had reminded him more than once that he couldn't absolve a sin Connor was only just planning to commit.

Chapter Eight

The harsh buzz of the alarm clock always made Ty jump a little as he pulled himself out of sleep. He fumbled around in the pitch black of his windowless bedroom until he found the right button to make it stop. Then, he pulled his arms back under the blanket and lay there for a few seconds while his brain started working.

He was sore. Not "got rubbed off a bronc" sore, but definitely a good "had to dig out a silt-clogged ditch for six hours yesterday." His fingers felt like overcooked hot dogs, and his ribs seemed to be attached to his spine with rusty wire.

And the new guy was coming today.

That thought was enough to propel him out of bed and into the bathroom that created the bottleneck "hallway" between the kitchen/living area and his bedroom.

The shower wasn't anything fancy; it ran off the same garden hose that somehow supplied plumbing to both bunkhouses, and the hot water heater had seen better days in somebody's little RV. But it was better than scrubbing himself off in a gas station sink by a long shot. Ty scrubbed himself off by the dull yellow glow of some battery-powered Christmas lights that had been zip-tied to the top of the shower by a previous tenant.

He decided to wait until it was daylight out to shave. Some things were just better done when you could see properly.

The new guy had gotten in around midnight in either a very quiet diesel or a gas truck with valve rods shot all to hell. Ty could hear him rattling around in the other bunkhouse, probably trying to find the lights and do some unpacking before their five a.m. rendezvous.

Ty had finally gotten a chance to go into Durley and get himself a few things for the kitchen. Among the most cherished of these was a little aluminum tea kettle and a jar of vanilla-flavored instant coffee. It didn't matter how nasty it was. Having something warm in your belly made daybreak more bearable.

Having dressed for the day, Ty went outside to wait at the patio table for his new coworker. He flicked on the lights above the table and took a gander at the newcomer's truck. It was a big, square domestic model that looked to be about Ty's own age, the exact color of its flat dark paint job indeterminate in the morning twilight.

At about ten minutes in front of five, a man emerged from the other bunkhouse. He was taller than Ty, fair-haired, dressed to impress in a clean plaid pearl snap and a newish pair of Wrasslers. His belt was adorned with a modest trophy buckle, well-scratched by time out in the sand and the grit.

"Good morning," he said, waving at Ty as he approached. "I'm Skip McCoy."

"Pleasure to meet you." Ty stood up and offered his hand in greeting.

"Pleasure's mine," Skip said as he shook Ty's hand. "Do we start with morning feed?"

"Yep, at six," Ty said. "We're getting started early this morning, so I can show you around the place a little before we get going."

***

77

The door to the horse barn had an arbitrary schedule. Sometimes you could open it without any damn drama, and sometimes you couldn't. This idiosyncrasy didn't seem to coincide with any weather condition, time of day, means of closing the door the previous time, or moon phase.

"Sometimes," Ty said with a labored grunt as he put his back into it, "You just gotta show it who's boss."

"Gotcha." Skip stood back and watched, a vaguely worried look on his face. He was handsome in a corn-fed, old-fashioned kind of way. Looked like he'd play football in a sweater and a leather helmet.

The door yielded, and Ty bit down on the urge to cackle at his own victory. "There we go," he said. "So, these are mostly Linda's barrel racing horses. She rides in jackpots with 'em, but some of them work on the ranch."

Twelve expectant heads poked out of their stall grates, big eyes glinting in the green floodlight that shone from the top of the barn.

"We start feeding in here because one, it's the furthest barn from the house so we'll make the least racket, and two, because Linda likes to have all eight of her barrel horses loped and put away as soon as possible." Ty walked inside and flicked the lights on. As the big glass bars hummed to life, he started walking along stall fronts and throwing hay inside. "As you can see, I like to get it set out in the evenings. Everybody gets three, four flakes at breakfast."

"Pretty classy digs when the lights are on," Skip remarked. He strode ahead to the other end of the barn aisle and started throwing feed in on that end. "Auto waterers!"

"Yeah, but they don't work right now," Ty said. "They're supposed to have an auto-water system set up for the whole ranch, but it's been offline since before I came here."

"Got it," Skip said. "Troughs out in their pens?"

"And buckets in their stalls for when they get shut in at night," Ty said. "We'll deal with all that later. Right now, we're just getting feed in front of faces."

After the horses came the rodeo stock, and after the rodeo stock came the breeding bulls, and after the breeding bulls they fed a pen of Charolais that were subject to a contract dispute with Mr. Briggs.

"This thing's burning a lot of oil." Skip poked his head out the window to survey the black smoke that was starting to pour out from under the feed truck's hood.

"It does that," Ty said. "Miss Linda's working on the boss man about getting the engine fixed or something. It's got a nasty oil leak dripping right on the exhaust."

"Exhaust shouldn't be hot enough to burn oil like that after operating fifteen minutes," Skip said.

Ty shrugged. "If you know how to work on diesels you can be our guest," he said. "Boss man might even give you a raise for it."

Skip laughed. "I wouldn't call myself an expert," he said. "If you all would let me look under the hood for a minute when we have more light, I wouldn't mind taking a peek."

"Like I said, be my guest," Ty said. "There's more work needs doing around here than we got hands to do it."

Fortunately, the new guy's hands seemed more than capable with the workload on this operation. Ty had worked alongside so-called ranch hands whose experience with livestock was confined to the mechanical bull. Skip McCoy, on the other hand, just needed to be pointed in the general direction of the tools he needed to get the job done.

"You said you did rodeo?" Ty hefted a big plastic tub of shit and shavings into the manure wagon in the horse barn's aisle.

"Team roping, mostly," Skip said.

"Ah, gotcha," Ty said. "Bet you were a header."

"Correct-a-mundo," Skip said with a winning smile. "Ran in the sevens until my good horse died."

"Aww, that sucks," Ty said. "I'm sorry."

"He was getting up there," Skip said, shaking his head and frowning. "Won't see his like again for what I paid for him, I can tell you that."

"They call 'em once-in-a-lifetime horses for a reason," Ty said.

"Yep." Skip nodded. "Figured it was time to settle down for a little while, save a few pennies toward something with some breeding."

"Yeah, I feel you," Ty said. "Can't say I'm mad about the steady paycheck here on the ranch."

"Beats the hell out of scrambling for a jackpot every week," Skip said.

"Kinda like being your own boss out there on the circuit, though." Ty picked his pitchfork and muck tub up and moved on to the next stall.

"Yeah, kinda," Skip said with a laugh. "Nobody likes traveling through Missouri by committee."

"Nobody winds up doing much travelling when the whole crew has to decide," Ty said.

Missouri, huh? Ty took a few seconds to study Skip McCoy's face through the stall bars. He'd gotten his bell rung more than a few times when he was on the road in Missouri, so it stood to reason that his memory was less than perfect. But there was nothing about Skip that looked familiar.

But Missouri was a big place, and Ty didn't like roping cattle enough to make it his rodeo event. It stood to reason that he wouldn't remember every team roper he happened across.

***

Like most well-to-do ranch families, the Briggses liked to at least keep a symbolic separation between work life and home life. The family lived in a quaint, two-story foursquare house built of bleached red brick. Ty had yet to be invited inside, but it looked well-kept enough from what he'd glimpsed during his tri-weekly lawn maintenance sessions.

Surrounding the ranch house was what had been, at some point, a lush orchard planted with enough fruit trees to keep a family well-stocked with pies and jams the whole year round. The trees themselves were still holding on despite the deadwood and the apparent lack of water. They'd even multiplied; Ty could see young apple and plum trees duking it out in there with the giant thistles and burdock plants.

When he'd started, the prospect of "doing something about those apple trees" had been a vague threat on the horizon. No way in hell, he'd thought, was Ty ever going to have enough spare time to tidy up the tangle of plant life that surrounded the house and lawn.

But with Skip helping, it was plain to see he was going to have time for some side projects.

He was working in squares. No, circles. He had to start with a shovel and an ancient scythe, hacking and chopping at the thickest and woodiest of the weeds so he wouldn't burn out the motor on the string trimmer.

The string trimmer itself was...hang on.

"...can't do a single fucking thing around here without you..."

"Do not take that language with me!"

The shouting was muffled, and it was definitely coming from the house. Ty checked his position. A barrier of weeds some six or seven feet tall was hiding him from view.

"Lord, you made me a lot of things," Ty said under his breath as he aimed his shovel at the base of a curly dock. "But thank you for not making me heterosexu...oh shit."

Glass seemed to sound different when it was being shattered in anger. His finely-tuned skinny queer instincts told him to freeze on the spot, and he did, crouched a little so nobody would be able to spot him.

"Twenty-five years! I been waiting for that ship to come in for twenty! Five! Years!" A woman, Mrs. Briggs by the sound of her, was screaming like a mountain lion in heat. Something else made of glass broke against a wall.

"You look like you been waiting a long time for something, you dried up old bitch!" Mr. Briggs's bellow was unmistakable to Ty by now. "Why don't you go on the computer and talk to your...shit!"

So, it was definitely Mrs. Briggs who was throwing the glass. Ty cringed as he heard three rapid volleys come one after the other.

Was he going to have to intervene in this?

Shit. Ty crept closer to the house, mindful of the plants above his head and the way they were moving as he passed through. He paused when Mrs. Briggs's voice once again reached a carrying volume.

"And she has never lost this much goddamn money!" Mrs. Briggs said. "That girl works her tail off trying to keep this place running so you can go wheelin' and dealin' and doing whatever it is you do..."

"Woman, are you accusing me of..."

"I don't know what I'm accusing you of!" Mrs. Briggs said, her voice mellowing slightly from its mountain lion screech to encompass shades of a scared calf stuck in a mud wallow. "I don't see you, I don't know where it is you're going, I don't know what these deals are..."

"Because it is not your job to run my business!" Mr. Briggs said. He'd taken on a nasty, mocking tone like a big kid about to take some lunch money from a smaller one. "My money is my private property, and the way I spend it is my goddamn business!"

Ty crept closer to the house, his heart thumping in his throat. He realized that he was clutching the scythe. He swallowed hard.

"My name is on the checking account you're draining!" Mrs. Briggs said. "It is on the credit score you're ruining!"

"And it's worth nothing! Without me!" Mr. Briggs said. "Do you understand that? You and your bimbo daughter do not exist! Without! Me!"

"Then I don't know how this ranch is still running, because we been doin' it without you!" Mrs. Briggs was crying now. "I just want you home, Marshall! I just want you to be here for our family!"

Ty couldn't hear Mr. Briggs's reply to that. He waited, hunched in the grass with his weed chopper clutched in both fists, for a long while for the yelling to start up again. It was an unpleasant reminder of living at Rob's house when he was a kid, truth be told. A really unpleasant reminder.

He had to get out of here.

Slowly, carefully, Ty crept back to the edge of the orchard. He would stop every few yards, listen, plan the next move through the weeds in such a way that he disturbed as little as possible. He didn't want to find out what new kind of crazy he could unleash from Mr. Briggs if they caught him eavesdropping.

Chapter Nine

Connor winced with exertion as he twisted the end of the baling wire back around itself, going entirely by feel. There was deep, unmitigated evil in what he was doing here.

"Do you think we could rig up, like, a coffee can or something to catch the oil as it spills?" Linda had crouched down on her hands and knees to peer up underneath the big semi-tractor. If she had any idea who Connor was from the few times they'd met, she hadn't shown it yet.

"Mmm." Connor shifted around so he could properly fondle the abomination he'd just created. "A bean can, maybe, but it might be leaking too much oil." Father Andrew might not be able to take care of this one for him. He wasn't sure he could bring himself to confess it.

"Well, let's see how it works before we try anything else." Linda walked around to the cab door and opened it up.

Connor grunted and shoved himself out of the shadow of the feed truck's engine compartment. Linda started the big hay baler up, and Connor listened to see if he'd managed to get baling wire or a pie plate involved with any of the motor's working parts.

"Sounds good," Linda said.

"Yep." Connor opened the other side of the cab door and hopped inside. Linda put the truck in gear, and they rolled forward in the darkness of the early morning.

Many years ago, when Connor had first admitted to his family why he just couldn't bring himself to date any of his female classmates, his father had been full of questions. What had he done wrong? Was it possible that Connor was just a late bloomer? Was there a way to help him get over this? Was this going to get Connor hurt?

And then, after several days checking on the herds in the hills with Luis and a bottle of scotch: How was Connor going to defend himself? What did his father need to do to keep him on the high school rodeo team? How was he going to keep from getting cheated by people who wanted to mess with him?

The day Sean Dougherty realized there was a practical and strategic component to being gay was the day Sean Dougherty realized that he was pretty much okay with having a gay son. Connor had been schooled in every aspect of "fending for himself" that his father could think of: horseshoeing, carpentry, even the odd bit of HVAC and appliance repair when it was relevant to the ranch.

And automotive repair. You could not forget automotive repair. If Sean Dougherty had not been born to the Dougherty Ranch, he would have been one hell of a mechanic. His art went far beyond identifying broken parts and replacing them. He'd been a physician for machines, possessed by an instinct for tracing a single failure through an entire web of affected system components.

He was not the kind of man who would wire a pie plate up underneath an oil leak to divert the leak off the exhaust. Luis would not have been able to talk him into forgiving that kind of transgression.

But the pie plate did its job. The aging diesel truck completed its slow, unhappy journey around the feed troughs without a puff of smoke to be seen.

"God," Connor said, crouched on one knee so he could see the steady, expensive drip of golden oil down to the rubber basin they kept underneath the truck. "That is just the most wretched thing I have ever done."

"Yeah?" Ty Gibson bent down next to him, hands on his knees. "Looks about right for a Triple V repair, I'd say."

"It don't have enough duct tape on it, from what I seen around here." Connor grinned up at the wiry young cowboy.

Apparently, Ty Gibson had been working here for about a month with no help from anybody except Linda. Mrs. Briggs reportedly had to pitch in on occasion, which was a little concerning considering both Mrs. Briggs's size and Mrs. Briggs's devotion to her time in the salon.

Gibson was a good hand. Nervous, awkward despite his good looks, and self-possessed in the same manner as a barrel cactus, he was every inch your typical rodeo cowboy who'd gotten sick enough of losing to get a real job. If Linda didn't see through Connor's ruse, then Gibson probably would.

"Hey, you boys are lucky my daddy even pays for duct tape," Linda said. "If I didn't get on his case about it, you'd be trying to fix everything with packing tape from the dollar store."

Gibson's laugh at that was a little more nervous than Connor wanted to hear. "Well, we appreciate the effort," he said.

"I'm glad someone does," Linda said. "Come on. We gotta get a move on morning chores if you boys wanna both shower before church."

***

Connor's job interview for the Triple V Ranch had been both brief and unorthodox. They had checked none of his references, asked to see none of his paperwork, and given him very little indication of what his job duties were actually going to be.

Linda might have mentioned, in passing, something about 'you have to go to church on Sundays.' Given the dubious legality of the rest of the job, Connor had paid it no mind. He might have paid it a little mind had Linda specifically mentioned that he had to go to church with her.

It wasn't that he minded Baptists or minded the Baptist service. It was something new and it was an hour or two in an air-conditioned church. Besides, Linda and the ranch hands went to the late morning service, which was for young and hip people who sang and danced and hollered and referred to themselves as "Cowboys for Christ."

Connor's problem with the service was that he had to go with Linda. Linda, who had definitely met him more than once. Linda, who when she'd seen him—two big rodeos in Las Vegas and a stock sale in Oklahoma City—had only seen him in his Sunday best.

Now, Linda was barely recognizable as Linda in her calf-length skirt and her nice blue blouse and cardigan with her hair piled high on her head. She wore tasteful makeup and a pair of sensible flats, and she spoke softly while she introduced Ty and Connor to her congregation. She sang enthusiastically—if not well—she shouted praise and affirmation back at the preacher when it was due, and she whispered instructions to Connor when it was plain he was looking for a cue to sit, stand, or kneel.

She had to know. She had to have figured it out. There was no way she was getting this far and buying Connor's act.

But here she was, trotting him up to her pastor and introducing him as Skip McCoy.

"Nice to meet you, Skip!" The pastor was a good-looking young gentleman with bright red hair and feet that never stopped moving. "I hope you'll find a warm welcome here in Grass Springs."

"It's a great little town," Connor said. "Looks like a bunch of the folks here are cattlemen?"

"A lot of the folks at our late service come from the feedlots and ranches around town," the pastor said. "It's a great crowd of the hardest-working young people I've ever met!"

He must have been introduced to Ty already. Ty had made a beeline for the donuts and coffee table as soon as the service had let out, and he was studying his paper plate closely while a young red-haired girl tried to talk to him.

"Skip's from Omaha, too!" Linda said. Was that a naive smile on her face or a shit-eating grin?

"Oh, yeah?" the pastor said. "Small world! I went to Falcon Ridge, class of '08."

Connor panicked. "Cool," he said. He had no idea what the high schools in Omaha were called. He hadn't actually expected to, you know, meet anyone from one of the biggest cities on the Plains. "I was, uh, homeschooled," he said, nodding sagely like his heart rate wasn't comparable to a rabbit's.

"I keep meeting more and more people out here who were homeschooled," the pastor said. "It just seems to work out better for some folks out in cattle country."

"It certainly does," Connor said, forcing a smile. Linda was just letting him walk into this, smiling as sweet as cherry pie. No way in hell was he actually getting away with this.

Before the pastor could tug any more on the strings composing Connor's web of lies, a young couple with several small children caught his attention. Connor did his best to dissolve entirely as he made his way across the church lobby to the line for coffee and donuts.

"Hey, no fair." Gibson appeared at his elbow. "He only held you captive for a couple minutes."

"He's from Omaha too," Connor said. "He knows I got just about nothing to talk about."

Gibson laughed. "That won't stop him."

"I'll keep that in mind," Connor said. "How's the coffee?"

"Not bad," Gibson said. Then, in a lower voice: "Truth be told, I'm surprised these folks drink coffee."

"I think that's Mormons," Connor said. "But I could be wrong."

"You a church-going man?" Gibson said.

"Depends on who's cooking at the barbecue afterward," Connor said. He realized as he was speaking that rodeo life was somewhat incompatible with having a regular church. "Uh, you?"

Gibson shrugged. "I don't mind the music or the company," he said. "But…" He looked around and shook his head. "Can't say I'm much of a believer."

"Kind of unusual in a cowboy," Connor said.

90

"Yeah, I've noticed." Gibson had a dry, flat smile that only appeared for a moment before his face returned to its usual watchful scowl. "I dunno. These people might just have a convert if they keep it up with the free breakfast."

"Catholics will give you a full brunch spread," Connor said. "Not that I'm biased."

"Shit, if there's breakfast here and brunch at the Catholic church, imagine what they got down at the Unitarian place," Gibson said. "I think it might be time for some spiritual growth in my life."

***

After church, Miss Linda had been generous enough to swing by the hardware store and pay for enough cleaning supplies, plywood, drain caulk, zip ties, and white paint to make Connor's bunkhouse habitable.

He supposed it was a good thing that the walls were made of particle board instead of drywall. Drywall would have made this situation more complex than it needed to be.

"What the fuck was that?" Gibson's voice came from the dinette area that occupied the less-decrepit half of the refurbished train car.

"That was supposed to be the floor." Connor tossed a piece of rotting particle board out of the bathroom. "Some dipshit didn't notice that the shower pan was flooding the bathroom every time he used it."

"Jesus," Gibson said, looking around the dimly-lit rooms. "This bunkhouse is even more of a dump than mine."

"You snooze, you lose, I guess." Connor reached down to grab some broken-off bits of plywood that

91

still remained screwed to the floor framing. At least that hadn't been rotted by the previous tenant's abuse.

"Cattle, auto repair, construction." Gibson chuckled. "You're a jack of all trades, Mr. McCoy."

"We aren't going to talk about what I did to that poor truck," Connor said.

"Hell, you did better than anybody else was gonna." A metallic pop and hiss indicated that he'd opened a beer. "Old Man Briggs doesn't seem to want to throw money at anything worthwhile. Lucky you didn't have to pay for your own supplies to fix this rat trap."

"Yeah?" Connor stood up and turned around. "I kinda figured from the interview that things were kind of lean around here."

Gibson offered him the beer; Connor took it.

"Yep, money is tight," Gibson said. "Can't figure out why, either. Not that it's any of my business."

"Their money's your salary," Connor said.

"Yep." He took another can of beer from his pocket and opened it. "And there's times when you kinda run out of rope to get the job done, know what I'm saying?"

"I think I'm starting to get a general understanding," Connor said, wobbling a piece of warped particle board that he'd leaned against the wall. "But if he's not spending his money on the ranch, what the hell is he spending it on?"

"Goes to Vegas and loses big, is the impression I get," Gibson said. He took a long drink of his beer and sighed. "Fights with his wife, spends more money sending her to the beauty parlor or the beach or wherever. And then of course he's got to be the big man of the house, so no business gets done without his say-so."

Connor nodded. "But if he's not home to give his say-so…"

Gibson raised his beer can to him. That dry, thin smile glimmered on his face for a moment.

"Oh, for fuck's sake." Connor shook his head and took a long drink of his own beer. "We're still getting paid, though?"

"As far as I know," Gibson said. "Miss Linda's a nice enough girl, but I'm not nearly sweet enough on her to work for free."

Connor was certain his tinny laugh gave away a lot more than he wanted to. "Don't she have some kind of boyfriend?" he said.

"More like a fiancé," Gibson said. "I haven't seen a girl that love struck since I was in the seventh grade."

"Is that so?" Connor took a drink of his beer. He could feel his palms starting to get clammy.

"Yeah, it's a whole long story." Gibson raised his eyebrows and shook his head. "But her daddy hates his guts, and I think he'll be dead in the ground before he lets the poor sap take her hand."

"What in the hell?" Connor said. "What year is it?"

"I just think he's a control freak," Gibson said. "The father, that is. She talks about her fiancé like he's the best thing since sliced bread."

"Well isn't that sweet?" Connor said.

Gibson rolled his eyes. "If you say so, man," he said. "I could never tie myself down to just one person. I've seen that shit go sour so many times out on the circuit."

"Well, if you're trying to date on the rodeo circuit, I imagine so," Connor said.

"Yeah?" Gibson laughed, his eyes darting to the side. "I don't see you talking to no girlfriend."

Connor gave him the flat, businesslike smile he'd perfected over the years. "Nah," he said. "I got bad luck with women."

"I'll drink to that," Gibson said. For some reason, he looked about as nervous as Connor was currently feeling.

Chapter Ten

"No, it was a nice little outfit." His mom's voice was harsh from cigarette smoke, but she was both calm and lucid this afternoon. "We built a little loft up top, and there was Wi-Fi from the burger place next door, so Harry brought me a laptop and we could stream movies and stuff."

"Right," Ty said, scanning the wide array of boxed macaroni products in front of him. "But then it caught on fire."

"Oh, for fuck's sake, Tyler," his mom said. "It wasn't anybody's fault!"

"Yeah, I'm sure it wasn't," Ty said. He found a five-for-two-dollars deal and started grabbing boxes of macaroni off the shelf. "I'm glad you and Rocky weren't in there when it happened is all."

"Rocky would have woken me up," his mom said. "Wouldn't you, baby? You're a good boy!"

Ty smiled. Even if she was smoking pot and living in storage units, it was good to hear that his mom was at least happy. It could be a lot worse. Shit, it frequently was a lot worse.

"So, you have your own house at the ranch," his mom said. "Did I hear that right?"

The welling of goodwill in Ty's heart stopped as it occurred to him that she might consider him her next source of housing. "It's a little fifth-wheel type thing," he said. "Moldy as shit. My coworker had to tear out half the floor in his because the last tenant fucked up the bathroom."

"You can fix it up, though," his mom said. "You've always been good at that kind of thing."

"Not as good as this guy," Ty said. "He's like a fucking robot. Fixes the feed truck. Fixes the pump on the auto-waterers. Fixes the bathroom. Pressure washes the stock trailers. He even goes to church and likes it."

"Sounds like a prick," his mom said.

"Yeah, I wish." Ty pushed his cart down the aisle to the mashed potato flakes. Sale or no sale, club card discount or no club card discount, he would accept no substitute. He was a grown man and a taxpayer, and he was stuffing his face with Idaho Maid Garlic and Butter Flavor tonight.

"Oh, no, baby, do you have a crush?" His mom was laughing. "You gotta be careful with these damn cowboys, Tyler."

"Yeah, I know," Ty said. "I don't got time for any of that shit right now, though."

"I'm sure you don't," his mom said, her voice gently mocking.

"Come on, Ma," Ty said. The next aisle was dangerous. The next aisle could eat half his paycheck if the stars aligned and he wasn't careful.

"I'm just giving you shit, baby!" She laughed. "Okay, I gotta run, Jason's here."

"Tell him hi from me," Ty said.

"I will. Love you, baby!"

"Love you, too, Mom." Ty hung up the phone and turned his grocery cart around the corner.

He did not need any more books. He'd just wired his mom most of the money he had in the world, and he did not need any more books. The crate he'd gotten last year was still only half-read, and his current employers were so bug shit crazy there was no telling how badly he was going to need that seven or fourteen or fifty-six dollars.

But it didn't cost anything to read the backs, did it?

"Space crusaders, huh?" Linda's voice seemed to come out of nowhere.

Ty jumped a full foot in the air and made a less-than-dignified sound. "Jesus!"

"Sorry." Linda laughed and picked up the book he'd dropped in his shock. "Hmm." She squinted at the back cover. "A secret investigation into the dark underbelly of a galaxy torn by eternal war, huh?"

"It's entertainment," Ty said.

"I didn't have you pinned as a spaceships and lasers kind of guy," Linda said.

Ty shrugged. "I got a milk crate full of books at a thrift store for two bucks," he said. "I kinda got hooked."

"Mmm." Linda flipped the book over. She took in the sweating, muscle-bound figure of Colonel Creed on the front cover and raised an eyebrow at Ty. "Looks like he's got a big, uh, gun," she said.

"Give me that." Ty felt a flush in his cheeks as he snatched the book out of her hands.

"I'm just messing with you, Gibson," Linda said, eyeing the rest of the goodies in Ty's cart. "Jesus. We have got to get you guys a fridge out there."

"Yeah?" Ty said. "You reckon maybe that McCoy's an electrician, too?"

Linda's smile got wider and wilier. She let out a slow, deliberate laugh. "Oh, good old Skip McCoy," she said, dropping the syllables of his name out of her mouth like they were a particularly funny joke. "He's got all kinds of tricks up his sleeve, doesn't he?"

"Not that I'm, uh, complaining," Ty said, looking a little sideways at Linda.

Linda snorted. "I'm sure you're not!" she said. "Just remember what I said about my dad. I'm not condoning his behavior, but..."

"Wait, what?" Ty said.

"Oh, he hasn't let on about it?" Linda's eyes got big. She scanned the aisle up and down and lowered her voice. "I had kind of figured you'd put the word out to him about the job. You all kind of know each other, don't you?"

"Uhh." Ty blinked a couple of times, his head tilted to one side like a dog listening for a sound.

And then it hit him. "Ohhhh," he said. "Wait, what?"

"Yeah." Linda was grinning.

"Are you sure?" Ty said. "I mean, a lot of straight guys talk a certain way, or..."

"No, I know," Linda said. "For sure. Trust me. I know a lot more about Skip McCoy than you might think." There was still something inside-joke funny about the way she said his name.

"Huh." Ty stood there for a second processing that bit of information. "Is there something you're not telling me?"

"Could be," Linda said. "But it seems to me like you like a little bit of mystery." She winked and turned around.

Ty sighed as he picked up the Creed's Crusaders book and put it back on the shelf. He was just gonna have to wait and see how much he needed that seven dollars in the next few weeks.

He'd be putting the potato flakes back over his own dead body, though.

***

Now, Linda had definitely been correct about one thing: all the gay dudes on the rodeo circuit more or less knew one another or knew one another through friends. It was entirely possible that word had spread through the grapevine that Ty Gibson had found a good gig on the Triple V Ranch with room for more.

But it was equally possible that Linda was, knowingly or unknowingly, completely full of shit. There were plenty of soft-spoken straight men out there, even on ranches and rodeo circuits.

And so, what if Skip McCoy was gay? Ty wasn't remotely in the same league as he was. With his square jaw, his broad chest, and his long legs, Skip McCoy was barely playing the same sport. Not only would he probably turn Ty down, but he'd probably turn Ty down in such a smooth and caring way that Ty wouldn't even have the luxury of hating him for it.

"You doing okay in there?" Skip had paused in front of the stall door, a tub of shit balanced on one shoulder.

Ty realized he'd been scraping at the same pee spot for about...well, let's not pay too much attention to how long. He jumped like he'd been slapped.

"Oh! Yeah," Ty said. "I'm just kind of tired."

"Can't blame you," Skip said. "Sounds to me like you been doing the work of two or three men out here."

"I don't know about three," Ty said. "But I tell you what, there's been more than one occasion where they sure could have used two of me around here."

Skip laughed and dumped the bucket in the big wagon. "I kind of feel bad for waiting as long as I did to apply," he said. "You should've sent out some kind of S.O.S. smoke signal."

"Boss man wouldn't have let me have the time," Ty said. He frowned as a thought occurred to him. "Say," he said. "How did you come to hear about this job, anyway?"

For a second, Skip McCoy froze. Ty saw his face go blank before he plastered a wide, winning smile on it. "Oh, you know how people on the rodeo circuit like to yap," he said. "Couldn't tell you for the life of me who in particular told me you all were looking for an extra hand."

Ty laughed. "Yeah, everyone kind of starts to sound the same after a little while," he said. Maybe Linda had assumed correctly after all.

"How about you?" Skip said.

"How'd I hear about this place?"

"Yeah." He was leaning against the stall doorway now, the muck bucket dangling from one brawny arm. Beneath the open collar of his shirt you could see a thin trail of sweat through the grime on his skin, making its way from his throat past the ridge of his collarbone.

"I was sleeping in this gas station's parking lot," Ty said. "I...I had a shitty night at the rodeo, my

100

money was gone, and the girl working there felt sorry for me, so she told me about someone she knew who was looking for a ranch hand."

"Did they spend much time on the interview?" Skip said.

Ty shook his head. "Shit, I went to what I thought was my interview and Mr. Briggs just hired me without a single question," he said. "It was the damnedest thing."

"You, too, huh?" Skip thinned his mouth for a second. "This place gets weirder and weirder by the second, I swear to God."

"Yeah, no kidding." Ty nodded and went to go pick horse apples out of a corner.

I know a lot more about Skip McCoy than you might think. Linda's voice kept echoing in his thoughts as he worked. She never said that they knew each other. It was entirely possible that he'd just gotten himself a reputation in certain circles, circles that Ty didn't run in since he was neither a team roper nor a barrel racer.

He was pulled from his thoughts by the sound of tires skidding on gravel outside the barn. Ty could hear the muffled sound of angry voices, which unmuffled itself shortly after the vehicle came to a halt.

In the other stall, Skip sighed. "Not this shit again," he said in a low voice.

"...no idea how much I have sacrificed for you!" Linda was either currently crying or had been recently. "If you would pay attention to anything but your..."

"You have no right to talk about sacrifice to me, young lady!" Her father's voice was raised so high it was cracking. "You know, that's all you and your mother do is take, take, take! I will never see a dime back..."

The car door slammed, and Mr. Briggs's shouting once again sounded like it was coming from under water.

Ty looked at Skip, and Skip stared back at him with his eyes bugging out. They stood frozen in place while the truck's engine roared and took off back down the driveway. The angry jingle of Linda's boots on the gravel grew steadily louder as she came into the barn.

"Get out."

He heard her voice before he saw her silhouette, burnt black against the bright square of daylight created by the barn door. Her hair was loose and messy, twisting around her head like smoke.

"Both of you," she said, her voice quiet and unsteady. "Take the afternoon off. You're finished. Get out."

"Are we fired?" Ty said, cursing himself even as he spoke for being less than sensitive.

"You're not fired, Gibson," Linda said. "Neither one of you. Just get out."

"Yes, ma'am," Ty said. He hefted his pitchfork and his half-filled shit bucket and made for the entrance of the stall.

"I will put the shit away!" The more words she was compelled to speak, the thinner and creakier Linda's voice got. "Just. Get out."

"C'mon, Gibson," Skip said. "Don't make her chase us."

"Do not start with me, McCoy." Linda walked into his stall and grabbed the pitchfork from him. "Go take your wise ass back to the bunkhouse and figure out exactly what it takes to shut you up for an evening, huh?"

"Yes, ma'am," Skip said.

Ty rolled his eyes and waited at the barn door for Skip to catch up to him. A whole lot of good all that charm and handsomeness was doing him right now, huh?

"Jackass," Ty muttered as Skip passed him by.

"Rather be a jackass than a horse's ass," Skip said.

"You can be both if you don't stop talking," Ty said. "Let's get out of here. I got a twelve pack of Gold Lite and there's a county reservoir about two miles on down the road."

"Nah, man," Skip said. "I ain't leaving these folks to their own devices with Big Daddy in a mood like this. I seen this movie before."

"Yeah, and you're not the goddamn starring actor!" Ty stopped in front of Skip, feeling very much like a corgi about to have a disagreement with a herd bull. "Trust me on this, McCoy. Linda can take care of herself. When her daddy snaps, it's gonna be our hides for sale outside a gas station!"

Skip's face twisted like he'd just taken a drink from the spittoon bottle. "Some kinda man you are," he said.

"It's not about being a man," Ty said. "It's about being smart enough to remember that no good deed goes unpunished in this..."

"No good deed, huh?" Skip said, his face darkening with anger. "You mean like giving a job to some piece of shit bronc rider who can't stay on a horse long enough to win a motel bill?"

"Hey, fuck you," Ty said. "I've been pulling three times my weight around here..."

"I thought I told you motherfuckers to leave!" Linda was standing in the barn door with tears streaking her mascara. "I don't care where you go! Just get!"

When she looked like that, there was no need to tell them twice. Skip and Ty booked it in their respective separate directions, shoulders hunched and eyes on the ground.

Chapter Eleven

Connor's head pounded with every step he took across the barnyard. On the plus side, he'd been much too exhausted last night to dip too deep into the flavored disinfectant he was obliged to drink as part of his disguise. On the minus side, he'd flopped down on his lumpy futon mattress without chugging the mason jar of water he was obliged to drink as part of being over twenty-three years old.

Ty Gibson's truck was back in its spot by the bunkhouses. For a couple seconds, Connor had thought about waking him up for morning feed. But no good deed goes unpunished, right?

Connor didn't mind doing morning feed by himself. It wasn't like they were running a feedlot operation, here, and Connor liked to have some solitude in the early morning anyway.

He got the feed truck started and popped the hood. The previous day's oil leak had deposited probably half a quart in the coffee can under the pie plate. Connor filled the coffee can to the line from the new jug, grabbed the funnel, and went about filling the engine back up.

This fucking place.

From the truck barn, it was about a hundred yards to the hay barn. Connor, not being a dumbass bronc rider who couldn't think five seconds into the future, had already stacked enough bales for the morning in a precarious position at the truck edge of the stack. Loading up was just a matter of pulling the truck up, swinging up the horizontal boards that held the haystack's truck-side edge straight, and delivering a few well-placed kicks. The bales didn't fall on the

105

truck terribly neatly, but they were all about four hours from being cow shit anyway.

He ignored the smell of mold that rose up out of the haystack while he was kicking. That was a problem for someone who signed the....

Had he left that light on?

Connor stood up straight and blinked a couple of times at the horse barn. He couldn't remember whether or not the tack room's window had been glowing in the pre-dawn twilight when he'd come out here.

His fists clenched reflexively when he thought of that electrical usage versus his paycheck, and in that moment, he knew his father's spirit was with him.

Or maybe that was just a wave of toxic shock from all the formaldehyde his liver was pumping into his blood. Either way. Connor jumped down from the haystack to the truck, and from the truck bed to the ground, and made his way across the barnyard.

His hackles started rising when he saw that the door was opened already - not the sensible, patient way, but just kind of ripped off the sliding track on one end with its corner resting in the gravel.

Reflexively, he reached for the holster that accompanied him always when he was working on his own ranch. He cringed when his empty hand reminded him that his $650 handgun didn't really go with his 'dirt poor ranch hand' persona.

He listened at the door for a second before slipping in. Whoever was inside the barn wasn't making much of a racket, which was probably a good thing. Unless someone had already broken in and stolen a bunch of shit.

Connor barely dared to breathe as he crept forward toward the yellow glow of the tack room's doorway. He tried to ignore the visions milling around in the back of his mind, of tweaked-out burglars and cartel musclemen desperate for cash and armed to the teeth.

There was really no way to prepare himself for what was actually waiting for him inside the door.

It was the mess, actually, that caught his eye first. Saddles and saddle blankets were thrown off their stands, piled up against walls in a careless tangle that made Connor's eye twitch. The whole medicine shelf had been cleared off; he could see iodine leaking out from the bottom of the pile that had fallen at one end.

If Mr. Briggs hadn't groaned and rolled over, Connor might never have noticed him.

"What the fuck!" Connor said, jumping so high he damn near hit his head on the door lintel. "Mr. Briggs?"

"Ngh?" Mr. Briggs was curled up on the floor, in front of some cabinets that had been flung open and gutted of all the medicine and equipment they contained. He was using a roll of bandage padding for a pillow, and he'd covered himself with an ancient and foul-smelling yellow slicker.

"Mr. Briggs," Connor said. "Are you okay?"

It took a couple seconds for Mr. Briggs's eyes to focus on Connor. "McCoy," he said. "What the hell are you doing here?"

"It's time for morning feed, sir," Connor said. "I...uh...I saw there was a light on in here."

"It's none o' your business what lights I leave on," Mr. Briggs said. Slowly, painfully, he picked himself up into a more or less standing position.

Every single one of Connor's instincts was telling him to book it, but he stayed put. It was like watching an anvil cloud spin slowly overhead, waiting for it to either drop a twister down or break up and blow away.

Mr. Briggs was looking around the destroyed tack room, frowning and nodding. After a couple of very tense minutes, he grunted and started searching through his pockets.

"I got some business to take care of in town," he said. His voice was calm and quiet, and he would not meet Connor's eyes. "I want this cleaned up before you do another goddamn thing around this place, you hear?"

"Yes, sir," Connor said.

Mr. Briggs walked up to Connor and thrust a wad of cash in his face. "We never had this conversation," he said. "There was never a light on in this barn. You never stepped foot in this tack room, and when I return from town you will still have a job at this facility. Do we have an understanding, Mr. McCoy?"

Connor took the cash and stuffed it in his pocket. "Yes, sir," he said.

***

All told, there was a sum of $795 in the wad that Mr. Briggs had given Connor. Most of it was in tens and twenties, with a couple of fifties in there and a flaky sheaf of fives.

It felt strangely heavy in Connor's back pocket, like it had been cursed. Connor kept reaching into his back pocket to check on it as he cleaned up Mr. Briggs's mess. The more he cleaned, the clearer it was to Connor what the purpose was behind the midnight destruction: he'd been looking for something, and he'd wanted it badly.

Connor was just finishing up morning feed when Linda's truck came rolling down the driveway, containing a bundle of sunglasses and dark hair and rodeo sweatshirt that had Linda inside it somewhere. She parked in front of the barn and sat on her hood, drinking coffee out of a gas station cup while she waited for Connor to put the truck away.

"Where's Gibson?" she said.

"He was sick this morning," Connor said. "I fed by myself."

"Took you a while." Linda took a noisy slurp on the coffee cup that necessitated tipping her chin skyward.

"I'm not feeling so hot myself," Connor said.

"Mmm." Linda got off her hood. "Go get my horses tacked up, starting with Banjo. Tie 'em to the inside of the arena fence when you're done."

"Yes, ma'am," Connor said.

"When you're done with that I'm gonna need you to get my trailer completely cleaned out and ready to go." Linda opened her driver's side door and hopped in. "That should take you a couple hours, and then I'm gonna need you to help me hose my horses off. We're taking off tonight and we oughta be back Tuesday."

"Tuesday?" Connor said. "You're...hold on, what's going…"

109

"There's a five grand jackpot in Torrington," Linda said, putting her truck in gear. "And I got myself a hot date."

She took off toward the bunkhouse just enough to spit some gravel out from underneath the truck's rear wheels. Somehow, that wad of cash in Connor's back pocket felt heavier than it had when Linda had shown up.

***

"Well don't give it *back*," Greg said. "You'll blow your cover!"

"Greg, you don't need to whisper," Connor said. "She can't hear you."

"Right," Greg said.

"No, I think she needs that money," Connor said. He was crouched in the back of Linda's horse trailer, peeking out the slats to make sure the coast was clear while he reconnoitered with his brother. "That's my point! The old man was looking for something in that tack room."

"For seven hundred bucks?"

"Look, Greg, I think you were right," Connor said. "That girl is definitely hiding something about what her family's up to."

"Why would someone like Mr. Briggs steal seven hundred..."

"That's what we've got to find out," Connor said. "I know the old man fights with Linda all the time, and I've heard it getting nasty more than once."

"Then, you and me oughta..."

110

"No, man, I think it's more complicated than that," Connor said. He dropped his voice even lower. "See, I've been thinking."

"Yeah?"

"Greg. Buddy." Connor pinched the bridge of his nose. "You don't need to whisper."

"Sorry," Greg said.

"No, but I was thinking," Connor said. "We gotta be careful with this, man. I'm starting to think Mr. Briggs is in, uh, some pretty deep financial shit."

"Oh, yeah?" Greg said.

"I mean, he's running this business into the fucking ground, man. He's not in his right mind." Like a periscope operator checking the surface, Connor rose up to peer out of the trailer slats. The coast was clear: Gibson was loping horses around the arena, and Linda was bathing the ones he'd already worked. "I don't know if he's drinking, or on drugs, or something worse, but we have to tread really cautiously here."

"You don't think he's in with a dealer or something?" Greg said.

"He might be," Connor said. "But we have to be super, super careful about how we find out."

"Maybe she'll tell me when she meets me in Torrington," Greg said.

"Why is she going all the fucking way to Torrington?" Connor said.

"Beats me," Greg said. "Maybe she just needs a change of scenery."

"Or maybe she needs a bunch of money in a hurry," Connor said. "See what you can find out from her. It's just going to be me and this Gibson kid here watching the place over the weekend."

"Be careful," Greg said.

"You don't have to tell me twice," Connor said. "I'll talk to you later. She's gonna start to get suspicious."

"Okay," Greg said. "I'll tell you as soon as I find out anything from her."

***

As soon as Connor came over to the wash rack, Linda abandoned the hose and the horse to him. With her back slumped and an expression on her face like somebody had died, she went to go haul saddles over to the horse trailer.

That wad of cash was not getting any lighter in Connor's pocket.

Instead of watching Linda, Connor turned his attention to the man loping her horses out in the arena. He might not have been much of a bronc rider, but Ty Gibson was elegant in the saddle and gentle with the reins. It was just nice watching him move, watching the relaxed focus on his face as he made circle after circle after circle around the sandy ring.

Truth be told, Connor didn't really know what to make of his new coworker and neighbor. He was friendly enough, but that shady rodeo cowboy attitude wasn't Connor's favorite thing to deal with.

Or maybe Gibson, too, had caught on to the real identity of Skip McCoy. That was always a distinct possibility.

There was a third possibility, too, and remote as it was, Connor couldn't quite keep himself from

112

wondering about what would happen if Gibson was watching him the same way he was watching Gibson. He caught himself looking for clues in Gibson's mannerisms, hoping childishly that he knew the exact tells and clues that would give Gibson away.

From there, if he wasn't careful, his imagination could run wild. It was better not to indulge those kinds of thoughts while he was trying to get his work done alongside that man.

All told, Linda was taking five of her eight horses to the jackpot in Torrington. In addition to their saddles and bridles and boots and blankets and rhinestone-covered odds and ends, she brought along enough hay, water and premium sweet feed to sustain her whole string through the road trip as well as the weekend of the jackpot.

She left as soon as she'd loaded the horses and double-checked that her brake lights were working. Connor and Ty watched from the top of the haystack as her rig went speeding down the driveway, leaving a plume of red dirt behind her.

"You'd think there would have been more fighting today," Gibson said. Stripped down to his undershirt with his hat tilted back on his head, he was particularly hard not to think about.

"Yeah?" Connor said. "Is it always this...uh..."

"Intense?" Gibson said.

"Yeah," Connor said.

"More or less," Gibson said. "You should hear the old man when him and the missus go at it. This daddy-daughter squabbling is nothing compared to that shit show."

"Huh," Connor said.

"I don't know how long this gig's gonna last, man," Gibson said. "Sounds to me like this girl's been trying to float the place winning money on barrel jackpots."

"You think so?" Connor raised his eyebrows, scanning the barnyard below him. "More power to her, I guess, if she can win."

"If she can win," Gibson said. "You know what it's like, gambling on your entry fees."

Connor's laugh came out a lot more nervous than he'd like it to sound. It occurred to him that he had not, in fact, ever really needed to make his entry fee back.

Gibson was giving him one of those looks he didn't quite know how to read, and it made a blush creep up his neck. "Yeah," he said. "I prefer a steady paycheck."

"Then you might not wanna hang around here much longer," Gibson said. "Me, I'm hoping to God that Miss Linda wins big out there."

"You and me both," Connor said. "She deserves something nice to happen to her."

Chapter Twelve

At a certain point in these dreams, Ty became aware that he was dreaming. Sometimes it made it a little less terrifying to drive his truck up a near-vertical road that kept getting narrower and narrower. It never got him to wake up, though. He just had to keep climbing and climbing, foot jammed down on the accelerator the whole way up, spiraling up a red mesa he only ever saw when he was asleep.

The horses were a new feature. The horses...

Ty sat up suddenly in his bed, tangled in his blanket and not sure why he'd woken up in such a terror. No, he was sure, those were hooves on the gravel outside his bunkhouse.

"Gibson!" Skip's voice accompanied a fist pounding hard on his front door. "We got loose stock all over the damn place! Mrs. Briggs is having a fucking meltdown!"

Ty was already awake with his jeans on. "I'm coming!" he said. One boot found its way onto his foot, then the other.

"Shit," Skip said. "You got a halter or something in there with you?"

"In my truck, probably," Ty said. He burst out the front door and almost collided headlong with Skip.

"Shit, you are awake," he said.

As he hustled to his truck, a few things occurred to Ty. Number one, it was nearly pitch black under the new moon. Two, there were a number of horses and cattle grazing on the crinkly grass in front of his bunkhouse. Three, he could hear a familiar voice screeching in the barnyard.

The dome light came on as Ty flung his truck door open, illuminating a scrambled mess of the belongings he hadn't seen fit to move into his bunkhouse. After a little searching, he managed to come up with a rope halter and two flat nylon halters, only one of which had a lead rope attached.

"Here," he said, slamming the door and turning around to find Skip. Skip was wandering over to him, looking and walking like a man who'd just been punched hard for no discernible reason.

"What in the fuck is happening, Gibson?" he said.

"Hell, if I know," Ty said. He squinted over in the vague direction of Mrs. Briggs's voice. "Shit, that's Blue!"

He tossed the other two halters at Skip and walked over to his horse with the rope one. It didn't have a lead, but it did have a little nubbin on the end he could use to get Blue over to a hitching rack.

"Easy, boy," Ty said. "Don't screw me over right now."

Blue picked his head up and took a few steps away from Ty, his ears pricked in a way that made Ty's stomach sink. But he let Ty catch him, and Ty hustled him on over to the horse barn.

"Go back to bed, boys!" Mrs. Briggs's voice came from over by the rough stock pens. "We're closing the ranch! Everything is over!"

Ty stuck Blue in a stall while he went and got his tack out. What he was dealing with here was a matter of priorities, and loose stock was always priority number one.

Apparently, Skip didn't feel the same way. Ty could hear his voice out there, too quiet to make out clearly.

"Well, you tell that to these goddamn debt collectors!" Mrs. Briggs was sobbing now, her voice high-pitched and broken. "At my door in the middle of the night, threatening me in my home..."

"Woman, who gave you the right to air out all our dirty laundry to the goddamn help?" Mr. Briggs slammed the door so loud it made Ty cringe all the way over in the horse barn.

Ty shook his head as he pulled his latigo tight. Loose stock was priority number one, which was precisely what Mr. Briggs was screaming at Skip. Ty got his horse bridled and out of the stall, swung himself on his back, and hauled ass back to the bunkhouse.

"Come on, Skip!" He waved his arms as he hollered toward the barnyard. "We gotta keep these horses off the septic system!"

But there was no reply from the barnyard, only incoherent yelling from all three combatants in this shit show. Ty heaved a sigh and started making a wide loop around the back of the bunkhouses.

It was easy to get the stock moved away from the whole living and parking area. The grass there wasn't good, there were spooky houses and generators and hoses lying around, and they knew there was a hay barn a little closer to where they'd come from.

Once they found the hay barn, though, the shit show began. Every cow, steer, horse, bull, and goat on the property had been turned loose, and they were not getting along like they do in the cartoons.

Ty wasn't dumb enough to try and do this by himself. He galloped over to the stock pens, fuming over the sheer stupidity of this entire situation. What the hell did Skip think he was going to do about this situation? He didn't know either of the Briggs well enough to do anything but escalate whatever bullshit was happening over there.

"Skip, what the hell is going on?" Ty had to yell at the top of his lungs to cut over the yelling in the barnyard. "Every head of cattle on this place is ransacking that damn hay barn!"

It worked. All three combatants turned to face Ty, wide-eyed like raccoons in the glare of a sodium lamp.

"Holy shit," Ty said. He'd just registered the fresh, bleeding bruise on Skip McCoy's face. "What just..."

"It was just a misunderstanding," Skip said. "Mr. Briggs was just about to help us get the stock back in." He gave Mr. Briggs a long sideways look.

For a split second, it looked like their boss was going to explode again. But then he took a sharp, deep breath and nodded. "That seems like it's for the best, don't it?" he said.

***

Herding horses was nothing like herding cattle, and herding both at the same time was nothing like a job that Ty wanted to do twice. He was out there with Skip and Mr. Briggs for the better part of two hours, cutting and sorting and herding and penning. In the feeble light of the moon and the floodlights, it was hard to tell one type of critter from another.

Eventually, they reached a point where the different stock pens more or less contained the stock they were supposed to contain. Mr. Briggs was slumping in his saddle, exhausted by the effort of keeping up with one of Linda's horses for three hours.

"Good work, gentlemen," he said before dismounting and handing his reins to Ty. "I think I'll handle morning feed. I need to assess the damage done in the hay barn and how much it's going to cost to fix everything that happened."

"Thank you, sir," Ty said. He got off his own horse and started leading both animals back to the horse barn.

Skip followed, grim-faced and sitting tall in his saddle. He said nothing until he'd dismounted, unsaddled his horse, and followed Ty into Linda's tack room.

And then he set his saddle on its rack, turned around, looked Ty in the eye, and said, "That crazy son of a bitch is going to get this whole place burned down if he don't start listening to his wife and his kid."

"Did he punch you?" Ty said.

"Backhanded me, actually," Skip said. "Which I did not tell you about, if anybody asks."

"Jesus Christ," Ty said. "You know, you can press charges for..."

"Look, Gibson," Skip said. "I don't know who this guy has been borrowing money from, what he's been spending it on, or what kind of bullshit these debt collectors are willing to do in order to get it back." He rested one hand on the feed counter, suddenly looking very tired. "I think it's in both of our best interests not to piss these people off or make any more of a mess of this situation."

"Oh yeah?" Ty said. "Well, pardon me for being flaky, but I'm not sticking around and waiting for my boss to take me out back and beat my ass." He hung his bridle on its hook and walked out of the tack room.

"What about Linda's ass?" Skip said.

"What about it?" Ty said. "Nobody's making her come home from Torrington, Skip. She's a grown woman, and at a certain point you gotta let adults make decisions for themselves."

"You don't have any idea what she's going through," Skip said, storming out of the tack room behind him. "If you were in her shoes..."

Ty whirled around to stop Skip in his tracks. "I been in her shoes, Mr. McCoy," he said, looking him in the eye. "Okay? I watched my mom go through this cycle for eighteen damn years, and I'm still watching her go through it to this day. You think you're the damn magician who can make everybody see the light and confess all their sins and go home?"

Skip didn't respond to that. He seemed to deflate a little as he took a step back from Ty.

"You cannot just butt into these people's business like that," Ty said. "I guaran-goddamn-tee you, after that bruise fades and your pride heals, that woman is going to be facing the consequences of you getting involved in her business." His fists were clenched at his sides.

"What the hell was I supposed to do, Gibson?" Skip said. "What kind of man sees that..."

"It's not about you being a man," Ty said. "When you got a situation like that on your hands, you either calm it down or stay the hell away. Like you said, let's try not to make the situation worse or piss these people off any more than they already are." He hung his bridle on the hook and walked out of the tack room.

"I don't see how walking off the job is going to not make the situation worse," Skip said. "Without us around, Linda can't get away…"

"Yes, she can," Ty said. "It's a choice you gotta make for yourself in a situation like this. It's not a damn picnic, trust me, but it's what you have to do." He unhitched Blue and started walking him back to his stall. "There's no worse pain on this earth than having to save yourself by walking away from your own mother."

Skip's footsteps behind him stopped. When Ty stepped back out of Blue's stall with an empty halter in hand, Skip was still standing there, looking vaguely like somebody had punched him again.

"What?" Ty said.

Skip shook his head and walked back to the hitching rail.

Ty rolled his eyes and walked out of the horse barn. Some things just weren't worth explaining to some people.

**

If he weren't on the verge of walking out of the first steady employment he'd enjoyed in two years, Ty might have gone into town and hit a bar. If he'd gone to that effort, he figured he might have had time for a few drinks before the place closed.

So, he figured he may as well dip into the cache of beer he was keeping in the cool crawlspace beneath his bunkhouse.

He had started a new book last night, a laborious political drama that felt like a bad cable show awkwardly shoved into a spaceman costume. It wasn't a long book, so he felt bad about abandoning it, but by God it was hard to see the point of writing an outer space story that had nothing to do with the trials and tribulations of being in space.

"How many of those things do you go through in a week?" Skip McCoy had returned from the horse barn.

"Depends." Ty didn't look up from the description of a ballroom that was taking three pages. "Some of them are good and I read them fast. Some of them suck and it takes me all week."

"Huh." Skip leaned down to squint at the cover. "Star Vikings."

"I don't see what makes them Vikings yet," Ty said. "But there's titties, if you like titties."

"What do you mean, if I like titties?" Skip's voice was oddly defensive.

Ty let his book fall a couple of inches and looked up at Skip. Truth be told, that phrase had just kind of fallen out of his mouth without any thought behind it.

"You want a beer?" Ty said.

Skip looked at the foam cooler next to Ty's chair. "I thought you were getting out of here," he said.

"I can't apply for no job at one in the morning," Ty said. "I got nothing to feed my horse on the road, I

122

got nothing to spend on rodeo fees. I wired my mom most all the damn money I had so she could pay rent on an apartment instead of a damn storage unit."

"Huh." Skip nodded and walked around the table toward the cooler.

"I am getting the hell out of here, though," Ty said. "These people are fucking crazy."

"And you think the next place is going to be any less insane?" Skip said.

"Look, man, you want crazy shit? Try hanging out with gay rodeo cowboys." Ty shook his head. "I know my crazy, and this right here is on a whole 'nother level."

He wasn't sure why he'd just said that. Probably a combination of the empty beer bottles in front of him and the way Skip McCoy's unshaven jaw looked in the chemical glow of the lantern.

"You did gay rodeo?" Skip said.

"No, regular rodeo," Ty said. "I'm just gay."

Skip burst out laughing. "Well, I'll be damned," he said. "This world gets smaller every day, don't it?"

Ty raised his eyebrows, watching Skip carefully as he sipped on his beer.

"I mean...you know," Skip said, gesturing up and down his long figure. "I, uh, I figured you'd already figured it out."

"That's not an assumption I like to make about people," Ty said. "'Specially with you being the church-going type and all."

"I'm what they call a Cafeteria Catholic," Skip said, pulling a hoof pick from his pocket to crack open the beer he'd pulled from Ty's cooler.

123

"What's that mean?" Ty said.

"It means I apparently have a thing for complicated relationships," Skip said. "With God, with some of the folks from my hometown." He took a drink and sat down in the unoccupied metal mesh chair.

"You're about to tell me about your mom, aren't you?" Ty dog-eared the corner of his book and snapped it shut.

"Not really," Skip said. "That wound's still a little fresh on my mind."

"Sorry," Ty said.

"It's fine. You didn't know," Skip said. He drank his beer and watched the bugs gather around the lantern. "Just remember you're not the only one who's had to make that particular judgment call."

"Hmph." Ty opened his book again to the page he'd been on. "And neither are you."

Chapter Thirteen

"Well, why the hell would you tell him that?" Greg said.

"I don't know!" Connor was reclining in the driver's seat of his truck, a MegaFreeze in his lap and his hat pulled low over his eyes. "I just...look, it's been a *long time*."

"Gross, dude..."

"Fuck you," Connor said. "It's fine when you need to get laid so frickin' bad I have to go into witness frickin' protection!"

"Sorry!" Greg said. "Sorry, that was rude."

"I shouldn't have told him," Connor said. "None of his damn business."

He was parked in the gravel lot shared by the liquor store, the grocery store, the Mr. Grill, and the laundromat. It was the laundromat that gave Connor the best excuse to go sit around in town and do nothing for a couple of hours while he waited for the washing machines to run.

With his AC blasting and his truck aimed away from the midday sun, this was almost a tolerable place to update his brother on the other night's shit show. This just wasn't the kind of conversation that Connor felt like he needed to have back on the Triple V Ranch.

"I'm sure it's gonna be fine," Greg said. "There's plenty of gay dudes out there these days."

"I just really don't want these people finding out who I really am," Connor said. "Your future father-in-law already came about an inch from beating my whole ass last night."

"Well, that just pisses me off," Greg said. "I oughta come down there and..."

"Let's see how Linda reacts," Connor said. "You know? Maybe this will just be the last push she needs to get out of here and take her mom along with her."

"Shit, I hope," Greg said. "She's so happy to be out here away from that situation."

"Well, let her be happy," Connor said. "She deserves it."

"Can't believe she hasn't picked up on your act yet," Greg said. "All she can talk about is Skip McCoy fixed this, Skip McCoy rode that, Skip Skip Skip."

Connor laughed.

"Hell, if you weren't gay I'd start regretting sending you on down there!" Greg clucked his tongue. "Anyway, there she is coming back from the gas station."

"Better help her load up," Connor said. "I want my boss in a good mood when she gets back here."

"Heh, well, I lent her about fifteen hundred bucks," Greg said. "That should help."

Connor sighed. "Well, I guess I can't complain," he said. "If nothing else, this adventure has given me a real appreciation for..."

The rest of his sentence evaporated off his mind instantly as he saw a familiar pearl-white pickup pull into the gravel lot.

"I gotta go," Connor said. "Mr. Briggs just rolled in."

"Oh, shit!" Greg might have actually had a reason for whispering this time. "Good luck, man!"

Connor hung up and ducked low to the side. In his back window, he could just sort of see the reflection of Mr. Briggs's pickup truck cruising around the parking lot. What was going to happen when he parked? What kind of story was Connor going to have for why he was crouching and hiding in his driver's seat like he was getting ready for an ambush?

But Mr. Briggs didn't park. Mr. Briggs made three circles around the parking lot. Mr. Briggs turned back out onto the highway.

When Connor sat up, he could see Mr. Briggs going back the way he came.

Connor didn't even have time to express his vague, surprised confusion before a black sedan backed up from its spot at the liquor store and peeled out of the gravel lot. It turned out without signaling, and it sped up immediately until it was cruising right behind Mr. Briggs.

"Oh, holy shit!" Connor had one hand over his mouth and the other one on top of his head, like his hat was so shocked by what it had just witnessed that it was about to up and leave. "Holy shit!"

Panic took hold of his chest as he watched the two vehicles disappear over the horizon. They were headed east, toward Copperville and away from the ranch. He hadn't noticed anybody in the black car. He had barely registered the black car on his personal radar. He'd just pulled into the parking lot, put his and Gibson's wash in at the laundromat, and called his brother. He'd thought he was the only one in town up to something remotely shady.

Maybe the driver of the black car was in the same position. He wouldn't have any reason to recognize Connor, would he?

"Guess I'll find out," Connor said to himself.

***

When he returned to the ranch with their laundry, Ty had finished repairing and re-stringing the clothesline that had been victimized by the other night's livestock escape. He had assumed his usual off-hours position: draped amongst the patio set, shirt off and hat pushed low, beer in hand, engrossed in some dime store book about hunks in space.

He looked up and waved his book as Connor got out of his truck. "Thanks, man," he said.

"No problemo." Connor grabbed the two laundry bags out of the back of his pickup.

"Those posts weren't set in concrete," Gibson said. "I found a couple of bags of concrete mix in the hay shed, though, mixed that in with the new post holes." He took a sip of his beer. "Don't tell the boss, though."

"You don't gotta worry about me," Connor said. "It's not dry yet, then."

"It'll be fine," Gibson put his book and beer down on the patio table and stood up. "The bottom of the holes is dry-set, plus I wound up driving an extra couple of rebar spikes down on either side of the posts and running some guy wires down."

"Whatever works, man," Connor said. It was going to pain him to abuse fresh concrete like that, but this clothesline was truly not his problem. At least, it wouldn't be for much longer.

Gibson grabbed his mesh bag of wet laundry and got to work on one side of the clothesline. There was a kind of nervous silence between them that felt like it needed breaking. Gibson hadn't made much eye contact with Connor since their conversation the other night, which made Connor feel both kind of bad and kind of hopeful at the same time.

"You talked to your mom lately?" Connor said.

"The other day, yeah," Ty said. "She's doing good."

"That's nice to hear," Connor said. "You said you found her an apartment?"

Gibson snorted. "I can't tell that woman shit," he said. "I just send her the money when she's doing shit she actually needs to do."

"Ah," Connor said. "Gotcha."

"No, I guess it's a nice place, though." Gibson nodded. His attention was fixed on the shirt he was pinning neatly to the line. "You know, she kind of bounces between boyfriends, but this one doesn't sound too bad."

"Yeah?" Connor said.

"He's got a job, now," Gibson said. "It doesn't pay him too good, because he's on disability and can't lose that, but now they've made that first deposit he can at least pay rent on the new place."

"Well, that's a step up," Connor said. "She's lucky she has you."

Gibson laughed. "Yeah, I guess this week she might feel like that," he said. "She's got some issues."

"I feel you on that one," Connor said.

"What, the queer rodeo cowboy's not the favorite son in your family?" Gibson's voice was teasing, but when he glanced at Connor his face fell. "Sorry," he said.

129

"Nah, you're fine," Connor said. "My dad and I used to be real close, actually, before he died."

"Aww, I'm sorry," Gibson said. "And you're not much older than I am."

"It was out of the blue," Connor said. "We were at a barbecue and he just collapsed. DOA from a heart attack." Even now, reciting those words made his blood chill a little.

"Shit," Gibson said.

"Yeah, it...it was hard on my mom." Connor shook out a wet, crinkled pair of jeans so he could figure out which way was up. "She just got depressed and never got un-depressed, you know?" He realized how that sounded, and cleared his throat. "She had a stroke," he said. "But...man, I just think she was so young for how fast she went downhill."

"That's like my grandma," Gibson said. "She was only fifty-six, but she was just mentally..." He shook his head. "It sucks watching that happen, though. It's like you watch someone die a little every day."

"You know, that's exactly it," Connor said. "And the whole time, people who aren't watching this happen keep butting into your business, acting like if you'd just do a *little more*..." He frowned bitterly.

"People like to micro-manage each other's suffering, don't they?" Gibson said, fixing a dry smile on Connor.

"Yeah." Connor glanced at the ground. "I guess they do."

"Did they know you were gay?" Gibson said.

"Who, my parents?" Connor laughed. "Yeah, I thought I was about to get caught in high school, so I told them before somebody else could."

That was close to the truth—even if "somebody else" was always and only a figment of his imagination.

"And they were cool, huh?" Gibson nodded. "Probably a good thing my dad never found out, man. That would have been ugly."

"See, my dad was the cool one," Connor said. "My mom..." He shook his head. He was realizing how much of his real, un-edited backstory he was giving out to Gibson here. Not that it wasn't cathartic, but he needed to backtrack sooner rather than later. "Well, I guess that's why I struck out on the rodeo circuit," he said.

"Yeah," Gibson said. "You wouldn't be the first."

Connor didn't reply; he was trying to think of the best way to bring up this next part. Maybe it would be better not to bring it up at all, since Gibson was so annoyed that Connor was trying to help Linda with her situation.

"Speaking of other people's suffering," Connor said.

"Yeah?" Gibson paused and turned to him, an undershirt dangling from a clothespin he was holding.

"Did Mr. Briggs tell you where he was off to this morning?" he said.

"Nope." Gibson shook his head. "He just went banging around Linda's tack room and left, cussing about something or other."

"Hmm." Connor pinned a pair of socks up, one on each side of the line. "Well, I was sitting in the laundromat, minding my own business, and I saw him come by and cruise around the parking lot a few times."

"Like he was checking up on you?" Gibson said.

"That's what I thought at first," Connor said. "But then he leaves, and another car peels out from the liquor store parking lot and tails him down the highway."

"In a completely non-suspicious manner, I'm sure," Gibson said. "See, you oughta think about getting out of here, too. I'm starting to think I need to do more drinking before he starts pricing out my liver and my kidneys."

"And what am I gonna do for work once I get out of here?" Connor said. "I'm just as hard up for work as you are. I'll be selling my kidneys in a few months anyway."

"We could go hit the rodeo circuit again," Gibson said. "You and me could be buddies, ride in the paired events together. I've got a good-sized stock trailer. We could do steer wrestling, or maybe I could heel for you."

"Oh, is that what you want to do for me?" Connor thought his tone was pretty gentle and teasing, but it made Gibson turn beet red and stare at the ground.

"Aw, I'm just messing with you," Connor said. "I mean."

"Look I'm not trying to...to sleep with you." Ty mumbled the last few words and kept his eyes on the shirt he was hanging. "Unless, you know."

"I'm not sure if I do know," Connor said. He was reminded why he preferred hooking up with city boys, who said what they meant the first time and generally meant it. "I wouldn't mind if you were trying to make a move on me, I'll tell you that."

Someone had once told Connor that the act of being observed has a way of changing something, on a level so small as to only be relevant to very smart people in research labs. As he looked Gibson up and down, he could see where someone had gotten that idea. Gibson seemed suddenly aware of his own body in a way that Connor hadn't seen before, standing taller and correcting the pessimistic slump that usually bent his shoulders.

Connor took a step toward him, and Gibson took a paranoid look around him. Connor paused.

"Not here, man," Gibson said. "I mean, I don't think anybody's gonna catch us in the bunkhouses or anything." He bent suddenly to pick up a pair of shorts and pinned them up to the line. "I mean, shit, I don't know," he said. "I didn't think you'd actually, uh…"

"You're a hard man to ignore," Connor said. "And this whole idea's a sight more interesting than hanging laundry."

"Yeah?" Gibson's eyes were big; he was looking Connor up and down with a faint smile on his face. "I mean…we can try," he said. "See…see if we like each other."

"You've got an interesting set of priorities when it comes to getting to know people," Connor said. "You're willing to go out on the rodeo circuit with me as we stand right here, but fucking…"

"Fucking makes things complicated," Gibson said. "You know that."

"It doesn't have to," Connor said. "We could, you know, just do some kind of friends with benefits thing."

"We could," Gibson said. "If I decide that sleeping with you is, in fact, a benefit."

Connor hadn't yet come up with something clever to say when he heard the sound of tires on gravel.

"Well, so much for that conversation," Gibson said.

"Yep," Connor said. He sighed as he watched the pickup make its way down the driveway of the ranch. Mr. Briggs probably had photos of himself in doctors' offices where they sent people with five-hour erections.

"You, uh, doing anything after evening chores?" Gibson said.

Connor shot him a wicked grin in reply. "I haven't decided yet."

Chapter Fourteen

It made perfect sense, in Ty's mind, that you'd want to be a little less careful picking a rodeo buddy than picking someone to rail you when the ranch owner wasn't looking. If you got sick of a rodeo buddy who wasn't working out, you could just ditch him and his horse behind a gas station while he was asleep and recovering from a head injury.

If something went wrong with the guy who was jacking you off behind the hay barn, though, then that could get dangerous.

Ty had known, deep down, that Skip McCoy had the kind of body you could get addicted to if you were careless. *There was no adrenaline rush that could compare to the feeling he got when he imagined those big hands taking hold of his hips, pushing his jeans down as they bent Ty over his kitchen counter. Skip would engulf Ty's chest with one powerful arm while he stroked Ty's cock with his free hand, laughing softly at Ty's desperate groans. He would know exactly how fast Ty wanted him to stroke, and he would go just slow enough to drive Ty insane.*

At the moment, in the privacy of his own bed, Ty was trying to replicate that masterful touch, the "my-way-or-the-highway" lazy stroking that could keep Ty on edge, and he couldn't come close. He halfway thought about getting out of bed and waking Skip early. Maybe Skip's morning was going about this way, too.

Their first night together was going to haunt him. If he were being honest with himself, Ty had always had a little bit of a thing for getting bossed around in bed. He wanted to get reduced to begging for someone's cock, to hear himself pleading for a guy

135

to fuck him while he teased his hole like he had all the time in the world?

Ty bit his lip and quickened his hand's pace on his own cock. *He could imagine every inch of Skip's skin, and feel Skip's teeth on his shoulder.*

He'd liked Skip to straddle him, let Skip stroke his massive cock while Ty lubed Skip's asshole and Skip gently ground himself against Ty's erection. Ty wasn't accustomed to topping; he was always nervous that he was going to explode as soon as his shaft had breached the rim of a tight hole.

Even in that position though, Skip was in control. He set the pace and Ty followed, plunging deeper and deeper inside Skip while Skip's cock twitched in his hands.

In his mind, Ty finally had the right mix of courage and lust-induced madness to follow through. *He pulled out of Skip, shoved him off balance so he could grip his sweat-damp shoulders and push him down on the bed.*

With his hand on the back of Skip's neck, Ty took his opportunity and thrust his cock back inside Skip, just pushing his head in before pulling out again and letting it rest on the cleft of his ass.

"*How do you like it now?*" he asked in his mind while Skip groaned and begged him to push the rest of his cock inside him. "*You want that whole thing?*"

In his mind, *he finally had mercy on Skip and started pounding him with his cock like it was his last day on earth. Skip loved it; Skip begged him for more of his big, thick shaft while he gripped the sheets beneath his heaving chest.*

There in his bed, Ty was panting as he stroked himself faster, pushing himself to cum all over his bare stomach. He relaxed, suddenly exhausted and weirdly embarrassed at having entertained thoughts like that about someone he knew.

But the weirdness passed as he sat up and grabbed some tissues from the box on his bed. If Skip didn't want Ty thinking about him while he jacked off, there were a few things he could have been doing differently.

***

It was possible that Ty's newfound fantasizing had kept him from noticing this week's developments in the Briggs family shit show. For all he was paying attention, there could have been a knock-down drag-out fight in the kitchen every night after evening chores.

But while he was paying attention, it seemed that the family had quieted down significantly. Ty was mowing the ranch house's lawn when it occurred to him how strangely calm his workplace had been as of recent. He hadn't even found the time to look for new gigs at less dramatic ranches.

He was coming around the side of the house when Linda stepped around the corner and waved him down. He stopped the mower and shut it off, and she walked toward him with a couple envelopes in her hand.

"Hey," she said. "It's payday, and I figured I'd catch you while you were up here."

"Oh, thanks," Ty said.

She handed him both envelopes, looking back at the house. Ty felt something hard in there, and the look on his face must have showed.

"Some of the prize money was in gift cards," Linda said. "Sorry."

Ty took the envelopes and put them in his back pocket. "Oh," he said. "Uh, don't worry about it."

"Thanks." Linda smiled. "How's, uh, Mr. McCoy holding up for you?"

Ty hoped that his face wasn't showing the flash of embarrassment that had just washed over him. "Uh, he's doing all right," he said.

"Good to hear it," Linda said. "I need you two to make sure all my horses stay in shape over the next week. I will put the names on the board of the ones I ride. All right?"

"Yes, ma'am," Ty said. "You must have done pretty well at the jackpot."

"I did all right," Linda said. She was looking out over the orchard, her eyes unfocused. "Question is, how long can I keep doing all right?"

"You've got some fast fuckin' horses..."

"Don't swear where my daddy can hear you," Linda said.

"Sorry." Ty looked around him, as if by cussing once he'd summoned the flossy-haired agent of every inconvenience presently in his life.

"It's not enough to have fast horses," Linda said. "You oughta know that."

"Yeah." Ty nodded. "Hell, I bet that's why you hire rodeo cowboys," he said.

"No, it's because ranch cowboys all know about..." Linda nodded her head toward the house.

Ty smiled. "Oh."

"Anyway, I want all eight of them rode and hosed off daily," Linda said. "I want you and Skip to watch their legs carefully and tell me the moment you see anything is off. You got it?"

"Yes, ma'am," Ty said.

"My project this week is getting those Charolais off our property if we're not going to breed them or feed them," Linda said. "My daddy won't get the certification for the pasture, and the owner won't graze them on pasture that hasn't gotten the certification, but there's language on the lease that says...anyway." Linda shook her head like she was clearing water from her ears. "We'll be getting a new load of hay in, at least, so make sure the stack's ready to take a new load."

Ty winced. That was going to be a project in this heat. "How long do we have?" he said.

"Depends on how long you and Mr. McCoy take to do it," Linda said. "Truck's coming Thursday."

∗∗∗

Ty and Skip started working on the stack Wednesday afternoon, with the aim of finishing by mid-morning on Thursday. It was a pain-in-the-ass job; the ranch fed small square bales even to the larger herds of cattle, and previous employees had left a long and low bank of bales instead of taking hay from one end of the barn like a human being.

Despite a late start Thursday—which did not involve any blowjobs if anyone asked—they got finished with the haystack around eleven in the

139

morning. Congratulating each other on their efficiency, the two of them proceeded to finish the regular morning chores they'd put off in order to get ready for the hay truck.

They took their lunch on the haystack and hung around there for a while, drinking lukewarm soda and speculating on when they might expect their delivery.

"I mean, Thursday isn't really a set time," Skip said. "Could be Thursday 7 PM."

"And you think Linda would be out here if she was expecting the truck," Ty said.

"Have you texted her?" Skip said.

"A few times," Ty said. "Haven't heard back. Don't see her truck around here."

"Could be that church thing she goes to, some production they're putting on," Skip said. "Seems to be more or less on random weekdays."

"Church on a fuckin' weekday," Ty said. "This whole family's crazy."

"No, man, weekdays are for shit like choir practice or softball league," Skip said.

"You're not making it sound any better," Ty said.

"See, this is what I never liked about rodeo," Skip said. "Nobody actually goes and enjoys themselves. Nobody has any real friends."

"Bullshit," Ty said. "You just haven't met the right people on the circuit."

Skip laughed. "And you have?" he said. "Seems like every time someone makes a friend out there, they make three new enemies."

"That's just the way the world is," Ty said. "Ain't no point bitching about it just because you didn't have a good time on the rodeo circuit."

"The world is what you make it," Skip said. "The people who most want you to accept that life is miserable, generally speaking, are the people who most like to make life miserable for others." He drained his soda and pitched his can at the garbage.

Ty watched it arc high over the metal can and roll out into the road in front of the hay barn. "Nice shot," he said.

Skip was frowning at his phone. "We got a message from Linda," he said. "Truck's been rescheduled for Monday."

"Hmm." Ty looked over the neat stack of hay they'd busted their asses for hours to accomplish. "Well, at least we've got plenty to get us through until then."

***

By the time Monday actually rolled around, the haystack didn't look quite as generous as it had when they'd first tidied it up. Ty and Skip got the morning chores started as usual, both of them keeping half an eye out for the hay truck coming down the driveway.

Linda came out while they were cleaning stalls, big sunglasses perched on her nose and her hair piled high in a bun.

"Ty, can you get Roxie and Bear saddled for me while I'm riding Bella?" she said.

"Yes, ma'am," he said.

"I'll give you guys an update when I hear back from the hay guy," Linda said. "He swears he's coming today."

Something about the cool tone of that last sentence made Ty shoot a glance at Skip. Skip grimaced and shook his head as he turned his attention back to the pitchfork in his hands.

Linda didn't say much as she went about taking her horses out and putting them through their paces. She rode like she was in a coma, reins slack and sunglasses pointed dead ahead. Her eyes could have been closed completely and Ty wouldn't have been surprised.

About halfway through her ride on Bingo, she stopped and pulled her phone out of the front of her sweatshirt. She rode to the far end of the arena to take the call, turned away from Skip and Ty as she spoke to whoever was on the other end.

"That doesn't bode well," Skip said, walking up next to Ty and leaning on his pitchfork.

"No, it does not." The day had dawned hot, and the line of clouds on the horizon was thin and distant, but Ty swore he could feel a storm rolling in overhead as Linda continued her conversation.

"I'm gonna go dump the wagon," Skip said as he watched Linda end the call.

"Good idea." Ty kept his voice low and pretended to busy himself with Scooter's latigo. For a few seconds, at least, there was no need. Linda held her phone in her hand and stared at it without turning around.

As a matter of fact, Linda went on to finish her entire ride and cool out without speaking another word to anybody. She got off her horse, led him to the barn, and handed him to Ty at the hitching rack.

"Hay truck's been rescheduled," Linda said. "I might need some help from you and Skip sometime later this evening or early-early tomorrow morning."

"What kind of help?" Ty said, untying a halter from the rack.

"We might just need to be moving some stock around," Linda said. "Nothing to make a big deal out of."

"Okay," Ty said. "Uh, we'll be ready."

"Thanks." Linda gave him a bitter smile as she led her horse out toward the arena. "I'll let you know what I need and when."

It was hard not to notice how much time Miss Linda spent on the phone during the next several rides. She made all her phone calls in the same location, at the far end of the arena where nobody could hear or see what she was talking about.

In between phone calls, she would lope fast circles around the arena. You could tell when her phone rang, because she'd sit up suddenly and her horse would slam on the brakes.

When she was done, she brought her horse back to Ty. Her jaw was set, and she held her head higher than she had all morning.

"Get your phone out and get some paper," Linda said. "I'm gonna need you to write this down so you know it, but I'm gonna need you to get rid of it afterward so I don't kill your ass. Do we have an agreement?"

"Yes, ma'am," Ty said. He got his wallet out and found a receipt; Linda handed him a pen before he could go looking for one.

"I'm going to need you to sort 653, 707, 719, 720, and 801 from the bronc herd," Linda said. "Do it on foot and don't draw too much attention to what you're doing. Vet's gonna be out around 7 to do some bloodwork on them. He's going to need to see the envelope I'm going to leave in..." Linda looked off to the distance. "It's gonna be taped up under the circuit board cover at the end of the alleyway," she said. "Got it?"

Ty nodded. "Got it," he said.

Linda smiled. It wasn't terribly convincing. "Thank you so much, Ty," she said. "I'll just wake you up if I need you in the morning. Don't worry about it if I don't."

Ty laughed. "Actually, I'm gonna try and forget about the whole thing as soon as the vet's gone," he said.

"That's a smart idea," Linda said. "I wouldn't let Skip in on any of this, either."

Chapter Fifteen

It occurred to Connor, as he traced the line of an old scar on Ty's shoulder, that he'd gone into this expecting Ty not to want him. Rejection was easy; well, maybe not easy, but at least familiar enough that Connor never had any navigational problems.

He had no idea how he was going to handle the situation as it had actually turned out.

"I should get going back to my bunk," Ty said, picking himself up and turning to sit with his feet on the floor.

"Good idea," Connor said. He rolled over and watched the shadows play on the wall while Ty got dressed.

Connor would never admit it in a million years, but Ty's appetite had a way of wearing him out physically that he just hadn't anticipated. The guy was a fucking freight train, and his addiction to Connor's cock had spiraled immediately out of control.

"Night," Ty said, switching the lantern off as he left the bedroom.

"See you in the AM," Connor said.

He rolled over again and watched the other cowboy's silhouette move down the length of the boxcar.

At a certain point, Connor realized, he was going to have to sit down with himself and come to terms with what he was doing here. Regardless of how enthusiastic Ty was about the situation, the fact remained that Ty wasn't signing up for a fuck buddy arrangement with Connor Dougherty. Sooner or later, he was going to learn the truth about Skip McCoy.

And what then? Was it illegal to fuck somebody under an assumed identity? Was it immoral? Was Connor taking advantage, here?

But what about some of the hookups he'd had when he was younger? Breathless, nameless, stealing two minutes of privacy in a darkened city far from home.

And maybe those weren't too innocent, either. You'd hear rumors, sometimes, about straight men with lives and families disappearing out of the blue and resurfacing in California with a secret lover of ten years. Connor always wondered if he hadn't by accident participated in the hidden corrosion of those marriages.

But who could blame those men for keeping those secrets? Their world was only starting to come out from the clutches of men like Mr. Briggs. Every week, it felt like someone needed to remind Connor how much worse it used to be for guys like him.

Fact was, though, it wasn't going to get better if guys like him kept living in the shadows. Yeah, it wasn't always worth it to be honest. In this situation, it might be particularly not worth it.

Which kind of brought him back to where he'd started with this debate. Connor pulled the blankets around him and rolled over again. It was going to be a long day tomorrow if he didn't get any sleep.

***

The new hay, when it had finally shown up, was mostly of the high quality that you'd feed to horses and other single-stomached grazing animals. Mostly.

Mixed in with the good bales, at random intervals that Connor could only attribute to spite on

146

the part of a long-suffering feed broker, were bales so blue-black with mold and moisture that they were barely fit to toss to the cattle. Sorting the good hay from the bad hay was going to be a side project enough to keep Connor and Ty busy for the rest of the week. Maybe longer, if Ty zapped any more of Connor's strength out via his dick.

"So, then I see the kid one morning, he's down at the store in town. Completely fucked up, his whole face, everything." Ty made a vague gesture around one of his eyes. "Looked like someone stuck him in a damn washing machine."

"Uh-huh." Connor coiled his back muscles for a moment so he could heave a bale on top of the stack well above his head.

"Won't tell anybody what happened to him. Not a peep. But the old hippie lady comes in, and..."

"...and you can just come find me when you get your fucking shit together!" This time, it was Linda's voice coming across the barnyard as smooth and serene as a fire hose on full blast. "Cause I'm done! I've had it with both of y'all and I'm out!"

Neither Connor nor Ty spoke a word. Like nosy spiders, they were up on top of that haystack in a good viewing position before you could bat an eye. Linda was storming down the walkway from the house to her truck, a backpack in one hand and her keys glittering in the other.

"Linda, you can't leave me!" Her mom came tottering out of the house behind her. "Baby, please just talk to..."

"I can't help people who won't help themselves!" Linda got in her truck and started the engine.

"You can't leave me, baby!" Linda's mom threw her wine glass down and leapt up on top of the truck's hood. "Linda, I have given you everything..."

It was damn near impossible to parse exactly what the two women were yelling at each other as Linda tried to back out of her parking spot. Her mother was shrieking like a child, both fists clenched and pounding on the hood of the truck as Linda tried to shoo her off.

"What in the fuck?" Ty said, looking at Connor for a second before returning his horrified gaze to the scene below. "Is she...?"

"Yeah," Connor said, nodding along as Linda started doing reverse donuts. "She oughta turn the wiper blades...ah."

"You think this has happened before?" Ty said.

"I mean, it would make sense," Connor said. "The way she's holding on."

"Ope!" Ty's hand flew to his mouth. "That had to sting."

"Well, what was she thinking was gonna happen?" Connor said. He got up and started monkeying his way down as Linda put the truck in drive and went speeding up the driveway. "Come on," he said. "We oughta help her out."

By the time he had gotten up to the driveway, Mrs. Briggs was sitting on the gravel with her face in her hands. She was bawling, shaking her entire body while she thumped her feet on the ground.

Connor approached carefully, looking around him for signs of an oncoming Mr. Briggs.

"Is everything okay?" he said.

"Nothing's okay," Mrs. Briggs said. "Marshall went out again, then my baby left me, and now I've got nothing! Nothing, absolutely nothing." She sobbed incoherently into her hands. "Don't even have a bottle of wine left to calm my nerves."

"Wait, Mr. Briggs took off?" Connor said.

"Mm-hmm," Mrs. Briggs said. She sniffled; her hands fell in her lap as she looked Connor in the eye. "I don't know when he'll be back. Hell, I don't know if he'll be back. He's in so deep with those…" She bit her lip and shook her head.

"With those who?" Connor said.

"It's none of my business," Mrs. Briggs said, burying her face in her hands again.

"Hey, now," Connor said, taking Mrs. Briggs by the arm. "Let's get you back in the house, ma'am."

"You're such a sweet boy, McCoy," Mrs. Briggs said. "Linda goes on and on about you. I'm so lucky we found you!"

"Well, thank you very much, Mrs. Briggs," Connor said. With one hand on her shoulder, he ushered her up the walkway into the house. "Um, if you don't mind my asking, do you know where Mr. Briggs went?"

"That's not important right now, sweetie," Mrs. Briggs said. She hurried ahead of Connor and opened the door. "I need to make a phone call."

The door snapped shut behind her, and Connor stood dumbfounded on the walkway.

***

When Linda returned to the ranch some five or six hours later, it was in a little red sedan that

149

dropped her off at the end of the driveway. She walked down slowly, a little dark dot moving down the expanse of green between the house and the highway.

She was about halfway down to the house by the time Connor had gotten in his truck and driven up to meet her. She smiled and stuck her thumb out as he approached.

Connor leaned out the window. "You need a ride?" he said.

"Sure." Linda walked around the hood of the truck. About halfway there, she made like she was going to jump up on it. Connor startled, and Linda threw her head back and laughed.

"Jesus," Connor said.

"I don't think he's going to be much help with my family," Linda said. "I've been asking for twenty years." She opened the pickup's door, swung inside, and fixed Connor with a bug-eyed smile.

"What happened to your truck?" Connor said.

"I sold it." Linda sat back and shut her eyes. "You've got a three-quarter ton, you can haul my trailer to races when it comes time."

"Wait, you *sold*..."

"Welcome to my world, Connor!" Linda threw her hands up. "I sell our broncs! I sell our vehicles! I'll be selling my mom's jewelry next, unless there's a really smart plan behind this stupid damn stunt."

Connor blinked, paused in the middle of a three-point turn in the driveway. "Uhh...you, uh, you know..."

"Connor, we've met face to face on at least three occasions," Linda said. "Now, is this Ty Gibson kid in on it?"

"No," Connor said, probably a little too quickly. "I'd never met him before I showed up here."

"So, what's your plan?" Linda said. "Why are you going to all this trouble to stack moldy hay for my dumbass dad? And why didn't either one of you assholes see fit to tell me about it?"

"Linda, we've been worried sick about you," Connor said. "Greg thinks it's worse than you've been telling him, and I think he's right."

"Greg can sit his ass down and wait until I have sorted out my own private business," Linda said. "So, you two are just lying to me because you don't think I can take care of myself?"

"Uhh..."

"It's a yes or no question," Linda said.

Connor sighed. "Will you believe me if I say no?" he said.

"Probably not," Linda said.

"Greg knows how stubborn you are," Connor said. "Look, I'm sorry..."

"Don't be sorry," Linda said. "Be useful. Do you actually have any plan other than snooping around my business?"

"It would be a lot easier to make a plan if everything around here wasn't shrouded in secrecy," Connor said.

"Look, my dad gambles," Linda said. "He gambles a lot. Sometimes he wins big, sometimes he wins huge, but most of the time he doesn't."

"Uh-huh," Connor said. "Kind of figured something like that was going on."

"I don't know what to do," Linda said. "He won't admit he has a problem. Won't talk to anyone at church about it, won't get help, if you say a goddamn word to him, he flies off the handle, and you saw what he gets like when he gets pissed off!"

Connor nodded. "And he's making you all pay for it?"

"Who else is going to pay for it?" Linda said. "This is what you and Greg just don't understand, Connor. We are responsible for our family!"

"I think we both understand that perfectly well," Connor said, shooting Linda a hard glare. "Look, I know parents can be difficult, but you know...you're your own person." He realized was sounding like Ty now, but this was ridiculous.

"I am my own person," Linda said. "And I am a person who does not walk out on her family when they're dealing with an addiction!"

"I wouldn't describe anything your father is doing as 'dealing' with his problem," Connor said. "Do you think I came down here to stage a surprise intervention or something?"

"I don't know!" Linda said. "I guess I just wanted to entertain some tiny hope that I could do better than a couple of little boys playing secret agent."

"Look, what do you want me to do?" Connor said. "I'm here. My cover is blown. All I want is for my brother to be happy, and he can't be happy if you're stuck here babysitting your parents."

152

"Oh, thank God there's a man's feelings involved here somewhere," Linda said. "I was beginning to think this would never matter to anybody but me."

"Linda..."

"Do not turn this around on me, Connor Dougherty," Linda said, twisting in her seat to jab a finger at him. "You are the one who is lying and double-dealing and getting into business that ain't yours, and you are the one who is going to be taking orders and helping make things right."

"Okay, okay," Connor said. He pulled into his parking spot in front of the bunkhouses. "I'll take orders."

"Good." Linda pulled a damp, multi-folded piece of paper from her pocket. "I finally gave up and went to our pastor about it." Her voice started to lose some of its angry clarity. "I..." She shook her head. "It's...kind of a big deal in our church for someone to be struggling with something like this," she said.

"Uh-oh." Connor winced. "Was, uh, was your pastor..."

"It's not Pastor Chuck who I'm worried about," Linda said. "Mama always said there's men of God and men of church, and Chuck's a man of God."

"At least you've got that going on," Connor said.

"But if anyone from the congregation finds out what's going on?" Linda said. "We're over. All our family's credit, all our family's good name, everything we have built up in this town over the years?" She sniffed. "It's bad enough that we drink."

Connor opened his mouth, thinking he was going to say something comforting about to hell with what your church thinks. But in the time it took for his jaw to move, it occurred to him what it would be like running his own ranch if his whole church turned on him. Fully half of their business relied on someone in the family "knowing a guy."

"So, I had a talk with Pastor Chuck, and we kind of came up with a plan," Linda said. "We...we have to get him to get help. We don't have a choice. He's on my mom's credit, he's on my credit..."

"Wait, he's on *your* credit?" If Connor had a drink he would have spat it out through his nose.

"Yes, he's on *my* credit!" Linda said. "Which means if your brother had his way, his credit would be ruined, too!"

"Oh," Connor said.

"But getting him help could be, uh, tricky." Linda frowned at the paper. "See, what we were fighting about last time, is I froze my credit. He can't take out any more shit using my name. No loans, no lines of credit, no five-dollar gift certificates to the Corn King Megaplex, you hear?"

"What the fuck is the Corn King Megaplex?" Connor said.

"You haven't been?" Linda's eyes got big for a second. "I'll take you both out sometime. Anyway, my mom's credit is trashed, so he can't use that."

"Oh, no," Connor said. "I see where this is going." Trashed credit and a gambling problem couldn't coexist for long without getting into some shady territory, especially if you were trying to keep it a secret where all your money was coming from and going to.

154

"Can you?" Linda said. "Do you know what those people's debt collectors are actually like? Do you know what it's like to live with this constant fear?"

"I..." Connor gulped. "Do the cops know?"

"If the cops find out how much shady stuff my dad's been doing to save face at church, he will lose this ranch," Linda said. "Okay? We are operating under the radar here."

Connor had a million different objections to that, and he was too smart to voice a single one of them. "Okay," he said. "And what, exactly, is our operation going to accomplish?"

"You're going to be putting this dumbass disguise idea to some good use," Linda said. "My daddy doesn't know you well enough to bother hiding everything he does from you. Maybe you can figure out exactly who he's seeing and where he's going."

"Okay," Connor said. "And once I find out?"

"That next step is up to me," Linda said. "Just keep an eye on him. Let me know if he seems...off."

"Oh, that reminds me." Connor held up a finger. "I have something in my bunkhouse that belongs to you."

Chapter Sixteen

"Okay, on the count of three we're gonna all pull as hard as we can. Got it?"

"Yes, ma'am," Ty said.

"You ready, Mama?" Linda said.

"Oh, Lord, I hope I am!" In her safety goggles with her husband's tool belt flapping about her waist, Mrs. Briggs looked like some kind of human-bumblebee hybrid. She clutched a bright green impact driver in both gloved hands. It had a big carriage bolt magnetically held in the tip, big enough that Ty really hoped she knew what she was doing up there.

"Okay," Linda said. "One, two,..."

Linda, Ty, and Skip all yelled "Three!" simultaneously, sinking low to the ground and hauling hard against the pulley ropes attached to the shed's new wall. Slowly, serenely, like a wing unfurling on a fantastic spacecraft, the big, clean rectangle of two-by-fours and corrugated steel rose up in the midday sun.

"Okay, mom," Linda said as Skip ran around to brace his big body against the metal wall. "Sink that first bolt in."

As Linda grabbed a cordless drill and sprinted up another ladder at the shed's other corner, Mrs. Briggs put in the first carriage bolt that would affix the new wall to its corner post. The impact driver's rapid tattoo accelerated into a harsh grinding noise, and Mrs. Briggs pulled it off with a little cheer.

"Mama, can you bring that over here?" Linda's cordless drill wasn't exactly screwing around, but she'd spent the money on some serious bolts to hold this shed together. Funny how that worked—when you didn't blow your whole budget on walls that took five days to build, you had money left over for hardware that made a building last.

"Coming, sweetie!" Mrs. Briggs was having the time of her life this morning, out here running to and fro as Linda and the guys turned a flatbed full of FarmList building supplies into a shed that could actually stand up to the ravages of a herd of cattle.

"Hey, a truck's coming down the driveway!" Skip McCoy was looking out to the horizon, his canteen held in front of his chest.

"Cattle pot?" Linda said.

"Looks like," Skip said. "Ope! We got another one."

"That'll be the MacAllisters," Linda said. "They're gonna lease that corriente herd at their facility in Oklahoma City for the rest of the summer, maybe into the winter to boot."

"Just like that, huh?" Skip said, a sly smile on one side of his face.

"Well, nobody told me not to do business with the MacAllisters," Linda said. She grabbed the impact driver from her mom and finished sinking the carriage bolt into the corner of the shed.

The sheet metal may have been freshly stripped off someone's roof, and the two-by-fours might have been painstakingly picked off the dry bottom of a stack of scrap wood, but when it was done the shed didn't look half bad. Skip had found the materials for just under five hundred bucks, and it was going to last a lot longer than the ones with battened siding.

Mrs. Briggs waved and ran across the barnyard to meet the two cattle pots pulling up to the stock pens.

"The loading chute's over here!" she said.

"Ty, sweetie, why don't you and Blue help these nice young men get these roping steers off our feed bill?" Linda gestured with her thumb toward the cow pens.

"Yes, ma'am," Ty said, striding off to the hitching rail where Blue was napping in front of a water trough.

Even when you took away the steep financial boon this posed for the ranch, the prospect of getting rid of eighty steers was enough to make Ty jump for joy. And these weren't exactly wild cattle roaming up on the high hill pastures, either. They were bred and raised to run in rodeos, which meant when they saw a horse and rider they got moving with no questions asked.

It occurred to him, as he swung up on Blue's back, that there was no reason for the MacAllisters to send two big cattle pots to pick up a single load of small, running-bred cattle. He could see Mrs. Briggs talking to one of the drivers; the other one was pulling around to the pasture gate. They were full of restless black cattle. Ty could hear their bawling over the usual afternoon complaining of the animals in the rodeo pens.

Linda was walking over to the pasture gate, and Ty caught up with her on Blue. "What's going on?" he said. "I thought we were getting some steers off our feed bill..."

"We are," Linda said. "These heifers are going up to Unit 230."

158

"What the hell is Unit 230?" Ty said.

"It's my family's code name for our secret lab," Linda said. "We're injecting alien eggs into cattle to see how they..."

"Miss Linda..."

"What?" Linda laughed, a genuine grin on her face. "I thought you'd appreciate that!"

"Come on, now," Ty said with a smile. "What is it?"

"It's a little stretch of pasture we lease from the government," Linda said. "We can't afford to give it up, but it's costing us money every summer we don't use it."

"Up in the hills?" Ty said.

"I don't know if you can still call that territory 'hills,'" Linda said. "It'll take you and McCoy a few days to move them on up there, but Sean tells me they're a pretty easygoing bunch. Been raised on his front pasture, his girls practice moving them around, so they shouldn't give you too much trouble."

"A couple days?" Ty's eyes got big. "Are you and your mom gonna..."

"We'll be fine," Linda said. "Now that we don't have all eighty of those damn corrientes on our lot."

"Are you sure about..."

"Of course, I'm sure about it!" Linda said. "I need to have every single one of those heifers up on Unit 230 as soon as humanly possible before my father gets back. Do you see what I am saying here?"

"Uh..." Ty nodded. "I think," he said.

Now, far be it for him to question the methods and motivations of his employer, but moving a hundred fifty head of cattle to pasture was kind of a large operation to carry out while your dad wasn't watching. Ty gave Linda an eyeball, which only made her smirk.

"You ever moved cattle across open range before, Gibson?" she said.

"I've moved them across a feedlot," Ty said. "I, uh, I know enough not to say it's pretty similar."

"You didn't do too badly cleaning up when the broncs and the mixed herd got out the last couple times," Linda said. She patted Blue on the butt. "You'll be fine. McCoy knows enough to keep both of you out of trouble."

"Does he, now?" Ty said, looking behind him at Skip. He was ambling over to the hitching post, looking bemusedly at the trucks about to disgorge a herd of cattle into the Briggs's pasture.

Linda didn't respond, but walked ahead to open the big green double gate so the cattle pots could pass through.

***

Ty's saddlebags hadn't seen much real use in the past nine months; the leather was hardened and warped from doing hard time scrunched up beneath his truck's passenger seat. He found half a tin of Neats foot oil in the back corner of his trailer's tack compartment and got to work, a glass of whiskey and a torn-up T-shirt on the table in front of him.

He looked up for a moment when Skip's truck returned from town. Skip got out with a couple sacks of groceries in one hand and a six pack in the other.

"Hope you like snack crackers," he said.

"I packed some instant potatoes," Ty said. "And a little mac and cheese."

"You got something to cook all that with?" Skip said.

"Linda let me borrow a couple of her mom's pans," Ty said. "All you gotta do is boil water to get it ready."

"Hmm." Skip frowned at the bag of munchies he'd brought home from town. He looked toward the house. "Do you think she knows?" he said, his voice low.

"Knows...oh." Ty shrugged. "I don't think she knows. I think she thinks she knows, but..."

Skip laughed. "I *think* I know what the hell you're saying," he said.

"What I'm saying is, it doesn't really matter what we do," Ty said. "She's figured out I'm gay, I'm pretty sure she's figured out you're gay..."

"She has?" Skip said.

"She's dropped hints, here and there," Ty said. "Not in an, 'I know what you're doing you sinning bastard' kind of way, you know, she's not like that."

"Thank God," Skip said.

"But, you know." Ty shrugged. "Nosy straight girls."

Skip laughed and started sorting through his bounty on the table. "Well, you know, some of these women who wind up managing these big places on their own," he said. "They don't like hiring single straight guys to help them manage the place."

161

"Huh," Ty said. "I never thought about it like that."

"I wouldn't let anything Linda says bother you too much," Skip said. "She just likes to talk a bunch of shit for fun. It's how she blows of stress, and she's got a lot of stress in her life right now."

"Yeah, join the club," Ty said.

"Did she bring the panniers over here?" Skip looked around the courtyard.

"They're on my truck bed," Ty said. "I packed everything on the list you left. Tried the hobbles on Blue. He seems to know what they are."

"We'll try and find some spots where we can do a highline if we can't make it to the cow camps at the right schedule," Skip said. "Linda gave me a map that shows the usual stopping points on the way to the pasture."

"You really think we'll be out there four days?" Ty said.

"If we move fast and don't fuck around." Skip walked over to the truck to grab the half-empty set of canvas bags they'd use to carry their larger gear. "And if the weather holds up."

"Sounds like a lot of 'if' to deal with," Ty said.

"Good thing we're a couple of tough sons of bitches." Skip set the pannier over the back of one of the deck chairs and started throwing food in. "If you can handle life on the rodeo circuit, you can sure as shit handle a cattle drive that doesn't even last a week."

"Hell, the cattle driving part of it is only gonna last a couple days," Ty said. "I mean. Depending on the 'ifs' involved."

***

Linda woke them up a couple hours before dawn with the promise of a hot breakfast in the ranch house. It was the best meal Ty had eaten in several weeks: he stuffed himself to the gills with pancakes, bacon, and scrambled eggs loaded with cheese and chili.

They didn't talk much as they ate, or as they got their horses ready and double-checked that they'd packed everything they needed. The eastern horizon was just starting to turn grey-blue as they made their way out to the pasture where the heifers had stayed overnight.

Linda accompanied them on her ATV for the first couple of miles, opening gates where necessary and directing them through the maze of wire fences that divided up the pastures closest to the house.

The very last gate between the Triple V Ranch and federal land was set over a dry creek bed. The heifers funneled through easily, complaining quietly to each other as Ty and Skip pushed them gently forward to the open range.

"Well," Linda said as she pulled it closed behind the last cow. "This is it for my part."

"We'll be fine from here," Skip said. "Looks like we'll have a long day of clear skies ahead of us."

"Looks like that so far," she said. "Be careful once you get higher in the hills. Those flash floods in the arroyos are nothing to play around with."

"Duly noted, ma'am." Skip tipped his hat to her.

"See you next week." Linda returned the gesture and sped off on her ATV.

It didn't take long after sun-up for the heat of the day to start bearing down on their expedition. The first leg of their journey took them up three fairly steep hills in a row, and both horses and cattle were sluggish to get on with the day.

They had brought one of Linda's barrel horses along to pack their gear, a stocky sorrel mare who had no problem sticking with the herd whether there was a pony rope on her or not. Better yet, she seemed to get the general gist of what they were doing, and would now and then chase a cow back to the herd of her own volition.

Their third climb eventually brought them up to a sharp, grassy ridge that made a crescent high above the lower hills. Ty could see the whole valley laid out in front of him, green and flat, with the little brown ribbon of highway running through the middle beside the river. From this distance, the trees seemed to be made of cotton wool; different crops or different plowing directions made a patchwork out of the fields at the valley bottom.

"You don't realize how hilly this country is before you get up in it, huh?" Skip pulled his horse up next to Blue.

"It's beautiful," Ty said. "Everything's so green."

"Mmm." Skip nodded. "The way the map looks, I don't think we'll see the valley again until we come back this way."

"Crazy," Ty said.

"You want crazy, huh?" Skip chuckled. "Wait until you see the section we gotta move these girls through in the morning."

Chapter Seventeen

Now that Connor was actually riding through it, Dead Horse Draw wasn't as bad for moving cattle as it looked. These heifers were still on the small side, ranch raised and clever enough to keep from getting stuck or injured in the thick scrub that covered the narrow, rocky valley.

He was glad to have a horse who did well barefoot. He could see that their pack horse had already twisted a hind shoe scrambling through the sandstone, and even with their farrier tools it was going to be a pain in the ass straightening it out and re-attaching it. Connor just had to hope and pray that the shoe didn't actually come off while he was looking the other way.

"Come on now! Come on! I said git!" Across the gulch, Gibson was shaking his rope at a pair of heifers who were curious about what lay up a game trail. His little roan pinned his ears and snapped at them as he scrambled to gain some high ground.

See, as long as you had high ground, it was pretty easy to keep the heifers going through this part of their journey. But getting and keeping high ground was a righteous pain in the ass on horseback. Probably had something to do with why this stretch was called Dead Horse Draw.

The second morning had come up cooler than the first, and Connor had woken to a couple flecks of rain pinging down on his face. He and Gibson had slept in shifts, which strangely enough had left Connor feeling kind of refreshed and optimistic about the day ahead of him.

The clouds overhead were thinning as the sun came up, but the heat had yet to arrive. Connor liked it. He hummed to himself as they climbed up, weaving switchback by weaving switchback, toward the high valley where the heifers would spend their summer.

"Hey, McCoy!" Gibson waved to him. "Is that the saddle you were talking about?" He pointed ahead of him, to a dip in the ridgeline where this valley joined up with another valley.

"Let me check." Connor pulled the map from the outside pocket of one of his pommel bags. As they moved through the area, he kept refolding it so he could always pull it out and have it be on the square they were in presently.

It took him a minute or two to get his bearings on where they were, just based on the steepness of the slopes and the Briggs's marks and the location of certain blobby rock spires around them. "Looks like that's it," Connor said.

They were high enough in elevation that the scrub oaks and yucca were being replaced by aspens and ponderosas, but the steep valleys cast rain shadows that streaked the forest with wedges of dry taiga. It was easy to get the impression, riding up one of these dry valleys, that you'd come out of the green hills and into a desert that was going to last as long as you could go.

And then you crossed over, and you were in a whole new world.

"Well, I'll be damned," Connor said to himself as he followed the herd down into a wide meadow that sloped down to a series of little kettle ponds.

Gibson was up ahead loping alongside the herd's flank. He was laughing, waving his hat in his free hand as the mass of stock spilled down through the lush grass. He didn't stop when he reached the first kettle pond, instead giving his horse his head and letting him take a flying leap over the bank and into the water.

"Now, that's more like it," Gibson said, turning around to holler at Connor. "Come on, Skip!" he said as his horse lowered his head to drink. "Water's just fine!"

"Bonito likes to roll in ponds," Connor said. He stuck along the back of the herd with their pack horse, gently nudging the heifers who had decided that this was just as good a place as any to get their snack on.

"We oughta stop here awhile and graze the horses," Gibson said. He moved his horse back to dry land and dismounted. "Starting to get hot."

Connor took the map out of his pocket again and studied the route ahead of them. They weren't even a third of the way to the next cow camp, and there was a lot of steep and tricky bullshit to get through yet.

"I don't know," Connor said, but when he looked up he saw that Gibson was already buck naked and running headlong for the next kettle pond. "Dammit. Gibson!"

It was too late. Gibson's leap carried him almost into the center of the pond, and the glass-calm blue of the surface shattered silver. Gibson resurfaced a couple moments later and a couple yards away, the same clear laugh rising out of him.

"Holy shit!" he said. "This is cold!"

"What the hell did you think it was gonna be like?" Connor said. As the herd coalesced about fifty yards off from the pond, he came riding over to the edge of the pond where Gibson was kicking around.

Bonito snorted at him, but lowered his head and drank deeply.

"It didn't bother Blue," Gibson said.

"Doesn't look like it's bothering you much, either." Connor made no effort to hide the approval on his face as he watched Gibson swim a lazy spiral around the center of the pond. "How deep is it?"

"This one's about five or six feet in the middle," Gibson said. "The other one's about three."

Connor dropped his reins and got off Bonito. He was in a bosal this trip instead of his usual bit, which made grazing breaks a hell of a lot more convenient.

"You know how these kettle ponds show up?" Connor said.

"Glaciers," Gibson said. "They leave these big chunks of ice behind, and they just melt and leave these little ponds."

"Isn't that just crazy to think about, though?" Connor looked from one edge of the pond to the other. "Just a chunk of ice the size of a house, sitting way out here?"

"What's crazy is the footprint stays here the whole time," Gibson said. "I'm swimming in ancient history." He had swum up to Connor's spot on the bank of the kettle, resting his elbows on the grass while his naked body drifted lazily in the deep water. He grinned up at Connor. "You oughta look less and swim more," he said.

"It's too cold," Connor said. "Besides, we gotta get moving."

"Shit, we got all day," Gibson said. "And this is good pasture for all the critters."

"I'm sure there's more than one good...aagh!" Connor yelped as Gibson grabbed at one of his ankles, sweeping him sideways and knocking him right into the frigid water of the kettle. He thrashed for a second to right himself, gasping for air as soon as he could see the sky clear above him.

"Son of a bitch!" Connor said, searching around for Gibson. "What the fuck was that?"

Gibson was halfway across the pond, cackling like a madman. "Guess we'd better wait for your jeans to dry out, partner," he said.

"You fucking asshole!" Connor heaved himself back up on the bank, soaked to his bones and shivering. "If I'da had my phone in there..."

"Maybe if you weren't so proud of yourself leaving your phone at the ranch house, I would have thought of that." Gibson came swimming back over to Connor.

"It don't matter what I have on me!" Connor had to unbutton the sleeves of his soaked shirt to pull it off his arms. "You're an asshole!"

"Come on," Gibson said. "It'll put hair on your chest!"

"I like my chest the way it is," Connor said. He stood up to get his boots off.

"That makes two of us." Gibson floated by on his back, a shit-eating grin on his face.

"If my boots shrink, I'm gonna kick your ass," Connor said. "Jesus!"

"I thought Catholics weren't supposed to take the Lord's name in vain," Gibson said.

"And Baptists aren't supposed to drink," Connor said, "And atheists aren't supposed to do shit that requires the intervention of their guardian angel." He was still struggling with his boots, and he could feel his blood pressure rising with each second he failed to get them off.

"You need a hand with that?" Gibson said.

"Go to hell!" Connor said.

"Come on," Gibson said. "You know how good I am at getting you undressed."

"Gibson, when I tell you to get fucked right now, I do not mean it in any way you are going to enjoy." Connor finally got his right boot off; the sudden give caused him to land on his ass on the bank of the kettle pond.

"Are you sure about that?" Gibson said.

"Fine." Connor stuck his ankle out toward the pond.

Gibson grabbed his boot, wrenched it off, and chucked it back over Connor's head. "There," he said. "All better?"

"You're still talking," Connor said.

"You know, there's things you can do about that." Gibson was lounging on the pond's bank again.

"Pretty bold words for a man who's already in a pond in the middle of nowhere," Connor said.

"Kinky." Gibson dove under the water and swam back across the pond. There was something hypnotic about the way he handled his body, like every limb's path had been preordained by some cosmic Renaissance painter. He surfaced without making any noise, then dove again and spiraled toward the bottom of the pond.

Now barefoot, Connor stood up to peel his jeans off and watched Gibson make a slow circle around the kettle. He didn't seem to need to kick or paddle to move through the water; he just glided from surface to bottom and back again.

"I can't believe how clear the water is," he said to Connor upon resurfacing a little closer to him. "Most places I've gone swimming, you're lucky if you can see your hand in front of your face."

"I don't imagine there's much going on here to disturb the water," Connor said. He lay his clothes out flat on the dry grass a few yards from shore. One of the other kettle ponds had attracted a couple dozen thirsty heifers, one of whom was wading out up to her shoulders.

"Ain't much going on out here to disturb us, either." Gibson hauled himself up out of the kettle, the smooth lines of his muscles glistening in the sun. He shook the water out of his hair and slicked it back as he gazed from hilltop to hilltop, a smile on his face.

"Excuse me?" Connor said. There was still enough annoyance in him to show on his face.

"Well, I mean, I figure I owe you an apology." Gibson grinned as he walked up to Connor. It was hard to ignore the way the water trailed down his naked skin, leaving silver tracks that slowly vanished in the sunlight.

"You owe me a dry pair of socks, is what you owe me." Connor frowned at Gibson, even as Gibson walked up close enough to wrap a hand around his waist. "You're freezing, by the way."

"You seem to be warming up just fine," Gibson said.

"Hard and warm are two very different things." Connor drew his face back from Gibson's lips, but he let him lay a gentle kiss on his throat.

"I could help you be both," Gibson said.

"I'm listening." Connor let the slightest smile grace his lips as Gibson drew him closer. Gibson's body was still cool and damp from the pond, but his skin raised an electric tingle across Connor's body where they touched.

This time, Connor kissed him back. Gibson was eager with his lips, tactile in a way that most country boys were afraid to be. His hands, too, liked to explore Connor's body, and Connor was happy to let them get the lay of the land.

"Is that better?" Gibson said, his voice barely above a whisper despite the empty sky around them.

Connor didn't answer. Connor wrapped his hands around Gibson's firm, round ass and pulled his hips close. He could feel their cocks swelling against each other, could feel Gibson gently grinding his pelvis against Connor.

"You're gonna be the death of me, Gibson," Connor said.

"Nah, I gotta keep you around." Gibson's nails traced a lazy path up the skin of Connor's back. "A cock like yours doesn't come around every day, you know."

"I could say the same thing." Connor reached down between them to cup Gibson's balls in one hand. He liked the way Gibson half-moaned, half-purred as

173

Connor caressed them, probed carefully at the soft skin behind them with a couple of fingers.

Gibson slowly turned his attention downward, using his fingers and tongue to trace the lines of Connor's collarbone; his pectorals; his ribcage. Connor took in a soft gasp as Gibson's lips made their way along the ridge of his hipbone. His cock ached with arousal, but Gibson would only loosely grasp it in one hand as he tasted Connor's skin on his hips, his thighs, the lower reaches of his stomach.

"Now you're just being mean," Connor said. He twisted his fingers in Gibson's hair.

"You haven't seen how mean I can be," Gibson said. He flicked the tip of his tongue around the base of Connor's cock, gazing up at him with mischief twinkling in his hazel eyes. He was stroking his own cock at the same time, slowly but firmly, with the hand that wasn't caressing Connor's leg.

"Some apology," Connor said.

Gibson chuckled softly. "Is this better?"

"Is what...nnnhhh." Connor had to shift his feet to stay upright as Gibson sucked the full length of his cock into his throat in one fluid motion. His tongue had a way of wrapping around his shaft in a soft, wet grip.

Meanwhile, one of his fingers had found its way to the cleft of Connor's buttocks. He idly probed and pushed at Connor's hole, just hard enough to make Connor's body recall the heft and warmth of Gibson's cock inside him.

"Oh, fuck..." Connor gasped, clinging to Gibson's shoulders to keep his balance.

Gibson seemed to be enjoying the show. The more fervently he sucked, the faster the noise of his hand on his own cock.

It was just as well that Connor couldn't really form words at the moment. If he could speak, what would he say? Now wasn't really the best time to beg Gibson to fuck him, to lay his cock so hard into Connor's ass that Connor squealed and pleaded for more.

But Gibson's finger was working inside him now, prodding, pulling out just long enough for Connor to whimper softly in the back of his throat.

Then it was two fingers, and Connor couldn't take any more. He cried out as his cock unloaded in Gibson's mouth, leaning on the other man's muscular shoulders for balance as his load filled Gibson's throat.

He heard a muffled gasp below him, and he saw that Gibson had finished all over his naked thighs. He released Connor's cock from his mouth and fell back on the grass, panting and grinning with a trail of cum still dripping down his chin.

"There," he said. "Do you forgive me?"

Connor kept to his feet, but that was about all his current powers were allowing him to do. "Uhh…" He blinked. "It depends," he said. "If I say no, are you gonna do that again?"

Chapter Eighteen

Unit 230 was about as far from a sinister government space lab as Ty could imagine. The gate to the fenced-off rangeland was right next to a wide, shallow creek that ran down from the steep and wooded hillside. Nearby was a set of rustic corrals and a loading shoot, all built of aged and rotted pine trunks that had been sawn from the surrounding forest.

"I count all one fifty," Skip said as he dragged the loose post of the wire gate back over to the closing loops.

"Same here," Ty said. "Have a good summer, ladies!"

The heifers didn't even have a slight bleat of complaint to offer in reply.

"Heh." Skip wedged the bottom end of the gatepost into the lower wire loop. "I wish I could spend the next few months in digs like this." He used the lower loop as a fulcrum on the gatepost, so he could pull the top end close enough to bring the upper loop down on top. It was a tight gate, built to last and to put up a fight to anyone trying to open it. Even Skip's experienced hands took a couple minutes to wrestle it closed.

"I dunno," Ty said, looking around. "Looks like it gets pretty cold at night. Now, down by those ponds..."

"There's no fish in those ponds," Skip said. "We'd starve."

"Nah, there's gotta be deer and elk around there," Ty said. "And..." He went quiet and cocked his head. Had he...?

"What?" Skip said.

Ty held a finger up and turned his ear toward the southwest. He didn't hear it again; it must have been his imagination. Sure, they hadn't been out that long, but the human mind...

No, there it was again, the sound of a man yelling. He thought he heard someone breaking glass.

"What in the fuck?" Skip said, cupping one hand to his ear. "Is there someone out here with us?"

Ty's heart pounded in his chest. It was one thing to take company with you when you went out to mess around in the boondocks; it was a completely different thing to find company once you were already out there. He checked his holster on his hip; the handgun Linda had lent him was still there.

"Hold on," Skip said, pulling the map out of his pocket. He undid a couple of folds to expand the well-worn rectangle of topo lines and years' worth of notes in various kinds of pen and handwriting. "Okay, so we are...here..."

It was still early enough in the morning that Ty could figure out their direction from the sun. He wasn't sure where those voices had come from, though.

"Could be some campers," Ty said. "Or someone else moving stock through the hills."

"If it's campers, they're in the ass end of nowhere without a trail in sight." Skip was looking up and down the map with his brows furrowed. "The closest public access isn't even on this map. The forest is fronted by private land for about forty miles behind us."

Ty heard it again: a man's voice, bellowing something unparsable on the morning breeze. He closed his eyes and pointed in the direction he thought it might be coming from.

"Southwest," Skip said. "That's out in Unit 230, probably, which is home to a whole lot of nothing."

"Could be other ranchers out here moving cattle." The sound had stopped. Had it really come from that direction, or was it bouncing off the wooded hills that surrounded them?

"Could be," Skip said. "Could be someone who knows it's just the two of us bringing these cattle up all this way."

"You got a gun on you, don't you?" Ty patted his pistol.

"Of course." Skip nodded. He walked over to the gate post leading into Unit 230. "We ought to make sure the pasture's safe before we leave a hundred fifty head of cattle here."

Ty sighed. "Yeah, you're right," he said. "I don't have a great feeling about this, though."

"No, neither do I." Skip's face was grim as he pried the gate open so Ty could bring the horses through. "Seems weird, doesn't it, that you'd leave a pasture like this empty but keep the lease."

"It does," Ty said, "but Mr. Briggs is a goddamn idiot."

"Mmm." Skip frowned. "He's fucking weird, I'll give you that, but I don't think stupid is his problem," he said.

"If stupid's not his problem, what is?" Ty said.

"Marshall Briggs has several problems to worry about without adding stupid to the mix," Skip said. "He's prideful, and he's got enough temper for three men twice his size, and he's actually smart enough that he's mostly been able to handle his own problems up to this point in his life."

"Jesus," Ty said. "Do you do this to everyone?"

"Not everyone," Skip said. "But no, I think I would advise against underestimating Mr. Briggs. I think it's more than a little suspicious that there's people out here in this pasture he's been losing money to keep empty."

"Shit, I guess it is," Ty said. "But, uh, I have to wonder what..."

He went quiet as another sound came drifting down the valley from a high hilltop. Not a voice, but an engine, juicy and steady. And definitely coming from the southwest.

"What in the fuck is that?" Skip said. "There's no kind of road anywhere around here to get a jeep..."

"Dirt bike, maybe," Ty said. "Or they figured out a way to get a generator in here." He halted Blue, frowned at the hilltop. "You know, I don't know if I want to be poking around in this country."

"I don't know if I want to be responsible for losing a hundred fifty head of..."

"What in the hell would cattle thieves be doing that they'd bother with getting a generator back here?" Ty said. "This is something a little sketchier than that, I think."

"Like what?"

"Like a fucking meth lab!" Ty turned Blue around and started walking back toward the gate. "No, man, I'm getting out of here."

But Skip was pulling the gate closed behind them. "If they got crooks hiding out up on the back pasture, it's our job to figure out what's going on and how to fix it."

"No, it's not!" Ty said. "Let's just tell Linda what we saw…"

Skip laughed as he swung up on his horse. "Don't be a chicken shit, Gibson," he said. "You wanna ride for the brand, bud? This is what it means to ride for the brand."

"Ride for the brand, my ass!" Ty said. "These people treat us like shit, and I'm not getting….shot…"

Skip had apparently not meant for that to be the beginning of an argument. Skip had just said that and galloped away past the herd like that was an acceptable way to punctuate a conversation.

"Fucking prick," Ty said under his breath. The pack horse, being fond of running by nature, was already in hot pursuit of Bonito. Ty spurred Blue forward and cussed his luck as he tried in vain to catch up.

***

In the end, their journey wound up taking them a couple of miles to the southwest, up a long valley and through an irritatingly thick forest before they crested a ridge that ran north-south above a meadow where some beavers had built a series of ponds.

On the other side of the ponds, nestled just deep enough in the trees that aircraft overhead wouldn't be able to see it, was a little shack built of corrugated siding.

"What the fuck did I tell you?" Ty said under his breath, glaring at Skip as they peered down from a rock overlooking the meadow. Their horses were hanging out a couple dozen yards away, browsing on the undergrowth.

The idea here was to not catch the attention of the guy with the AR-15 walking up and down in front of the ponds.

"You can gloat later," Skip said. "Do you have a camera on you?"

"No," Ty said. "Shit. Maybe we should've brung our phones."

"I don't think we can take everyone in that..."

"We aren't going to be taking anybody!" Ty pulled Skip away from the rock and started scrambling down below the ridge. "We're going to pretend we never saw this shit, and we're going to go back where we came from and we're going to keep our skin attached to the rest of our bodies!"

"We have to at least tell Linda what's going on," Skip said.

"Are you for real?" Ty said. "Do you understand what happens to people who snitch on meth heads?"

"They have no idea we're here," Skip said.

"And they're not gonna." Ty hurried over to Blue and jumped back in the saddle. "I'm getting the hell out of dodge. You can stay behind to play hero if you want."

Apparently, Skip didn't feel brave enough to hang out and watch these people cook crank for the rest of the afternoon. He and the packhorse caught up quickly with him, and they maintained a good ass-hauling speed for the rest of the way through Unit 230.

"We ought to try and cut some time off our trip back," Skip said as Ty got off to work the gate.

"I told you, we need to stay the hell out of this bullshit," Ty said. "Telling Linda isn't going to help anything..."

"She needs to know!" Skip said. "Come on. She's trying to get this place out of the gutter, and she needs our help..."

"Yeah, I'm sure she does," Ty said. "And we're gonna help her, and help her, and help her, and mark my words the moment she's on her feet enough again, she'll screw the both of us so hard we won't know what hit us."

"It ain't gonna be like that," Skip said. "Trust me."

"Why would I trust you?" Ty said. "I know you and Linda have some history between you, and neither one of you respects me enough to tell me what the hell it is."

"What?" Skip said. "Me and Linda..."

"She's been teasing me about it since you showed up," Ty said. "I don't know what happened between you or what kind of dealings you've done..."

"We've run into each other when I was working feedlots," Skip said. "It's what people do when they work together and put effort into making friends instead of acting like paranoid crackheads."

"If there's nothing sketchy about you two, then why doesn't either one of you tell me what the fuck is going on here?" Ty was pissed off enough that the gate had come open easy. It didn't seem quite as eager to close.

"Look, right now is not the time to air all of my personal business to the world." Skip took a granola bar out of his saddlebag and opened it up. "Besides, you keep talking this big game about how you're gonna take off and you don't trust nobody and you're nobody's friend around here." He took a bite and nodded contemplatively while he chewed. "Doesn't exactly inspire my confidence in you, bud."

"Confidence?" Ty said. "You just told me you've got something to hide..."

"Everyone who's lived a life worthwhile has a couple things they'd like to keep close to them," Skip said through a mouthful of granola bar. "You, me, Linda, those fine people cooking meth back there in that kitchen."

"I know that, Skip," Ty said. "And you know what? Part of working with someone else is filling them in on things you need to know."

"I am filling you in on everything you need to know," Skip said. "Trust me. You don't need or want to know anything else."

Once again, he decided that galloping away from a conversation, pack horse hot on his heels, was something that a grown man could just do.

Ty didn't bother pushing Blue any further than Blue felt like going. Irritating as he was, Skip possessed a certain sense of self-righteous pride that would keep him from abandoning Ty. He could go ride

183

on ahead and sulk all he wanted, the last real cowboy in a world of dinks and snowflakes.

Well, fuck him.

Ty grabbed a box of snack crackers from his saddlebag and had himself an early lunch while Blue found his way down the valley. How long had he been threatening to leave this madhouse, anyway? He should have been long gone weeks ago.

He hadn't asked himself why he'd failed to make good on that threat, but the answer occurred to him anyway: did he really want to give up what he had with Skip? After all, that irritating pride and condescension didn't matter when they were tangled up with each other.

But when were they not tangled up with each other? Jesus, did it matter that they didn't consider this to be a romantic attachment? They sure spent all their time together, sharing their meals and their living space and a fair part of the free time the ranch allotted to them.

Ty glared at the hillside stretching out in front of him. They were following the curve where one low peak started rising out of a gentle ridge, and now and again Ty could catch a glimpse of Skip and the packhorse making their way through the woods up ahead.

Maybe it was just his imagination, but he thought he could see Skip checking back behind him again and again. He smiled. What was that smug son of a bitch going to do without Ty for an audience?

And that came with another question: What was Ty going to do without Skip's constant yapping to distract him from his thoughts? Did he really not have any thoughts that didn't concern Skip?

184

"You know what, Blue?" Ty said. "I think that man is hiding something from me."

Blue did not reply; he seldom did.

"And you know what's worse, buddy. What's worse is I know I'm going to have to figure out what he's hiding." Ty pried another snack cracker from the cellophane packet and shook his head. "Which, when you think about it, makes me just like him."

At that one, Blue snorted.

"Yeah, buddy," Ty said. "I know. Fucking pathetic."

Chapter Nineteen

If Linda had heard Connor the first time, she didn't respond. Another saddle pad came flying out of the tack room into the stack in his arms.

"Miss Linda, are you listening?" he said. "There is a…"

"I don't want to hear about it right now," Linda said. "Whatever you boys did or did not find…"

"Linda, this is serious!" Connor peered around the technicolor stack of wool pads and blankets in his arms. "If the authorities…"

"And I'm gonna praise!" Linda clapped as she picked up the song she'd been using to drown out Connor's attempts at being reasonable. "I said I'll praise!" Clap, clap. "Sing my praise, upon the mountain, gonna sing! And! Shout! My! Praaaaaise upon…"

"Linda!" Connor turned around so he could look her in the eyes. "Do you know how much trouble we can all get in about this?"

"Yep," Linda said. "Ain't shit I can do about it right now."

"You could call the cops," Connor said.

"And now it's *you* who doesn't understand how serious this is," Linda said. "What was it you promised me you were gonna do?"

"Not fucking this!" Connor said. "Linda, this is honest-to-God dangerous, and…"

"And it's gonna get more dangerous if whoever is out there figures out we called the cops." Linda came at him with two more saddle pads and reached over his head to pile them on the stack. "Our number

186

one priority is going to this jackpot. You are just going to have to trust me."

"You're asking for a lot of trust here," Connor said.

"Greg would trust me," Linda said. "Ain't that good enough for you?"

"Don't do this to me, Miss Linda…"

"Here's the last one." Linda slapped a checker-patterned blanket on top of the stack. "Shove those into the trailer or the truck, any which way they'll fit."

Connor had a smart-ass response to that somewhere buried in his throat, but it didn't really want to come to him at the moment. That was just fine, he guessed.

Linda's trailer was already hooked up to Connor's truck. Its gooseneck contained a tack compartment and a little-bitty living quarters, both of which had been flung open to accommodate as much equipment as they could stuff into it in a six-hour period.

Now, it had been a while since Connor had done rodeo for real, but to his knowledge these things were typically planned in advance. He assumed that you didn't usually surprise your ranch hand with an upcoming four-day jaunt out of town, especially when they'd just gotten back from one of their own.

"Just drop all those on the tarp in front." Gibson leaned out the tack room door, a tangle of halters in his free hand. "I have a method here."

"I'm sure you do," Connor said.

"Did Linda find the stretchy ties?" Gibson said.

Connor dropped the stack of saddle blankets in front of the trailer. "The what-a-what?"

"Ask her if she found the stretchy ties." Gibson's eyes were glazed over; he spoke with the robotic determination of a man far too gone in a task that only he could understand.

"Yes, sir," Connor said. It was probably a good thing he was driving. He seemed to be the last sane person left out here on this ranch.

***

The Daniel Brown Cooper Memorial Rodeo and Green Chili Festival was one of those surreal bright points in a high plains summer calendar, a three-day bacchanal soaking up one of those interminable sticky weekends between Fourth of July and the county fair. A small carnival had set up across the fairgrounds parking lot from the tent city of the chili cookoff; the smell of sugar and fryer grease carried across the entire town of Elk Creek. The sun was setting, and with the lavender dusk came a migration of people from the tent city of the chili festival to the grandstands overlooking the rodeo arena.

"Are you pre-registered?" A tired blonde woman in a safety vest leaned up against the window.

"We should be under Linda Briggs." Linda leaned across Connor's lap, thrusting a sheaf of yellow and white papers at the parking attendant. "I have Coggins and health certs for all six horses."

The blonde woman checked the paperwork against the list on her clipboard. In the grandstands, the crowd roared as the announcer narrated a bronc rider's eight seconds of fame. "Do you have your vaccine records?"

"Yep, each horse has all their papers in a little packet paper clipped..."

"Oh, I see!" The attendant smiled. "Let me just go back and check real quick."

As the attendant walked around the trailer to make sure Connor wasn't hauling stolen or plague-ridden horses, Linda grabbed her coffee from the cupholder and sucked it dry.

"Damn," she said. "We're gonna have to hit up the gas station after we get the trailer set up."

"You have drunk your entire body weight in caffeine since we left..."

"I gotta keep moving, Skip!" Linda was damn near literally bouncing in her seat. "It's all about the adrenaline."

Connor sighed and checked the time on his cell phone. They were gonna have to move fast, but they had time to get at least three of Linda's horses tacked and warmed up before her first run.

"Hey, wake up." Linda reached back to nudge Gibson, who had been solidly passed out in back since his driving shift ended five hours ago. "Wake up!"

"Mmf...What?" Gibson thrashed in the back seat for a few seconds and righted himself. "Jesus. What's going on?"

"We're at the rodeo," Linda said. "My first run's gonna be in about forty-five minutes."

"All your paperwork looks good, Miss Briggs!" The parking attendant returned with her clipboard and the sheet of papers. "You're in Lot B. The attendant will direct you to your parking spot."

"Thank you!" Linda waved as Connor pulled the rig forward.

Their rig had been assigned to a patch of hard-packed dirt between a couple of big stock trailers. Both of their neighbors had already unloaded and tacked their horses. A dozen or so big-eyed, low-built cow ponies watched them with their shaggy ears perked up as they parked.

The cotton candy energy in the air was infectious. Connor felt the electrical prickle in his veins as soon as he stepped out of the truck.

"Smells like money," Gibson said as he swung out of the cab.

"Let's hope so," Connor said.

Linda already had the trailer open and was guiding one of her barrel horses backward out of it. "Why don't you grab tack for Scooter, Bella, and Roxie and set it out on the truck bed?"

"Yes, ma'am," Connor said.

"Hey, I can grab the saddles," Gibson said. "Why don't you go and get us all checked in at the rodeo office?"

Connor paused in his tracks. It had been a long time since he'd taken care of paperwork at the box window. "Uhh..."

"You do remember how to check in at a rodeo, don't you, Skip McCoy?" He was grinning as he walked up to the tack room door.

"I'll do check-in myself," Linda said, walking up in a hurry with a horse in each hand. "I have to talk with Lorraine about my entry check. Just get these girls ready, okay?"

"Yes, Miss Linda," Connor said as he took Roxie's lead rope. "You heard her, Gibson."

"I don't want any bullshit from either of you this weekend, you hear?" Linda paused to turn and wag a finger at them as she made her way toward the grandstand. Behind her, another wild cheer rose up as a bronc rider's score of 92.8 flashed on the big electronic screen above the crow's nest.

"I'm not bullshitting nobody," Gibson said.

"I'm serious," Linda said. "We're here to work hard, run hard, make money, go home. In that order. No ifs, ands, or buts. Am I making myself understood?"

"Perfectly clear," Connor said.

Linda gave him a dangerous wall-eyed look before turning around and walking off to the rodeo office.

Connor turned to look Gibson in the eyes. "What in the hell was that about?" he said.

Gibson shrugged. "Nothing to get offended over," he said. "You and Linda need to come up with a better cover story than trying to convince me you were a rodeo cowboy, is all I'm saying."

"What the fuck are you talking about?" Connor said.

"Look, I don't mind you two playing your weird-ass little secret identity game," Gibson said, "but it would be nice if you didn't treat me like I was born yesterday."

"Man, I told you," Connor said. "This is not something you want to be involved in. It's not about you being stupid. It's about you having the common courtesy..."

"Don't fucking talk to me about common courtesy!" Ty said. "I don't think I even know your real name..."

"Why does it matter?" Connor said. "You're the..."

Gibson was staring over Connor's shoulder. He shook his head and made a throat-cut motion.

Connor turned around to see a young couple leading a couple of toddlers back to their trailer on mini ponies. He turned back to Gibson and raised his eyebrows.

"Like Linda said." Connor moved to tie Roxie to one of the metal loops welded to the side of the trailer. "We're here to work hard, run hard, win money, and go home."

"In that order." Gibson rolled his eyes and led Bella to one of the other trailer ties. "I'll believe that when I see it."

***

Now, it was clear from the prize list that someone had been making some *phone calls* in the weeks preceding the Daniel Brown Cooper Memorial Rodeo and Chili Fest. Three thousand added to the bull riding, five thousand added to the open barrel jackpot, a trailer for the weekend's high point winner, a thousand added to novice barrels with a saddle to the winner of each division.

"Just think about the money, Miss Linda." Gibson was standing outside the living quarters door, alternately pleading and pounding.

"And think about it fast!" Connor said. "You've only got twenty runs in front of you!"

"Tell them I'm scratching," Linda wailed. "Fuck this shit! I'm just going to sell these damn horses and go home!"

"Miss Linda, you just hit one barrel," Connor said. How, exactly, did Greg put up with this shit?

"One more barrel than I could afford!"

"Your first time was under fifteen seconds!" Gibson said. "Come on. You probably already won your entry fee back times…."

"There are four hundred people in this race, asshole!" Linda said. "I need to do better than…"

"Then get out there and do better!" Gibson said. "Come on, Miss Linda! Can't you just picture the look on your daddy's face when you come home without your horses?"

"Ty, shut up," Connor said under his breath.

"Fuck you," Gibson said. "I tell you what, Miss Linda, that mean old bastard is gonna be smug as a snake in a prairie dog town lookin' at you coming home empty handed."

The weeping inside the trailer grew louder. Connor rubbed his temples with his forefingers.

"Are you gonna just let him have that, Miss Linda?" Gibson said. "Are you gonna drag me and this…this Skip McCoy critter up and down from hell to breakfast just so your daddy can rub it in your face that you lost the goddamn barrel race?"

"Shut up!" Connor said. "You are going to get us fired so fast…"

"Good!" Gibson said. "I've had my fill of this crazy bullshit." He banged on Linda's door again. "Come on, Miss Linda," he said. "At least have the balls to come out and say you tried. You know he'll know you spent your last run crying in your damn...."

The trailer door burst open; behind it, Linda was at her most raccoon-like and thirsty for blood.

"Ty Gibson, if you don't get out of my fucking face right fucking now..."

"The time to get out of your face is behind us, Miss Linda!" Ty put his foot in the trailer door. "In your own goddamn words! What was it...."

Connor couldn't watch this anymore. He turned and walked toward the bubblegum nightmare of the carnival across the parking lot. Fuming and tight-lipped, he pulled his phone from his pocket and dialed his brother.

Greg picked up after one ring. "Hey, man," he said, shouting over the noise behind him.

"Greg," he said. "You at the Back Cinch?"

His brother hiccupped. "Maybe," he said. "What's up?"

"Linda has lost her ever lovin' mind," Connor said. "She's locked herself in the trailer and she's throwing a shit fit..."

"Ohhh, did she nick a barrel?" Greg said. "She fuckin' hates that."

"You mean she just *does* this?" Connor said.

"Well, yeah, on the opening night," Greg said. "Did she slam three gas station coffees and a can of Ravager before the first run?"

194

Connor stopped in his tracks and blinked. "Umm."

"Yeah, man," Greg said. "You gotta, you gotta watch out with her and the caffeine on the first night. I always switch out her coffee with..."

"Is that your brother?" Mama Jade's voice screeched over the din of the barroom. "Give him kisses from me! He needs to come home!"

"Hi, Mama Jade," Connor said.

"He says hi," Greg said.

"Tell her..."

"Looking for Rider Four-Nine-Two, Miss Linda Briggs on Lil Tricky Puppet!" The announcer's voice was a kindly rumble echoing from every speaker on the grounds. "Rider Four-Nine-Two, we are waiting for you in the main arena!"

"Awww, shit!" Connor said. "She's gonna miss her run!"

"What, you just left her back at the..."

"No, no, the other ranch hand is there talking a raft of...shit." Connor stopped dead in his tracks.

"What is it?"

"Uhhhh...." Connor's hand fell to his side as he saw a familiar silhouette hauling ass through the parking lot. Linda's barrel horse was white-eyed and slobbering at the bit. His hind legs danced and his forelegs pawed; his rider's face was a mask of rage and adrenaline. Ty Gibson's grip on his reins was the only thing constraining the hot mess from breaking into a full-on dead run.

In the rodeo arena, the crowd of waiting riders parted in the middle.

"Let him go!" Linda yelled. "Let him go, let him go, let him yaaaaaaaaaaaaaa! Yayayayayaya!"

Connor's hand flew to his mouth. He had just watched a woman and a horse transform into a fucking bullet. He realized he was running toward the arena. He heard himself yelling Linda's name, cheering her on like he or anyone on earth had power over that woman right now. She kept up her shrieking as she ran through the cloverleaf, ass in the saddle and hands at her horse's ears.

Her horse rounded the final barrel, and Linda's voice was joined by the rest of the crowd in a wild yell as the time appeared on the screen.

"And it looks like it's better late than never, ladies and gentlemen," the announcer said, "because Miss Linda Briggs just burned up the sand in here with a Thir! Teen! Point! Two! Six!"

Connor put his phone back to his ear. "Did you hear that, Greg?" he said, his voice suddenly hoarse. "Did you...thirteen point two six!"

"Holy...hey! Hey, y'all! Linda just got a thirteen point two six!"

"Jesus Christ!" Connor said. "Jesus Christ! That was fucking insane!"

The cheering in the Back Cinch was fixing to rival the cheering in the rodeo grandstands.

"I'm gonna marry that girl!" Greg said. "You hear me? I'm gonna...I'm gonna just...just marry the hell out of that girl, Connor."

Connor was walking toward Linda, who was trying to convince her blowing-hot horse to walk out a little bit after the run. "Shit, man," he said. "You'd

196

better. I don't think I can survive another rodeo with just her and this Gibson kid."

Chapter Twenty

The old man walked around the shiny aluminum trailer with his arms crossed. The desert had whittled him down over the years to nothing but his strongest components, and though time had bent his back, he moved with the grace of a man half his age.

He returned to where his daughter was standing and shook his head as he muttered to her in Spanish. His daughter rolled her eyes.

"He wants to know why you're selling it so fast," the daughter said. "He looked at the title, and it says you've only had it since Sunday."

"Uhh." Ty rummaged through his brain for the right parts he needed. "Um. Mi prima, la neh-sess-sita dinero mucho rapido," he said. "Ella me, uh, ven-day estuh, uhhh…"

The daughter muttered something more coherent to the old man, who chuckled and responded under his breath. The longer this conversation went on, the more desolate and isolated this truck stop seemed to Ty.

"Mmmm." The daughter shook her head. "It's too expensive. You can't sell it fast."

"No, ma'am, my cousin had to sell it fast," Ty said. "I got all the time in the world to move this bad boy." He slapped the lightweight, state-of-the-art siding hard enough to make the whole trailer echo.

"Hmph." The old man was frowning. "You trade?"

"No trade." Ty shook his head. "Cash only."

"He has a good rodeo horse for trade," the daughter said. "Ropes both sides."

"I'm sorry, but I just can't do a trade," Ty said.

"Okay," the old man said. "It's too expensive."

The daughter gave Ty an apologetic smile. "Sorry," she said. "Good luck, though."

"You can make an offer," Ty said. The daughter turned to him to translate.

"Three thousand and five hundred," the old man said.

Ty looked at Linda's trophy trailer, featherweight and freshly painted, gleaming in the sun looking like it had just rolled out of the showroom. Which it had.

"Look, man, thirty-five isn't even half of what we're asking," Ty said. "It's worth ten as-is..."

"But then we have to repaint it," the old man's daughter said. "I don't like this deal. Who is your cousin?"

"Now, if you offered closer to six, we could start talking..."

"And the dividers," the daughter said. "The dividers are no good."

"I give you four thousand." The old man's back straightened. He crossed his arms and looked Ty in the eyes.

Ty looked up and down the highway, rubbing the back of his neck like he was in any position at all to argue with these people. At least they were indulging him enough to haggle. The last three prospective buyers had all but cussed him out over asking this much for a secondhand trophy trailer that only fit two horses.

He wanted to go back to the ranch. He wanted to sleep in a bed. He wanted to get laid, Skip's attitude be damned.

Ty narrowed his eyes at the old man. "Forty-five," he said.

The daughter rolled her eyes. "Fine," she said. "You want cash?"

"If you got it," Ty said.

"Yes, cash." The old man extended his right hand to Ty as his daughter went back to her truck.

Ty shook it and managed to smile. "Thank you very much, sir," he said. "It's a great trailer. You're gonna love it."

***

Linda's face could have curdled milk. She went through the stack of hundreds twice, like there was going to be a miracle on the second count-through.

"Forty-five?"

"And I was lucky to get that," Ty said. "You can't just sell a brand new horse trailer out of a gas station with a three day-old title."

"I guess not." She leaned back in her lawn chair and stuffed the cash into her front pocket. "Thanks, though."

"Any time." Ty looked around the back patio of the ranch house, and out to the orchard beyond. "What do you guys do with all that fruit?" he said.

"Jam, mostly," Linda said. "A little pie filling. It's the most exciting part of my mom's life, every September."

"Huh." Ty shifted his weight. Now that it was on the tip of his tongue, this next part of the conversation didn't feel like it wanted to come out after all.

"What is it?" Linda picked up her glass of iced tea from the table.

"I noticed McCoy's not here," Ty said. "Neither is his horse."

"Is that so?" Linda said.

"Now, his rig is still here, making me wonder where he's ridden off to." Ty cleared his throat.

"He's running an errand for me." A thin, vague smile crossed Linda's features for a second. "He'll be back tomorrow."

"An errand," Ty said. "With his horse."

"Yeah," Linda said.

"You know, Miss Linda, I really do enjoy working for you," Ty said.

"That's good to hear," Linda said.

"Well, I just hope that you would tell me if there's anything going on here that I need to be concerned about it," Ty said. "I'm not in a position to be playing games."

"Neither am I," Linda said. "The moment you need to be made aware of something, you'll be made aware of it."

"Skip McCoy's not even his real name, is it?" Ty said.

Linda gave Ty a long, cold stare. "I thought you liked working for me, Mr. Gibson," she said. "I don't appreciate being accused of lying to my crew."

"You're the one who's been acting like there's some big, juicy secret behind the scenes here," Ty said. "I don't want…"

They both turned their eyes to the driveway when they heard the sound of a diesel engine. Ty swallowed. Mr. Briggs's truck was speeding down the narrow dirt lane, raising a plume of dirt behind him.

"Mr. Gibson, if I give you three hundred dollars will you drop this subject?" Linda waved part of the cash wad at him, suddenly looking like she hadn't slept in days.

Ty sighed and snatched the cash. "For now," he said. "You'd better not be getting me into any shit, Miss Linda."

***

With more than half the cattle leased, sold, or otherwise removed during Mr. Briggs's absence, evening feed was pretty much a one-man task. Sure, there was plenty of stopping and walking around the truck and climbing up on the truck and climbing back down again. But the evening breeze was cool, and hard work had a way of occupying Ty's entire brain at once.

He was tired of his mind wandering. When his mind wandered, it inevitably made tracks back to Skip—or whoever the hell he was. To an extent, Ty thought that was perfectly understandable. It had been a long time since he'd had someone to keep him company at night, and Skip's company was addictive in a way he'd never encountered before.

See? He was doing it again, thinking of Skip when he needed to be thinking of literally anything else.

Ty finished feeding by himself in a little under an hour. He shut the truck off and made his way back to the bunkhouse, half-listening to the screaming match that had been raging since Mr. Briggs returned.

Nobody came to disturb him as he made himself dinner (hot dogs and mashed potatoes, the feast of kings). Nobody came to disturb him as he got a couple beers from the cooler and went out to the patio table with a new book.

The night was sticky and threatening storms. It was hard to make himself focus on the opening to this one: the main character was a sober, civic-minded family man who seemed to pride himself on being less interesting than anybody else in the magical kingdom.

Skip would probably be into this guy. Skip would be exactly the kind of self-righteous law-mongering know-it-all who went to a wizard HOA meeting. He might not be this guy, though. This guy sucked.

Ty put the book down and opened one of his beers. Why had he grabbed two? The second one was going to be warm and disgusting by the time Ty had finished the first.

"You know damn good and well why you did that," he said to himself. "Idiot."

Was he, though? Honest or dishonest, irritating or enchanting, Skip was his lone ally out here. Linda was okay, as far as bosses went, but Ty had been around long enough to know better than to put his trust in his boss. Especially when his boss's nervous breakdowns were only marginally less destructive than her parents'.

Tonight's fireworks in the ranch house were dying down, actually. Mr. and Mrs. Briggs were still exchanging the occasional volley, but Ty hadn't heard anything shatter. Maybe Mrs. Briggs had run out of projectiles.

Ty was listening so carefully for the next development that he wasn't sure when he started hearing hoofbeats in the darkness. Someone was riding toward him, and riding hard.

"McCoy?" Ty called.

Of course, the silhouette of horse and rider went rocketing past the bunkhouses and up to the ranch house. But then, Skip McCoy wheeled his horse and rode away, back to where Ty was now standing on one of the patio chairs.

"McCoy, is that you?" Ty said.

"Gibson!" Skip came trotting over to Ty, breathing hard. "Shit. Mr...Mr. Briggs is back early. He knows."

"He knows what?" Ty walked up to Skip, his unopened beer in one hand. "I got you a beer."

"Shit." Skip launched himself out of his saddle and bent his knees as he landed. "Uhhhmm..." He took the beer from Ty and looked over to the ranch house for a second. "Oh, what the hell," he said, his voice heavy with defeat.

"What did you do?" Ty said.

"The Briggses..." Another long sigh, another long-suffering shake of the head. "The Briggses were behind on payments," Skip said. "Now they're not. But Mr. Briggs knows the payment got made."

"Payments?" Ty said. "What...what the fuck is going..."

"He's a compulsive gambler," Skip said. "As soon as any money comes in that could pay his debts off, he throws a fit and takes it off to Vegas and blows it trying to win big." He pulled his pocketknife from his pocket and opened the beer. "Literally. That is what 'compulsive' means here. The moment he has money, assets, anything to gamble with, he gambles. He has ruined his family's credit, he's been borrowing money from shady motherfuckers…"

"Is that why there's a meth lab on his lease pasture?" Ty said.

"Was. Was a meth lab on the lease pasture." Skip took a long drink of his beer. "Those jackpot winnings, plus a little help from the pastor, was enough to get these guys to back off and let the Briggses have their land back."

"It wasn't the Briggs's land to start with," Ty said. "It's…"

"Look, I know," Skip said. "I'm doing what I can, okay?"

"Is this what you two been hiding from me?" Ty said.

"Pretty much," Skip said. "Linda's a pretty private person, you know, and she doesn't want her family's business getting aired all over the place. Especially with Mr. Briggs involved with drug dealers and loan sharks and all kinds of fucked up individuals."

"What, and you don't trust me to be cool?" Ty stepped back.

"It's not about trusting you," Skip said. "It's about protecting everybody involved here. I don't want you getting fuckin' fired when Mr. Briggs finally snaps and grills you about you getting involved."

"Man, I don't care," Ty said. "I'm not gonna be staying here much longer anyway."

"Yeah, right," Skip said. "You're just as invested in this shit show as I am, and you've only known Linda for a couple months."

"It's not..." Ty bit his tongue. What the fuck, exactly, did he think he was going to say after that? He turned around and went to go grab his beer.

"It's not what?" Skip said.

"Look, man, I get sick of living like a fucking criminal," Ty said. "Everybody keeps secrets, everybody owes each other money, everybody's always after each other." He took a drink of his beer. "What happened to the damn....you know, all that cowboy code and shit?"

"There never was a cowboy code, Ty," Skip said. He walked over to him, a puzzled look on his face. "People wind up riding for a brand because they got nothing else going for them in life. That's the way it's always been. Maybe the way it always will be."

"I'm fuckin' sick of it!" Ty said. "It's like everywhere I turn, there's more fucking bullshit drama to deal with! I can't trust anybody, I can't be friends with anybody, fucking forbid I try to help someone out!" He drained his beer and hurled the bottle into the darkness, where it fell in the grass with an unsatisfying thud. "Fuck! I just...I can't take this anymore, man."

Skip nodded. "It's lonely as hell, isn't it?"

Ty paused, frozen to the spot. Something about the thought of applying the word "lonely" to his situation was...well, it was profoundly scary. Lonely was not something Ty did. Lonely was not something Ty was.

But he knew that Skip's hand on his lower back was pretty much the opposite of the feeling he'd just described.

"It's starting to feel like home here," Ty said, his voice barely above a whisper. "I don't like it."

"Starting to feel like home?" Skip said with a laugh. "That's not what I just heard."

"Not here...here on the ranch," Ty said. "Uhh." He cleared his throat, stepped closer to Skip's body.

"Oh..." There was faint surprise on Skip's voice as he took Ty in his arms. "Oh."

Ty's heart was pounding; he didn't have any idea how to continue this thread of conversation. He didn't want to be having this conversation in the first place.

So he reached up to take Skip's head in one hand, and Skip leaned down to kiss him on the lips, and for a second it felt like everything was actually just fine in Ty's corner of the universe.

Chapter Twenty-One

Some of Linda's barrel horses were what you might call "all round working horses." They had speed when Linda needed it, but for the most part they were easygoing fat-asses who were content to do whatever the hell you suggested.

Bella, on the other hand, did nothing but race and get in shape for races. Sitting on her was a little bit like getting on board a medium-heavy artillery piece and asking it to please do its homework out in the hot sun.

Connor straightened himself in the saddle when he saw Linda walking up. There was no need for her to see how hard he was panting after fifteen minutes working her mare.

"Howdy, Miss Linda," he said, waving at her as she made her way to the arena.

She leaned on the fence and nodded acknowledgement. Still, she said nothing as Connor made a few more circles around the arena on Bella.

Connor could only take so much of this. He stopped on the rail to let the mare snoof at his owner's face.

"What's up?" he said.

Linda pulled a folded sheet of glossy paper from her back pocket. "This coming weekend," she said.

"Hmm?" Connor took the paper and opened it up. It was a promotional poster for a rodeo outside Texarkana, neon green and hot pink, in the ugliest edgy wild-west font Connor had ever laid eyes on. "Holy shit," he said.

"They got Cargill Chemical to sponsor the open barrel jackpot," she said.

"I can see that!" Connor was trying to do the math on the winnings here. "They're giving away a damn dually?"

"Yeah, well, there was a little accident at the Cargill plant this winter," Linda said. "Their P.R. people have been shitting money all over that area like they just got tubed."

"Wow, Linda," Connor said, shifting in his seat and wincing. "You do know how to turn a phrase."

"There's a slight problem, though," Linda said.

"And what is that?" Connor said.

"My dad pawned my fucking trailer." Linda kept her voice and face calm while she said that, but you could see that it was taking a good deal of effort. "He said if I can play around with his property, he can play around with mine."

"How..."

"I've stopped asking myself how I could have let this shit happen, Skip," Linda said. "The only 'how' I care about right now is how I'm going to get back out of this shit."

"Umm." Connor raised his eyebrows. "Uhhh, Greg could loan you a..."

"No, we are not letting my dad near any more assets," Linda said. "That's rule number one about dealing with someone's gambling problem."

"Just put your entire life on hold?"

"I'll only be putting my life on hold if you don't help me, dumbass," Linda said. "It'll be four days' drive to Texarkana. I need to take five or six horses with me."

"Five or six?" Connor said. "Uhhh..."

"I know Gibson's trailer can fit three, and yours can fit two," Linda said.

"That's gonna be a long way for Gibson's truck with three horses behind it," Connor said.

"Mmm." Linda raised her eyebrows. "Let's say I know a guy who can meet me at a gas station not far from here. He's got a nice rig. Borrowing it from his brother, who is out of town for some unfathomable reason..."

"Oh, hell no," Connor said, hissing under his breath. "This mess is complicated enough. I am not getting Greg involved."

"Neither one of you really has a choice in this matter," Linda said. "Just play it cool. Pretend like I don't know anything. I don't want any more drama blowing up in my face."

"You don't have to tell me twice," Connor said. "Gibson's starting to catch on to me."

"Well, make him stop catching on to you," Linda said. "If there's the slightest chance that my dad figures out what we've been pulling on him..." She shuddered.

"I'll do my best," Connor said. "But I'm not letting you have a drop of coffee on that first night of the rodeo."

***

He had forgotten the unique joys that came with working alongside Mr. Briggs. He'd responded about as gracefully as one might expect to Linda's management of the ranch while he'd been absent.

"Sir," Connor said. "We have to move the moldy hay out of the barn before we move the new hay in. Mold will spread, and..."

"I don't give a good goddamn about a little mold," Mr. Briggs said. "When I have investors coming by this property, I want them to see that we run a high-class enough operation that we keep our damn hay in a barn where it belongs!"

Gibson spoke up: "We could use the indoor aren..."

"You could learn to speak when spoken to," Mr. Briggs said. "I want that nasty tarped-up mess out of the barnyard by tomorrow morning."

"Yes, sir," Connor said.

As Mr. Briggs stormed off, Gibson sighed. "How the hell are we gonna get all that hay moved by morning?"

"We aren't," Connor said. "It's physically impossible. Best we can do is get a good start, see if we can wake up early enough to get it done before he wakes up."

"Figures you'd have that kind of attitude," Gibson said.

"Oh, I'm sorry," Connor said. "Do you want to find out what he'll be like in the morning when he sees that hay still sitting there?"

"Not particularly," Gibson said. "Don't particularly want to find out how well my lungs work in the morning after shuffling black-moldy hay bales all night, either."

"Well, we signed up for this gig." Connor stuck his hands in his pockets and turned to go back to the stall he'd been cleaning.

"You know what your problem is, Skip?" Gibson was standing there with his head tilted to one side, leaning on the pitchfork heavy enough to bend the plastic tines.

"Early-onset male pattern baldness," Connor replied. "Brought on by the stress of..."

"You think that just because you're one bad break away from being on the street means you're also just one good break away from running the show," Gibson said. He shook his head. "You know goddamn good and well we don't actually have to move that nasty goddamn science project by hand, and so does Mr. Briggs."

"Man, I'm just trying not to get fired," Connor said.

"I know you are," Ty said. "And I'm trying to tell you this job ain't fucking worth it."

Connor swallowed. There was a desperation in Ty's eyes that he hadn't seen before. Or maybe had seen it, and just refused to acknowledge it. That kind of expression spoke of feelings that tended to get complicated.

"Ty, what are you talking about?" Connor said. "If you or I get a bad reference from Mr. Briggs..."

"This isn't about Mr. Briggs!" Ty said. "It's...oh, fuck it. Fuck you." He turned around and shook his head as he re-commenced cleaning the stall. "One of you assholes is gonna pay for my E.R. bill if I get mold pneumonia again."

***

The nearest Catholic church was a forty-five minute drive away, and they didn't do confession by appointment. Connor doubted that he'd have the balls to explain his situation anyway, not to a priest he'd never met before in his life. And it was going to take a lot more than a few Hail Mary's and an Our Father or two to absolve his soul of this sticky mess.

He bent his knees and twisted his fingers tight in the baling twine. At least the bales were getting lighter as the powdery black mold ravaged their insides. It was hardly any effort to pitch them high above his head, onto the third iteration of the Moldy Stack.

This time, Connor had a little bit of a plan. He'd made kind of a "quarantine area" for the worst of the moldy hay at the far end of the barn, where the worst bales were available to be fed out first before they rotted away completely. At the east end of the quarantine area, he'd made a little wall out of some dry, sun-bleached bales and a few pieces of plywood.

Not much you could do to stop airborne spores, of course, but maybe this way the poor cows would get to spend a little less time picking moldy spots out of their fodder. And maybe Connor could spend a little less time listening to Ty complain about his lungs.

He did have to admit he felt bad for the guy. Hell, if he didn't feel bad for the guy, he wouldn't be out here bucking bales under the light of the moon.

But the feelings had to stop there. Connor wasn't out here to solve his own romantic problems. Of which he'd had none, as a matter of fact, until he'd gotten tangled up with Ty.

And could you really call the Ty Gibson situation "romantic?" Where was the romance in two grimy, irritable cowboys taking years' worth of sexual frustration out on each other? Hell, even a "friends with benefits" situation required that there be some kind of friendship between the two people involved.

It wasn't like they disliked each other. It was just...well, Skip McCoy wasn't a real person, and there wasn't going to be much good feeling left between him and Ty once the truth came out.

Connor could try, he guessed. He'd rehearsed his confession to Ty more than once, while he was bored riding fence or half-awake in the shower or restless in his bunk on a hot night. He'd painted heartbreaking portraits of his brother's love for Linda, of how badly Linda needed a way to get out of her crazy family, of his own lifelong devotion to anything that would make his brother happy.

In Connor's head, of course, Ty thought that this was all understandable. Noble, even, and a little heroic in the manner of a quick-thinking scoundrel with a heart of gold. There was maybe a little arguing, a little how-could-you-not-trust-me, but at the end of the conversation they made out and made up and rode off into the sunset together and....

"What the fuck, man?" Connor paused in the middle of grabbing two more bales. This wasn't like him.

Besides, in real life, when you told someone, "oh, by the way I've been lying my ass off to you since we met about everything I've done, said, or been," they typically weren't too impressed. You can give them your justifications, you can come up with a whole trial's worth of evidence that you were picking the lesser of two evils, you can talk all day. It doesn't matter. Telling a lie is a little like pissing in a spring trough: no matter how much you clean it up or how much time passes, you can't ever get it really clean enough to drink from.

Connor's phone started buzzing in his pocket as he was chucking the bales up to the top of the Moldy Stack. He stepped out of the dust-choked shed and took the damp bandanna off his nose and mouth so he could answer.

"What's up?" he said.

"Sorry it's so late," Greg said on the other end of the line. "Luis got into town and we been shooting the shit."

"Oh, yeah?" Connor said. "How is the old buzzard?"

"He keeps shrinking," Greg said. "Says it makes the fish look bigger. He was showing me some muskie pics from his cabin up on Lake Erie, and dammit." His brother whistled.

"The cancer still keeping away?" Connor said. Last time Luis had come back from retirement in the Great Fishy North, it had been so Antonio and his sister could take care of him through a round of chemo.

"As far as I can tell," Greg said. "He looks great. Even has a little girlfriend up there at the senior center."

"Good for him," Connor said. "You all go out to the Back Cinch?"

"We'll go tomorrow for breakfast," Greg said. "He's been driving all day."

"How long is he gonna be in town for?" Connor said.

"Couple weeks, he says," Greg said. "He's flying his brothers up from Mexico and they're gonna go fish the Chalmath for a few days."

"They oughta see if Ricky will let them in the tailwater up at Ecker's Dam," Connor said.

Greg chuckled. "That's his plan exactly," he said. He went quiet for a second, cleared his throat quietly. "So."

"So." Connor cleared his throat. "I, uh, need you to do me a favor," he said. "Miss Linda's gonna give you a phone call here in a day or two."

"Is she now?" Greg said.

"Don't sound so excited," Connor said. "Her daddy is in some deep shit, Greg."

"I know that already," Greg said.

"Well, be careful." Connor sighed. "I know she's real special to you, buddy, but damn. There's a lot of sweet little barrel racing girls out there in the world."

"Well, if you know so much about women why don't you…"

"I'm just saying," Connor said. "Anyway. She's gonna call you in a few days, because she's gonna need you to haul her to a rodeo in fucking Texarkana."

"She's gonna what?" Greg said, suddenly sounding more like he was gonna take Connor's warning to heart.

"Yeah, I guess the local pesticide plant poisoned a few people's water supply or something," Connor said. "They're offering a jackpot like you wouldn't believe."

"In Texarkana?" Each syllable in "Texarkana" was a little more panicked than the last.

216

"Look, her daddy's crazy and her mom's crazy, and apples don't fall far from trees," Connor said. "I thought you knew what you were getting into with this girl."

"No, I'll do it," Greg said. "Texarkana, though." He made a small, perplexed noise on the other end of the phone. "Texarkana. Shit, Connor. We're gonna have to go that whole drive pretending we don't know each other from a hole in the ground!"

"Oh, good, you figured it out yourself," Connor said.

Greg laughed. "Bet this will be one hell of a good time, though!" he said.

Connor winced. "I'm starting to feel like you and I have a different idea of what a good time entails."

Chapter Twenty-Two

In the past several weeks, Ty had become an expert in burying his face in a hymnal and muttering non-words while he shuffled side-to-side along to the beat of the worship music. Not church. Church wasn't quite sinister enough for these people.

He had taken to positioning himself between Skip and Linda all through the Sunday service. That still meant he had a dancing, hand-clapping Hallelujah generator next to him on either side, but at least there was a person he knew somewhere in there. Maybe. Depending on how excited the congregation got during the service, the Skip and Linda that Ty knew could disappear completely for an hour or more.

Today, at least, there had been no miracles in the rodeo arena and no prayers answered on the open range. No relatives had been crushed by a defective vehicle, and no herds were threatened by an unknown epidemic. The congregation sang and danced and shouted its praise, and it was done, and Ty got to go get his donuts.

"It's Gibson, right?"

Ty turned around to see a tall, smiling mass of cowboy in front of him in a blue striped pearl snap.

"Uh, yeah," he said, extending his hand. "Ty Gibson."

"Ned Murphy," the cowboy said as they shook hands. "I came in third after you at Sugar Beet Days last year."

"Steer wrestling?" Ty said.

"You betcha!" The big cowboy grinned. "I knew I'd run into you somewhere!"

Ty smiled as if he couldn't hear his own heart beating louder than the whole congregation stomping and clapping at once. Had they met? If they had met, how much had they talked? Did he know?

"Small world," Ty said with a lame laugh.

"You working for the Briggses, then," Murphy said.

"Yes, sir," Ty said.

Murphy had a funny kind of smile on his face as he nodded, like he'd been watching this shit show go down for a while. "Linda's good people," he said. "I like her mom, too."

"It's a good gig," Ty said with a curt nod. "Good family." He said that last bit a little firmer than maybe he needed to. Whatever. He didn't know this kid from a hole in the ground, and it didn't take a psychic to see how badly he wanted to gossip about Linda's family.

Miss Linda was talking with the pastor, removed a little from the rest of the congregation. Though she was smiling, her eyes were serious, and her gaze kept darting around the room.

And Skip, of course, was laughing it up with a couple of young guys who appeared to work at a local feedlot. Ty ignored the combination of nausea and rage in his belly as Skip said something that made both the punchers nearly double over laughing.

There were still two Boston Cream donuts left when he got to the table, though, so that was something.

***

"Don't we usually, uh, turn left here?" Skip looked out the passenger side window, then back at Linda.

"Usually." Linda had her big sunglasses on, and she'd crammed a ball cap down over her Sunday hair.

Skip made a faint sound of surprise and went back to looking at the highway ahead of them. The warble of the singer on the radio took over the SUV cab. This was Linda's mom's car, or at least it was for the time being.

After a mile or so, Linda pulled over on a turnout and put the SUV in park. She leaned the driver's seat back, turned the AC up, and slumped backward with a heavy sigh.

"We're meeting with a church friend of mine," she said. "I need to talk to him about watching the ranch while we're in Texarkana. Won't be long."

"We were just at church," Ty said.

"And so was fucking Ned Murphy," Linda said. "Trust me. It's better to just stop out here and have a little...chat." She perked up when she caught sight of a car coming in the rearview mirror. "All right. Everybody out and start messing with my right front tire."

"Yes, ma'am," Ty said, unbuckling his seatbelt.

As Ty and Skip got to standing around looking useless, a little black sedan pulled up. Linda went over to talk to the passenger, a round black-haired woman who had to interrupt her conversation a few times to tell a kid to settle down. The conversation didn't last long, and it didn't seem to Ty like it was dramatic enough to necessitate going through this whole drug deal scenario. But what did he know?

After a couple of minutes, the black sedan rolled its windows up and pulled out of the little gravel patch.

"What was that about?" Skip asked.

Linda smiled. "That was about getting someone to help on the ranch while we're gone," she said. "They covered for us last time, but this time's going to be a little trickier."

Ty and Skip both answered that with a unanimous "Ummm..."

"My father is adamant that I stay home from this thing," Linda said, leaning against the passenger side of the SUV's hood. "The way he sees it, I'm being irresponsible with the way I go and earn my paychecks, because my entry fees are money he could be blowing at a roulette table somewhere." She glanced down the highway; the wind had begun to pick apart her carefully coiffed church hair.

"So, reading between the lines here," Skip said. "Is he, uh, gonna..."

Linda smiled. "Tomorrow night, I'm gonna talk to him about the notices we been getting from the mortgage company," she said. "He's been trying to hide them from me..."

"Shit, the mortgage company?" Ty said. "You mean, you guys are gonna lose the place?"

Linda went slack for a second as she stared at him through her bug-eye shades. "Gibson, we've *been* gonna lose the place," she said. "The only reason they're cutting me any slack is because..." She looked up and down the highway, like a jackrabbit was gonna listen in on the conversation.

"Because why?" Skip said.

"Because our pastor's brother works for the bank," Linda said. "And I've been making payments, little ones, but I've been making payments on this mortgage he took out a few years ago." Her voice was getting a little louder and a little less steady as she spoke. "And my dad would lose his fucking kittens," she said, "if he knew that I was embarrassing him in front of the congregation like that, when he thinks he's just one fucking lucky roll away from winning enough to buy this whole shitty town!" Her clenched fists beat a little at her sides.

Skip nodded. A distant, knowing look came over him as he watched Linda walk back around to the driver's side door, arms stiff and jaw clenched.

Ty raised his eyebrows; Skip waved his hand briefly like he was shooing a fly.

"All right," Ty said as he got back in the rear passenger seat of Mrs. Briggs's car.

Once both Ty and Skip had gotten in, Linda started the engine and signaled to pull out. She took a long, deep breath and licked her lips before speaking.

"Anyway," she said. "Tomorrow night, I am going to start some shit with my father about the statements he's been hiding from me, yelling at us about not paying what we owe on that mortgage."

"Mm-hmm," Skip said.

"At some point, I am going to get him off the property," Linda said. "The second he is out of that driveway, I want you boys hooked up with all my horses and all my shit, and I want you to meet my fiancé at the gas station out on the highway."

"You want us to *what*?" Ty said.

222

"I know it's dramatic," Linda said, "but I can't afford not to go to this rodeo. Okay? My fiancé's even gonna spot me my entry fees. If my dad wants to raise a fuss with his damn pride, he can do that to himself, but he's sure as shit not gonna keep getting away with doing it to me!"

"What are we gonna do if your dad figures out we're running off with your horses?" Skip said.

"That's a good question," Linda said. "My plan was to piss him off at me so much he'll be miles away by the time you get everybody loaded."

"So, what, are we supposed to hide our trailers…"

"I'll wait until the sun goes down, how's that?" Linda said.

"I don't like loading horses in the dark," Ty said, as if the lack of light was a real problem or even close to being the central issue here.

"I don't like this either, Mr. Gibson," Linda said. "I'll give both of you five hundred dollars."

"If you're doing this after dark, why don't you just have your fiancé wait down the highway and come get the horses after your dad leaves?" Skip said.

"Because if you're on his property he can shoot you," Linda said. "And my daddy would like nothing more than to shoot Greg and teach me a lesson."

Ty looked at Skip. Skip looked at Ty. They both made a "hmming" noise that was higher-pitched than either would acknowledge.

"Okay," Skip said. "Wait until dark, hook the trailers up, wait for your daddy to leave, and pull a grab-n-go with your horses."

Beneath her bug-eye shades, Linda's mouth smiled. "Why, Mr. McCoy," she said. "I don't believe I could have phrased that any better myself."

***

It had been Monday night that Ty had finally snapped and taken the weed whacker to the banks of tall grass and flowering ragweed around the bunkhouses. His primary aim had been to go all night without suffocating on the pollen. The grill iron he'd found in the cut grass (along with two rusted snaffle bits, a fairly new spur, and a partial raccoon skeleton) was just a nice little bonus.

The grill iron was just big enough to fit over the 55-gallon steel drum that sat in the courtyard by the lawn furniture. Some prior ranch hand had already done the drilling and fiddling and cutting necessary to put a fire-building platform about a foot down into the barrel, and there was no shortage of fuel around the Triple V Ranch.

And they'd run a big sale on the good hot dogs and bratwurst.

"What do we have tonight?" Skip McCoy sauntered out of his bunkhouse, hair still wet from the shower. Before Ty could put his spatula up and stop him, he'd picked up Ty's book from the table and started reading the back.

"Rich in gems and precious minerals, bone-dry Scarpithia offers the life of a king to the man brave enough to terraform it," he said, reading in the melodramatic tenor of an announcer in a movie trailer. "But when young Saul..."

"Give me that." Ty bounded over and snatched the book away from Skip.

"What? I wasn't…"

"Just leave my shit alone, okay?" Ty said, turning away so Skip wouldn't see his face flush. "It's none of your business what I entertain myself with in my free time."

"I…aww, shit, I wasn't making fun of you," Skip said.

"Okay," Ty said. He stuffed the book in his back pocket and picked up his spatula again.

"I just don't meet a lot of cowboys who read like you do." He sat down in one of the lawn chairs and put his feet up on the table.

"You ought to meet more cowboys," Ty said.

"I mean, with all the aliens and wizards and shit," Skip said.

"Yeah, well, y'all spend your whole day in church for your aliens and wizards fix," Ty said, his voice a little sharper than he wanted. "Then you go and get offended when people write about aliens and wizards for fun because they're not real." He looked at Skip, waiting for a reaction.

To his surprise, Skip looked like he was weighing that statement for a couple seconds and then broke out laughing. "Yeah, okay," he said. "I don't think I've heard it phrased like that before."

Ty cocked his head.

"No, you're right," Skip said, nodding. "I mean, that's kind of what I meant when I said it's funny to see a cowboy reading about space wars and magic kingdoms and shit. I mean, you see people getting…" He snorted. "Yeah, offended. Turn that shit off!"

"I mean, I know not all religious people are like that..."

"You wanna complain about religious people?" Skip said. "You're talking to a gay Irish Catholic."

Something about the phrase "Irish Catholic" stuck in Ty's mind. He couldn't for the life of him figure out where it was supposed to stick—it just hung out on that big old "to be filed" bulletin board in his brain's front lobby.

"And, I mean, it's not just religious people, I think," Skip said. "It's people who don't want to be questioned. You know, I mean, I'm happy with my faith, as a gay guy, because I like asking questions, and I like having to challenge myself. Like, why does it mean so much to me to be openly gay? Why does it also mean so much to me to believe in God? What is me, anyway?"

"Isn't it 'who am I?'" Ty said with a faint smirk.

"No, it's 'what is me?'" Connor said. "'Who am I?' is a completely different question."

"Whatever you say," Ty said. "That, uh, sounds like a shitty kind of existence, if you ask me."

"I mean, it was, for a long time," Skip said. "I dunno. I think...I think you just get to a point where you either give up and die, or you resolve to keep yourself going and realize that part of 'keeping yourself going' is saying 'fuck it' and making yourself happy. Somehow."

"Yeah," Ty said. He thought about that last fight with his mom, about yanking that wallet out of her hands and speeding down the highway as fast as his engine would take him. "Yeah, I guess at a certain point you gotta...gotta say you're worth it."

"And for a lot of people of faith, you know, that's...not good," Skip said. "On a moral level."

"Then why would you keep your faith," Ty said, "if it's gonna come with people who are, you know, against loving yourself and taking care of yourself?"

"That's a good question," Skip said. "See, before I came here, my theory was I stuck around for the community." He stood up and walked over toward his bunkhouse. "But see, going to these Baptist services...okay, so Catholics and Protestants have some big differences in the way they look at God and church, all right? Like, we believe Jesus is physically present at the church service, and Baptists, like Miss Linda, they're about his spiritual presence."

Ty blinked. "I follow, I think," he said.

"And then Baptists got this whole 'fellowship' thing going on, which I don't fully understand." Skip had stepped into his kitchen, where he was reaching for the mini fridge he'd acquired in Mr. Briggs's absence. "But it's much more of a community worship thing, you know?"

"I don't think I know," Ty said. "But I think I get what you're saying."

"So, I'm thinking, here I should actually be much happier with the Baptist service than I am with the Catholic service, and I'm wondering, why is that?" Skip returned to the table with a couple of beers in hand. "It's a good question."

"Huh." Ty started picking up brats and flipping them over. "Gotta say, I don't hear that a lot from religious people," he said.

"You'll have better luck if you don't compare believing in God to believing in wizards and aliens."

227

Skip sat back in his chair and cracked his beer open. "Well. For the most part."

"I'll have to tell you about the winter my mom spent in Sedona," Ty said. "The wizards and aliens thing didn't come out of the blue."

Chapter Twenty-Three

It was really a shame that some unseen power had appointed Connor to be some kind of Destroyer of Catholic Stereotypes. The puddle of guilt beneath the swamp cooler of his mind had grown into a reservoir large enough for a thriving walleye fishery and a marina that rented pontoon boats.

It was the guilt, more than any actual possibility of being caught, that propelled him all the way out here to make this phone call.

"Hey, man," Greg said. "I'm about ten miles down the highway from the gas station."

"Sounds good," Connor said. "And Linda went over her plan with you?"

"Yep. I've got hay bags up for all her horses. You and your partner just gotta unload 'em and tie 'em to my rig, and we'll be all set."

"Now, she hasn't told us how she plans on meeting up with your rig," Connor said. "Am I gonna be in for any unpleasant surprises?"

"Not as far as I know," Greg said. "But, uhh, she hasn't told me. I'm just gonna take off for Texarkana and wait for her to call, I guess."

"Can I ask you something?" Connor said.

"About Linda?" Greg said.

"Yeah," Connor said.

"Man, I know she's a handful," Greg said. "But she is good people, Connor. Look at how loyal she is to her folks."

"Oh, I'm lookin' at it," Connor said. "Well, kid, as long as you're happy." And completely in control of who got to inherit the ranch.

"I'll be happy when I get to put a ring on her finger," Greg said. "I appreciate you helping me out, I really do."

"Anything for my little brother," Connor said.

"Okay, I gotta go," Greg said. "I'll see you after dark. Linda's gonna call me when it's time."

"Got it," Connor said. "Good luck not blowing my cover."

"Yeah, same to you." Greg laughed as he ended the call.

***

Connor and Ty took shifts getting all their equipment together for the rodeo. One of them would pack, and the other would lounge around the courtyard or mess with the barbecue and act natural. They'd hauled Linda's saddles over to their pickup trucks one at a time, over the course of the day's chores. She'd stuffed all her other tack into duffel bags, and there was no telling where those had gone.

By the time it was dark enough that they could hook up the trailers unnoticed, the air was electric. Connor paced back and forth across the courtyard while Ty prodded at a low fire in the barbecue. They weren't making conversation.

Connor had to wonder how much of the tension was his own fault. He didn't have to go rib at Ty for his love of cheesy sci-fi, and he certainly didn't need to turn it into an awkward conversation about subjects best not discussed around the grill.

And he definitely...

A loud, furious "WHAT!" came from the ranch house, followed by something Connor couldn't discern.

Both he and Ty scurried to the corner between the bunkhouses where they could get a decent view of the ranch house and the yard without looking too suspicious.

Linda was yelling something now, and her mom was squealing too.

"Here we go," Ty said, shaking his head slowly as he watched shadows move behind the curtains.

"You think we ought to head to the barn?" Connor said.

"I'll go first." Ty nodded. "You follow in a few minutes."

Connor stayed behind and watched the storm develop inside the ranch house. Linda did most of the initial screaming, but it didn't take too long for her father to take over. You could see them stomping around after each other inside the house, until eventually Linda's shadow stopped and rushed at the bigger silhouette.

"What the fuck?" Connor said to himself as he watched the two shadows tussle. If he needed to go in there...

But the smaller shadow broke free and bolted for the door. Connor held his breath as he watched Linda sprint out the house with a small, dark object held above her head. She leapt into her mother's car and started the engine. As soon as the headlights were turned on, she whipped out the parking spot in reverse as her daddy came out the door behind her.

"You thieving little bitch!" He stumbled on the front stoop but recovered to run down the rest of the walk toward his truck. "I'll whip you until you regret the day you were born!"

Well, here it was. It was happening. Connor went over to the barbecue and dumped the five-gallon fire bucket all over it, sending ash and steam hissing up into the twilight.

Mr. Briggs started his engine. Connor waited until he heard the tires skidding out of the driveway.

By the time he got over to the barn, Ty had already loaded two of Linda's barrel horses into his trailer. He had two more in hand, one of which he handed to Connor.

"I'm gonna throw Roxie in and go," Ty said. "Hasta luego, good buddy."

"See you at the station," Connor said. He went around to the back of his trailer and opened it up.

Fortunately for him, Linda's horses were well-trained enough that they got into any kind of trailer as soon as you pointed them in. It only took him a couple minutes to get both horses in his rig, shut the door, and get out on his merry way.

His hands were sweaty on the steering wheel by the time he was pointed up the driveway. These past couple days had been spent trying not to think of the myriad things that could go wrong tonight. Every single pair of headlights he saw was a harbinger of doom.

When his phone buzzed in the cupholder, he almost went off the road.

"Linda!" Connor said as soon as he'd answered the call.

"I'm pulling in at the street to get to the ATM," Linda said. "He's right behind me. You guys are totally fine."

"We'd better be," Connor said. "And you be careful."

"Gotta go," Linda said, and she hung up the phone.

"Jesus, I hope she knows what she's doing," Connor said to himself.

The night was cool, cloudy, and moonless; the gas station was a neon oasis on the right side of the highway. Connor pulled his rig up next to a familiar trailer—a six horse slant load with a full living quarters and a title in Connor Dougherty's name. His brother was leaning up against one side while Ty loaded Roxie.

Connor got out of the truck and walked around to the back of his trailer to open it up.

Ty came out of the big trailer. "Greg, I'd like you to meet my, uh, coworker here on the Triple V, Skip McCoy. Skip, this is Greg Dougherty."

Connor and his little brother sized each other up across the parking lot. Greg gave Connor a tough-guy reverse nod and an unimpressed stare as he walked over to him.

"Nice to meet you, Mr. McCoy," he said, extending one hand.

"And you as well, sir," Connor said. His ability to keep a straight face was well enhanced by his brother's iron handshake. Behind the mean mug, Connor could see a gleam of mischief.

"Hope you been mighty careful with my Linda's horses, now," Greg said, putting a gruff edge on his voice that was never there in real life.

For fuck's sake. The little shit was going to milk this opportunity for everything it was worth, wasn't he?

***

They picked Linda up on the on-ramp to the interstate. Mrs. Briggs's car was nowhere in sight, just Linda standing there with her thumb out and a backpack slung over one shoulder.

She jumped into Greg's truck before Greg could even get it stopped.

"Come on, let's go," she said. "I swear I saw my daddy's truck out looking for me."

"Miss Linda, what happened?" Ty said.

"I started depositing all his cash into my bank account," Linda said. "He wasn't too happy about that, so I threw his wallet into the bushes out back of the bank and he went running after it."

"Holy shit," Connor said.

"You watch your mouth in front of my fiancée, boy," Greg said, glaring daggers back at Connor.

"Sweetheart, he means for the best," Linda said, touching Greg's arm. Connor swore he could see a smirk behind the concern on her face. "Anyway, I booked it over to my friend's house, she dropped me off here, and her husband brought my mom's car back home."

"You've got some real devoted friends, Miss Linda," Ty said.

"We like to help each other out." Linda smiled back at them before turning to Greg. "Did you bring me any food?" she said.

"Gotcha some cherry flavor pocket pies and a four-pack of Ravager at your cousin's station," Greg said.

"You really do love me," Linda said. "Deb wasn't working, was she?"

"Oh, no, it was some red-headed guy." Greg reached behind him to grab a plastic sack from the floor in front of the middle seat.

"Good," Linda said. "By the time my daddy figures out what happened to him, we'll be halfway back from Texarkana with two saddles and a boatload of cash money." She tore open the cardboard box of energy drinks and cracked one of the tall neon orange cans. "These two didn't give you any trouble, did they?"

"They were fine," Greg said. "That McCoy's a slow worker, though."

Connor fought the urge to slap the back of his brother's head. "Apologies, sir," he said.

"Don't be sorry," Greg said. "Be faster."

"Yes, sir," Connor said. He glanced over to Ty, who was looking more than a little bewildered.

Damn. Asking Greg to stick to a lie was like asking a plough horse to cut and sort fresh steers from the range. No matter how willing he was, there were just some things he was not cut out by nature to do.

***

Connor was just waking up when they stopped for gas in Amarillo, in a little run-down truck stop watched over by a plaster cowboy some fifty feet tall. The sun was rising through a thick haze that promised to turn into afternoon thunder.

It was weather that made him wish there was nobody else in the truck with him and Ty.

But that was beside the point. Linda was finished with her four-pack of Ravager and talking a mile a minute.

"So, then I guess Amy texted Marsha the next morning and said, you know what just don't come up here, so what did Marsha do? She just stayed home and went on with her life." Linda shook her head and reached up to take her hair out of its ponytail.

"Like you do," Greg said. He pulled up to a diesel pump and shut the truck off.

"So, then I get a text from Marsha, and she's complaining to me about how Amy went and threw her under the bus, and she has to deal with all these nasty old church ladies complaining about the chafing dishes not being matched to the damned heating elements, and Amy can't even do her the courtesy of being there to get yelled at." Linda flipped the mirror down in front of her and started fishing in her purse.

"Uh-huh." Greg flipped the button to open both fuel tanks and got out of the truck. "Sweetheart, I'm gonna be right back. Do you want anything in the..."?

"Oh, I'm gonna go in and pee and get some snacks just as soon as I don't look so homeless," Linda said. "Ty and Skip, can you please check on the horses and offer them some water from...oh, fuck, we didn't bring a water tank." She sat back in her seat. "Shit."

236

"I brought water from my well at home," Greg said. "We can always put Fighterade in it if they won't drink."

"Okay, try that," Linda said. "Or we can try distilled water."

Connor was already out of the truck. He hoped that Greg had at least remembered to drain the nasty moldy water out of his trailer tank before setting out on this strange little journey. If Linda had been on the phone with him, he might not have had time to think that one through.

He was looking through his tack room for where Greg had put water buckets when Ty came up behind him.

"Jesus!" Connor startled a little.

"Sorry," Ty said, his voice low. "Oh, Greg had me put the buckets up in the living quarters."

Connor's jaw clenched. He had just cleaned that carpet a week before he'd left. "Thanks," he said through gritted teeth.

"Can you believe Linda's fiancé?" Ty's voice dropped to a whisper. "He's crazier than she is!"

"He's a weird little dude, for sure," Connor said. He couldn't look Ty in the eye as he went out of the tack room, where equipment belonged, and went next door to the one clean and civilized place they were going to have access to for the duration of this rodeo.

"Rich as hell, though, it looks like," Ty said. "Kind of makes you wonder why he don't help Linda out a little."

"Yeah, this is a nice living quarters," Connor said, grabbing the whole stack of buckets as best he could without smearing horsey filth all over the place. "Don't know why he's using it as a storage shed."

"I mean, the old man can't owe that much," Ty said. "He could at least help them get ahead on the mortgage."

"I get the feeling that helping Linda out involves talking sense into Linda," Connor said. "And we both know how easy that is."

Chapter Twenty-Four

It was getting to be that point in the summer when the late afternoon inevitably brought a thunderstorm along with it. The thick, grey sheets of rain made it hard to drive a full rig anyway. Trying to drive a full rig through an unfamiliar town while trying to find a Murphy's Feed was what you might call "damn miserable."

Ty kept his eyes on the slick, hazy world outside his window. Skip might be dumb enough to try to get in between these two lunatics, but Ty was just trying to ignore the fight escalating in the front seat.

"I'm trying to maintain my speed!" Greg was saying, swatting away Linda's phone.

"We're gonna hit a construction zone in…"

"I see the damn construction zone, sweetheart!" Greg said. "Can you let me focus on the road?"

"I'm trying to tell you there's a back way in," Linda said. "Can't you just listen to me for once in your…"

"Guys, let's just all sit back," Skip said. "We have plenty of time. We can…"

"It is not your place to tell me what to do!" Greg turned his head for a moment and glared at Skip.

"I'm not trying to tell anybody what to do, sir," Skip said through clenched teeth.

It was the damnedest thing with these two. Skip could not say anything without provoking some kind of weird chest-puffing from Greg, and it only took Greg a remark or two to completely scrape off the veneer of civility that Skip liked to keep about him at all times.

"Eyes on the road!" Linda said. "I swear to God, if you can't keep your temper in check..."

"My temper?" Greg said. "My temper's the problem here..."

"Take the left two lanes to exit on..."

"Dammit, what left two lanes?" Greg raised his voice and pounded on the steering wheel in frustration. "Fucking Christ, I hate this town!"

"Let's just get off at the next exit and turn around," Skip said.

As Greg opened his mouth Linda made a hissing noise to cut him off. "We are taking the back way," she said. "End of the fucking discussion."

***

Not one of them said a word as they finally pulled into the Murphy's parking lot. The rain was easing up, but Greg still had to have the windshield wipers on full blast for them to see anything.

"I'll stay out here with the truck," he said, not looking at Linda or behind him as he put the truck in park.

Ty was eager to get out of the cab. With nobody talking and everybody tight-jawed, it was starting to get claustrophobic in there. Even the wet and the rain was preferable to listening to three people argue over something that you didn't care about in the slightest.

He, Skip, and Linda all hurried into the feed store, slickers pulled up close to their hat brims to keep the wet out. A rush of cool, dry air met them as the automatic doors sensed their approach. It smelled like bird shit and molasses.

"I have to pee," Linda said as soon as they'd cleared the entryway. She handed a list to Skip and patted him on the shoulder. "Go on and grab a cart," she said.

Before Skip could respond, Linda had hurried off to the ladies' room.

"So that's her dearly beloved, huh?" Ty said, shaking his head. He grabbed an orange cart from a stack by the door and pulled it along with them.

"I guess it is." Skip's voice was brittle.

Ty watched him as they walked through an aisle of garden hoses and sprinkler accessories. After the chaos of the journey and the storm outside, the store felt weirdly quiet. He thought he could recognize the voice of the singer on the store radio, but he couldn't quite place the melody or the lyrics.

Skip grunted as he stopped to survey a display of expanding coil hoses. His eyes were narrowed, and his lips were pursed. "There's gotta be a hose in that trailer," he said.

"Just get it anyway," Ty said.

From the way Skip looked at him, it seemed like he thought he'd been talking to himself in his head. "Yeah," he said. He reached up and grabbed a ten-footer and stuck it in the cart. "Grab a multi-spray nozzle, too."

"A what?"

"One of those plastic ones like we use to hose the horses off with," Skip said, waving his hand. He was glaring at the list, shaking his head.

Ty grabbed one of the nozzles he needed and walked over to the cart. "Hey, you doing okay?" he said.

"Yeah, I'm good," Skip said. "Just fucking tired of being on the road."

"I hear that," Ty said. "I don't know what fuckin' Greg's..."

"Look, enough about fucking Greg," Skip said. Anger flashed across his face for the briefest of moments. "I just wanna get our shit, get to the rodeo grounds, send the damn lovebirds to their hotel, and lay down in that living quarters."

"That sounds like a decent night," Ty said. "What's next?"

"Bucket hangers," Skip said. "Because I guess we're too good for baling twine."

Ty chuckled as he grabbed the cart and started heading toward the horse supply section of the store. "Sounds like she's just trying to spend his money," he said. "Wonder where they go out to eat tonight?"

"That little shit better..." Skip shut himself up suddenly, looked down the aisle as if Greg Dougherty was walking up behind them.

Ty licked his lips. "Huh."

"What?" Skip glared at him.

"Just odd, is all," Ty said. "You're usually a little more, uh, reverent toward the gentlemen lucky enough to employ us."

Skip snorted. "I don't really consider that gentleman to be my employer," he said.

"Duly noted." Ty kept pushing the cart forward.

It was all coming clear to him now. Skip McCoy's quiet feud with Greg hadn't started at the gas station back by the ranch, and it hadn't started in the truck on the way down to Texarkana. It had started long before Linda had started making sly remarks, teasing Ty with something she knew and he didn't, bribing Ty to keep his mouth shut and not rock the boat.

It was plain as day; Ty couldn't believe he'd been fool enough to miss it this whole drive down here.

Skip and Greg were no strangers. They were exes, and it hadn't been pretty.

Now, Ty wasn't sure how that worked out with Linda's involvement, but he was starting to get curious. Had she been the other woman? Was Greg straight now? Had Skip been an unfortunate experiment for him, a foray into dark and sinful waters from which he'd been reluctant to return?

Or—and this was a juicy possibility—had Skip seduced him? He'd heard stories before, of lonesome gentleman ranchers who'd become intrigued by the lifestyle of their sturdy young cowpunchers. It could...

"Where the hell do you think you're going?"

Ty realized he'd cruised well past the horse supplies and was now wandering amongst the woven wire and the plastic caps to dull the sharp ends of T-posts. Skip was walking behind him, weariness written deep on his face.

"Oops," Ty said. "Sorry."

"Hold on," Skip said. "We do need to get rope. That should be over with the chain and the, uh, bulk hardware in that aisle." He shook his head as he looked over the list again. "Jesus. You'd think we'd

243

packed for this thing in a hurry in the middle of the night."

***

The rodeo grounds were about an hour outside of Texarkana. You took a turn off the highway and went up the frontage road a ways, right to a little town called Rudy that boasted three feedlots and the glittering hulk of a Corn King Megaplex. Ty could swear that he'd seen the same rickety carnival rides set up outside the last rodeo Linda went to.

Greg had been either kind enough or smart enough—or both—to rent Linda's horses some stalls to stay in while they were at the rodeo. It took the four of them the better part of an hour to get all five horses put up for the night. The rain did not let up the entire time they were working. It roared on the metal rooftops, making everyone shout at each other and cup their hands to their ears.

"Hey guys, there's a tornado watch for the area," Linda said as she came down the barn aisle with a bale of hay. "I want you to keep a radio or something on for the night."

"Yes, ma'am," Skip said.

"What do we do if there's, uh, a tornado?" Ty said.

"Let 'em run," Linda said. "They all got brands."

"Yes, ma'am," Skip said. "What do we do?"

"Get in a ditch and pray to Jesus, McCoy," Greg said. "Didn't they teach you that in grade school?"

"Greg, would you shut the hell up?" Skip's voice matched a couple of recent lightning strikes for its sharpness.

"Skip!" Linda said.

"Sorry." Skip shook his head. "Long day."

Ty was watching Greg, waiting for the explosion of temper that would be perfectly rational from a pain-in-the-ass employer. But Greg waved him off and said, "you're good."

"Come on, Greg!" Linda said. "Our reservation does not say 'ish' on it!"

"I'm a comin'," Greg said. "I'm a comin'."

Skip watched them for a long while as they walked down the barn aisle. Overhead, the lightning had gotten so frequent that you couldn't pick out the individual thunderclaps anymore.

Ty walked along the stall fronts, double checking that all the latches were shut and all the horses were chowing down on something. The whole while, Skip kept watching after Greg and Linda. He had a pensive frown on his face, and his jaw worked gently beneath his stubbled cheek.

"You okay?" Ty said, walking up behind him.

"Yeah," Skip said. "You know, I'd kind of hoped that the boyfriend was going to have, uhh, some kind of calming effect on Miss Linda."

"Yeah?" Ty laughed. "Wishful thinking, bud," he said.

"I don't think I've seen them do anything but fight the entire time we've been out here," Skip said.

"Some straight guys like that," Ty said. "Makes 'em feel like, I dunno...like..."

"Nobody *likes that*," Skip said.

"Well, it makes no difference to me who likes what in that situation," Ty said. "Don't know why you're cut up about it."

"I ain't cut up about anything," Skip said, turning around. "Just tired of dealing with Linda's damn drama."

"Are you, now?" Ty said.

"I..." Skip glanced toward the other end of the barn aisle. He sighed. "Jesus. You know, I've been wondering what exactly the Corn King Megaplex is."

"I think it's some type of arcade thing," Ty said. "Looks like a big, obnoxious waste o' money."

"Don't you wanna go see what it is, though?" Skip said. "I'll buy."

Ty looked at the horses, looked at Skip, looked at the chaos outside. "Linda told us to stay back here and..."

"What happened to screw the Briggses and screw this fuckin' job?" Skip said. "Come on. You know they got onion rings or something over there."

***

Technically, the Corn King Megaplex did have onion rings on the menu. When they showed up, there was indeed a ring of onion in there somewhere. But here was the thing about the Corn King Megaplex.

Long ago, when fertilizer was expensive and people still owned their own farms, there had been a rumor floating around parts of Arkansas. The rumor went that the federal government, in collusion with certain other nefarious forces around the nation and the world, was going to undermine the entire corn growing industry and drive corn farmers out of

246

business as part of a plan to defeat the Reds by competing with Asian nations in the production of rice.

Now, this particular rumor had more evidence to it than anything concerning reptilian involvement in the assassination of JFK. It did not, however, have as much evidence to it as any of the stories that had come out of the incident in Roswell.

The evidence situation did not matter in the slightest to one R. J. Eckert of East Clattimer County, who responded to the rumor by creating a one man pro-corn propaganda machine that kept running until his death—and subsequent corn-themed funeral—in the early 2000s. Eckert's legacy included billboards, television ads, a radio jingle, a Sunday cartoon strip, and a chain of indoor theme parks compelled to include corn as a main ingredient in every single menu item.

Including the damn onion rings.

"You gotta try this, Gibson," Skip said, chewing on a bite of what appeared to be a pregnant corn dog. "It's actually not that disgusting."

"No. No, I will not." Ty could put up with the cornbread-flavored onion rings. He was actually looking forward to the mess of fried green tomatoes and breaded catfish on the big plate in the middle of the table. He was not going to touch an ear of corn on the cob deep fried in corn batter.

"See, the real abomination here, is they have to have corn in the beer formula." Skip took a long guzzle of his drink. "So you start with bottom-shelf beer, right?"

"I don't know about bottom shelf," Ty said. "They don't have Klump in a can here."

"Okay, well." Skip shrugged. "Anyway, the beer is bad to start with, and then the fact of being corn-themed makes it, I don't know..." He took a drink. "Special. Like how a mug with a horse on it is worth three dollars in Cheyenne but seven dollars at the gas station with the wild horse preserve out back."

"I think it might be more like how gasoline is worth two-fifty a gallon in Cheyenne, and five-twenty a gallon at the station with the wild horse preserve out back and nothing else for three hundred miles." Ty raised his own glass and drained what was left. "Look around us, Skip. Do you think any of these dads are in a position to turn down a cold beer?"

"The one with the seven identical kids..."

"No, we are not paying him any mind," Ty said. "You look at those families too long, you disappear and they got nine identical kids instead of eight."

Skip's muted laughter came out as a painful-sounding wheeze.

"You all right, bud?" Ty put his beer down.

"You have to warn me when you say shit like that, Gibson," Skip said. "I could have choked!"

"Don't do that," Ty said. "You die here? This is where your spirit stays for eternity."

"That sounds almost religious."

"It is religious." Ty gestured around him. "You brought me here and I said to myself, I believe now."

"You what?"

"A human being did not come up with this place on his own, Skip," Ty said, leaning conspiratorially across the table. "There was something darker at work."

Skip couldn't quiet down his cackling in response to that. He waved Ty away and shook his head, grinning and red in the face.

Now, it occurred to Ty that he could take this moment to ask Skip what the big deal was with him and Greg and Linda. If he asked now, he might get an answer. It might even be an answer that satisfied the gnawing curiosity in his gut.

But now that he had a chance, he didn't want to take it. Skip's smile was infectious, and his laughter addictive. Making either one stop was the exact opposite of what Ty wanted to do right now, his curiosity be damned.

Chapter Twenty-Five

The woods around the rodeo grounds were big and dark, and they seemed to grow slightly as the color faded from the sky overhead. With the twilight came a weird, damp chill like dying air conditioning in an old car.

Connor was certain they'd seen this carnival company at the last rodeo. There was a very distinct misrepresentation of Elvis Presley airbrushed on the side of the Galactic Spin. The encroaching trees meant there was less room at this rodeo grounds; you couldn't get from the showers to the stables without walking through the electric mess of lights and voices.

The showers here at the fairgrounds were a sight nicer than the showers he had back in his bunkhouse on the Triple V Ranch. He'd spent a good fifteen minutes in there, scrubbing off the dust and sweat and remembering what it was like to have his own bathroom back home. Back home, he could run the water cold if he wanted with no retribution.

At least, he could if he got Linda to marry Greg.

Connor paused, standing at the side of the thoroughfare across from the Captain's Cruise. He watched a young couple contemplating a ride that strapped you into a metal spider and flung you skyward about thirty feet. They leaned to and away from each other as they debated, now and then gently laughing or prodding at each other.

Last he could remember, that was what Greg and Linda had been like. Yeah, they'd had their squabbles. Linda was a ranch girl, of course, and a rodeo cowgirl to boot, and that made her by nature somewhat squirrely and strong-headed. That was fine.

Greg needed someone a little strong-headed in his life.

But whatever they had between them this weekend was different. Ty was right. They weren't just poking fun at each other at a carnival ride. What waited for Connor back in the rodeo stables was approaching World War Three.

"Sst!"

Connor turned his head at the sound as another young cowboy materialized out of the twilight. He was thin, a little taller than Connor, carved out by the weather a bit here and there. A three-day beard shadowed his cheeks and his long, sharp jaw.

"Yeah?" Connor said.

"You been travelling with Ty Gibson," the cowboy said. Not with any particular slant to his tone, just like he was remarking the fact.

"Lately." Connor nodded. As he looked the cowboy over, Connor realized he was being looked over himself. He narrowed his eyes. "You know him?"

"I know him some." A momentary half-smile at that. A barely perceptible nod. "Not really my type."

Connor's pulse picked up a little. Was he being hit on? At a rodeo? By a mysterious cowboy and/or funnel cake genie who'd appeared from between two nightmarish carnival rides? This was something that only happened to attractive people. Attractive and interesting people.

The cowboy chuckled. "You busy?" he said.

"Uhh." It occurred to him just then that when somebody hit on you, they expected you to actually respond in a tangible yes-or-no manner. That was frankly outrageous and unfair. Right now, Connor felt like he had the right to get some positive attention from a stranger without having to make any decisions. "I, uh…"

"Don't tell me you're all shacked up with Ty Gibson," the cowboy said. His voice was low and his lips were barely moving; his glittering green eyes scanned the darkness like a satellite array.

"I'm not shackin' up with nobody," Connor said. "I just…" Something had soured deep in his mind. He suddenly wanted to be far away from this conversation. Away from this guy, who was asking questions he had no business asking.

The cowboy chuckled as he turned and walked away. "Don't mind me," he said. "I won't bother you."

Connor's first instinct was to lunge after the cowboy, to protest, to clear his name of whatever cloud had just come over it. That instinct did not give him anything to actually say.

So he turned around, and he scuffed the red dirt with his boot, and he stuck his hands in his pockets as he walked back to the rodeo stable. "Shacked up with Ty Gibson," he said to himself under his breath. "What in the hell kind of bullshit is that?"

And why did it bother him so much?

***

The barrel race was the second to last event on tonight's show bill, just before the bull riding—which tonight was a big fiasco sponsored by none other than the Corn King Megaplex. Since this was a fancy, high-budget affair, there was a long and wide alley connecting the mouth of the arena with the warm-up pen where tonight's contestants waited their turns.

With Greg involved, it was no trouble getting Linda where she needed to be. At least, it was no trouble for Connor and Ty. Greg was leaning against the railing overlooking the arena, looking more or less like he'd been run through a laundromat.

"You okay, man?" Connor said, approaching him with two beers.

"Yeah, I'm good." Greg's voice was deflated. "She's just a little wound up tonight."

"No shit?" Connor looked at him with big eyes.

"Aww, she don't mean nothing by it," Greg said.

"Greg, I have never seen someone treat you like that in public and get away with it," he said. "I mean, I'm glad you're there for her..."

"You'd be upset, too, if you were in her situation," Greg said. "For all that our mom was cruel to you, she never went and got us into any legal trouble or nonsense like that."

"It's one thing to get stressed out over family drama," Connor said. "But when you start punishing the people who are trying to help you, I think you cross a line."

"Well, thanks for telling me what you think," Greg said. "You haven't been around for most of Linda's and my relationship. Remember that, bud."

"I'm not saying she's like this all the time, Greg," Connor said. "I'm saying this is a red flag. Okay?"

"Just 'cause you can't handle women..."

"This has nothing to do with being able to handle anybody," Connor said. "She...look, Greg. Your boyfriend, or your girlfriend or what have you, is

253

supposed to just, automatically treat you nicely. You're not supposed to 'handle' them into being nice to you."

"Kind of funny that a single guy's telling me what I'm supposed to do with my fiancée," Greg said. "Leave her alone, Connor. You just focus on your part, and this is all going to work out."

"I..." Connor saw the determination on his brother's face and sighed. "Fine," he said. "Have it your way." He, too, leaned over the arena railing to gaze at the race down below. "How many more runs until Linda goes?"

"How should I know?" Greg said. "She didn't tell me the order of go."

Connor decided not to open his mouth about that. He waved his hat at the popcorn girl and whistled until he caught her attention.

"Boo." Ty's voice came from behind him.

Connor only jumped a little. "Oh, there you are," he said. "Did you get my..."

"Yeah, they didn't have wasabi salt so I got you the regular salt," Ty said. He handed Connor a pretzel from the cardboard flat box full of carnival food he was cradling in one arm. "And I got Nachos del Jefe for el jefe." He handed Greg a red and orange printed takeout container with an ominous, greasy swelling in the bottom.

"Thanks, man," Greg said. His eyes grew wide with greed as he opened the top of the container. "Holy shit, they put five whole strips of..."

"...we have Miss Linda Briggs!" The announcer's enthusiastic rumble set off another wave of applause in the grandstands. Someone had gone on the computer and made word art of all the competitor's names to put on the big TV, and L I N D A B R I G G S shimmered as it rotated against a galaxy background.

Beneath the neon monitor, Linda came down the alley like a fighter jet getting slingshot off an aircraft carrier. Her big sorrel flattened out and got low as they came in for the curve around barrel one; Linda counterweighted him effortlessly against the turn.

"Get 'em, Linda!" Greg said, cupping his hands around his mouth as he hollered over the roar of the crowd.

There was fire in her eyes and steel in her neck as Linda rounded barrel number two, all her focus fixed on the next can ahead of her. Above her, a smaller Linda and a smaller horse performed in miniature.

"Yeah, baby!" Greg's voice raised to a scream as Linda shot across the gap to barrel number three.

Her horse curled its haunches up so tight it could have run in a sardine can; Linda opened her mouth to whoop encouragement at it. She leaned back to leg him out of the turn, he got in the pocket, and...

The barrel wobbled a couple of times and fell to the ground. A buzzer sounded and a bright red N O T I M E flashed across the big TV.

"And that is no time for Linda Briggs," the announcer said. "No time for Linda Briggs. And, by the way, I was just down talking to our good friends at Ed Richter Truck and Tractor down on Highway One-Fifty-One and they asked me to pass the word on you folks tonight, because..."

"Aww, Jesus Christ!" Ty threw his hands up in the air as he stared at the monitor, which was now airing an ad for the truck dealership. "The last barrel?"

"You say that like tipping number one would've been better," Connor said.

On the other side of Ty, Greg sighed and shook his head. "I'd better go down there," he said.

"Good luck," Ty said. "I'll keep the paramedics on standby."

Greg made a joyless effort to laugh as he shuffled toward the stairs leading down from the grandstand.

"Rough draw," Ty said.

"Getting real hard to feel bad for her." Connor glared at the television, now displaying R H O N D A V A S Q U E Z in blue metallic block letters that bounced like gelatin.

"We could always just walk off the job," Ty said.

"Tempting, isn't it?" Connor shook his head.

"Of course then, she might spill the beans about your, uh, little secret identity you got going on there." Ty's voice was casual, almost joking. He had a smile on his face as he watched the girl below them whip around the barrels on a little black and white paint.

"My..."

"So is he your ex, or what?" Ty turned to face him. "I've heard him call you Connor more than once," he said. "And I know you two are..."

"My what?" Connor's voice cracked as he squeaked the words out. "My...God! No!" He lowered his voice and glared at Ty. "He's my little brother! How did..."

256

"Look, I'm not stupid," Ty said. "You apparently think I am, but..."

"I don't think you're stupid," Connor said. "Look. It's a complicated situation. I...I meant to tell you."

"Did you really?"

"Yes!" Connor said. "I mean...eventually..."

"Oh, that's nice." Ty took a sip of his drink and turned around to walk out of the grandstands.

"Hey, wait!" Connor had to duck and dodge between people in the crowd. "I..."

Ty Gibson was nowhere to be seen when Connor reached the top of the stairs. He had to search the crowd for a while before he saw him, striding off toward the stables with his head held high like he'd just won the whole damn rodeo.

"Hey! Get back here!" Connor shoved around a couple of disgruntled bull riders, who were shockingly correct in their shouted guesses as to why Connor was in such a hurry. "Come on, man!"

But the back of Ty's hat didn't even bobble. He was making a beeline for the trees with his arms full of concession stand food.

"You gonna get a ride back from Bigfoot?" Connor yelled after him. "Huh? You gonna get a skinwalker to come take you back to the Triple V?"

Ty's footsteps slowed a little bit. Connor was, at this point, all too familiar with the way his thin shoulders raised and lowered when he was particularly fed up with a situation. Slowly, as if under threat of violence, he turned around to glare at Connor.

"Bigfoot, skinwalkers, grey aliens, el chupacabra..." Ty raised the straw in his cup so the

257

drink rattled and wheezed as he took a long sip. "They're all about as real as Skip McCoy, aren't they?"

"Ty, just let me explain..."

"You don't have shit to explain to me, Connor," Ty said. "I don't know what kind of bullshit scam you and your brother and Linda are trying to..."

"There's no scam!" Connor said. "You don't know the full story!"

"What full story?" Ty said. "Local idiot gets lied to for a few months, learns nothing?"

"Look, you were not part of the plan," Connor said. "Shit, even Linda wasn't supposed to..."

"Wasn't supposed to what?" Ty said. "You trying to rob that poor girl on top of everything else?"

"I ain't got a need to rob anybody!" Connor said. "That's my fucking trailer we been sleeping in, dumbass!"

"Keep your voice down," Ty said. "You're gonna get us hate-crimed on top of all this..."

"Look, Ty," Connor said, stepping closer so Ty could hear him. "The only person I'm setting out to screw over here is Mr. Briggs, and even then, I'm not really trying to rob anybody."

Ty narrowed his eyes, but instead of saying something he nodded faintly for a few seconds. "Is this about Miss Linda marrying your brother?"

"Look, I had no idea it was this bad," Connor said. "I...man, Linda said her family hated our family, said they wouldn't let her visit, say they wouldn't let Greg have *nothing* to do with her."

"So, you didn't know what a damn lunatic she is when they're together?" Ty said.

"Look, there's a lot I didn't know about," Connor said. "Look, I...the plan was just to figure out what Linda was hiding from Greg, but then Linda caught on, and then the plan was to try and get Mr. Briggs's debts under control without anybody from Linda's church finding out." He rubbed his forehead and shut his eyes for a second. "I just...it was complicated enough," he said. "I didn't want to get you involved on top of everything."

"Well, you got what you wanted," Ty said. "Because this whole thing is bat shit crazy, and I ain't gonna be involved with it for another minute more."

Chapter Twenty-Six

Boomer Collins wasn't a bad-looking man by any stretch of the imagination. He was a little sun-weathered, yeah, but that was kind of part of the territory with cowboys.

It was the stare that had always unnerved Ty. If Boomer's eyes had been set a little closer together he might have had a way of looking through you. The way his face was set up, though, you got the impression that the left eye was looking around you to your left while the right one took the territory to your right. You were somewhere in the middle, unseen and yet somehow definitely observed.

"We're gonna have to stop over in Wichita." Boomer was standing beside his SUV, ruminating on some chewing tobacco while he squinted at his back tire. "Something's up with this valve stem."

"We could move the tire up to the front," Ty said. "It would have less weight on it."

Boomer shook his head. "If it blows back here, we at least have the trailer to stabilize the rig," he said. "Somewhat."

Ty swallowed and leaned back against his seat back. Without the benefit of a highway breeze through the window, the SUV was about as comfortable as a brick kiln.

"You still mad at your boyfriend?" Boomer sauntered over and leaned against Ty's window. "Because if he could come by on his way and..."

"He ain't my boyfriend," Ty said. "And he won't lift a finger to help anybody unless there's something in it for him."

"Neither will the mechanic in Wichita." Boomer sighed. "Well, if you won't make nice with him, maybe I could. Seemed when I met him like he doesn't get out much."

Ty grunted. "Suit yourself," he said, scowling through the driver's side window at the wheat fields stretching out past the Interstate.

"If he ain't your boyfriend, I don't see why you have a problem with me talking to him," Boomer said.

"I would just like to go to one rodeo where I know a guy you haven't tried to fuck," Ty said. "Just one."

"Fortune favors the extroverted, my friend," Boomer said. "Anyway, you ought to see if you two can't kiss and make up. He can't be near as much of a pain in the ass as having a blowout on the Interstate with two horses in the trailer."

***

As it turned out, they never found out how much of a pain in the ass it would be to get a blown-out tire. Boomer's SUV made it to Wichita, where he deposited Ty outside a dive bar with his duffel bag and the remains of his most recent paycheck.

Ty wasn't sure what the bar was called, unless "Neighborhood Bar" was indeed the full name. He went inside and scouted the dim barroom until he found a booth with an electrical outlet in the wall above the table.

"Can I help you?" A tall butch lady in a faded Sturgis T-shirt appeared from behind the bar top.

"Can I get a Gold Lite?" Ty said, pausing halfway across the floor.

"It's ten in the morning," she said.

"Can I get a Gold Lite and some toast?" Ty inclined his head toward the table. "I need to charge my phone."

"Just sit down," the lady said, rolling her eyes and gesturing with her cleaning rag toward the booth. "We got a pay phone in back, too."

"Thanks." Ty's whole body and soul relaxed a little as he walked over to the booth. The barkeep returned to the back room, and Ty set his duffel on the seat opposite from his. He pulled his cell phone and charger out of his pocket and plugged it into the wall.

It took a few minutes for the battery to regain enough life to turn on. When it finally did, the phone buzzed and jolted non-stop for the better part of a minute. Ty let it do its thing face-down while he searched his duffel bag for the bag of pretzels he'd stashed in there.

He jumped when the speakers in the barroom came on, playing some old honky-tonk tune he vaguely recognized. When he glanced behind the bar, the lady waved at him through the doorway into the back room.

"Let me know if you wanna change the station, sweetheart," she said.

"Thanks." Ty smiled. He realized he hadn't called his mom in a dog's age.

And with that, it was time to look at the phone. It buzzed even as he picked it up. He heard a soft whine come from the back of his throat as he brought the screen to life and looked at the damage so far.

He'd missed thirty-four calls, and he had twenty-five new texts from seven different people.

Ty put the phone down for a second and breathed. Linda. He needed to deal with Linda's damage first.

And Linda was furious. She had sent him an essay in six texts, calling him every name in the book and blaming him for everything from her sloppy barrel runs to her father's financial problems. To hear her put it, she'd found him floating down the river in a basket and taken a chance on him when nobody else in their right minds would have hired him.

Oh, but then ten hours later she'd sent him an apology text. And another text expounding on the apology. And three texts begging him to please respond so she'd know if he was okay.

Ty shook his head and closed that window. Skip—Connor—whatever the fuck his name was, he'd been less verbose than Linda.

Where are you?

Pick up your phone...Linda's PISSED

Please call...need to talk to you

The next morning, he'd sent more:

Hey man it's Connor. I know you're mad and you have a right. Never meant to hurt you or do you wrong...please call.

Leaving the rodeo now. Hope you are OK. Just want to talk to you. Sorry again.

And that was it. The rest of his texts were spam, drunken complaining from his mom, and a group chat he didn't care about with some drinking buddies he hadn't talked to in months.

Ty let his phone skitter across the table and fall to the vinyl seat below. He put his head in his arms and shut his eyes while the weight of the last few nights came crashing down on him. Wichita was a long way from where he needed to be. He had no money, no vehicle, no horse, no ride to the Triple V Ranch to get his vehicle and his horse.

"You okay, buddy?" The barkeep came out of the back again. When Ty looked up, he saw she had a glass of water in one hand and a sandwich on a plate in the other.

"I'm fine," Ty said. "Just...dealing with some drama."

"How old are you, bud?" She set the glass and the sandwich down in front of him.

"Thirty-three come October," Ty said.

"Libra or Scorpio?" The bartender narrowed her eyes as she sat down across from him.

"Fuck that garbage," Ty said.

"Scorpio, then." The barkeep raised her eyebrows for a moment as she put Ty's phone back on the table.

If she'd been wrong, he would have told her. But she wasn't, so he gritted his teeth and picked up the glass of water. He hadn't realized how thirsty he was until he'd chugged the whole thing.

"Least you're of age," the barkeep said. "Most cowboys wind up on my doorstep, turns out they're teenage runaways and I gotta go take 'em to the youth shelter."

"Nah, I'm old enough to know better." Ty shook his head. "Just gotta make some phone calls. Used to

264

have a ride back to the ranch I'm working at, but he got a call and he's gotta go straight up to Duluth as quick as he can."

"Well, shit," the barkeep said. "Where's the ranch?"

"About three days' drive west of here," Ty said. "I just gotta go get my truck and my horse."

"Well, you're welcome to stick around here and see if you can find a ride," the barkeep said. "I don't have any work for you right now, but I know a few places you can stay while you're in town."

"Thanks," Ty said. "It's been a wild week."

"Looks about like it," the barkeep said. "What in the hell happened to you to get you stuck all the way out here?"

*　*　*

The story of how Ty got out here, slightly abbreviated in some places and slightly embellished in others, was good for getting sympathy and beer from the various people who wandered into the bar. It wasn't good for much else. Nobody really wanted to take a chance on bringing him home and giving him a place to sleep, and Ty could understand that. He was a dirty, sketchy cowboy on the best of days, and tonight didn't find him looking or smelling remotely close to his best.

Which is how he came to find himself standing in the alley outside the bar, sitting on his duffel bag with his back against the brick wall while he stared at his phone. He didn't want to do this. He might not have much in this world at the moment, but he did have his pride, and that pride might not make it through another encounter with Skip-Connor-Whatever.

Then again, his pride wasn't going to get his damn truck and horse back to him either.

"Dammit," Ty muttered to himself as he pulled up Skip-Connor-Whatever's contact and dialed him.

One ring, and Connor picked up. "Hello?" he said.

"Hey, it's Ty." He glanced down the alley. "I'm in Wichita."

"Well shit," Connor said. "We just left Albuquerque."

"Good for you," Ty said. "I need to get my truck back. And my horse."

"Is that Ty on the phone?" He heard Linda's voice. "Give me..."

"Hey!" Connor said. There was the sound of a scuffle; the call dropped.

Ty rolled his eyes and ran his hand over his face. "Bunch of damn children," he said to himself as his phone buzzed in his hand. He picked the call up.

"Yeah?" he said.

"Sorry," Connor said. "Um. I can get you a bus ticket back here?" he said. "Or, uh, I can just, uh. Bring you your rig."

"My spare key's in a magnet box under the left front fender," Ty said. "You'll see the little rusted spot you gotta reach through in order to get to it. And be careful accelerating on hills so you don't lose fifth gear, which then you gotta stop the truck and let it cool down and restart it. And if it still don't restart, you gotta go and unhook the battery so the computer resets."

"Got it," Connor said.

266

"And don't give Blue any alfalfa when he's hauling," Ty said. "He's used to long trips but he does tend to stock up some in the heat."

"I'll stop somewhere to walk him out," Connor said.

"Ty, please don't…"

"Sst!" Connor said, cutting Linda off. "You want me to bring you your final paycheck?" Something about the way he weighted "final paycheck" made it sound like there'd been a couple disagreements between him and Miss Linda.

"Yeah, that would be nice," Ty said. "And if I left anything in the bunkhouse or the tack room."

"Got it," Connor said. "I oughta be there in five days. You got a place to stay?"

"I'll figure something out," Ty said.

"I'll go ahead and call the Larkspur," Connor said. "It's a decent place. I'll put you up for a few nights."

"I can figure something out on my own." Ty frowned at the darkness in front of him. He hoped Connor-Skip-Whatever would really go through with it.

"Just take the damn hotel room," Connor said. "We don't want you wandering around Wichita for a week with no place to stay."

"Fuck what you guys want," Ty said. "I've already seen where that gets me."

He hung up the phone and stood up, shouldering his duffel bag and looking out into the street. There was a little fleabag motel not far from here, and he was still sober enough that he could more or less walk there without incident. He didn't have enough cash for more than one night, but maybe the morning would bring with it a way out of Wichita.

Shit, if he hitchhiked tonight, and if he caught a ride with the right truckers, he might even make it back to the ranch before Skip-Connor-Whatever made it back. Maybe he'd walk on up to Mr. Briggs and tell them what his family was up to behind his back. Wouldn't that be some entertainment to walk away from with no fear of repercussion?

Not really. Pissed off as he was at both Linda and Connor-Skip-Whatever, he didn't even want to think about what the fallout was going to be when Mr. Briggs found out what Linda had done.

Hell, he didn't even want to think about what was going on at the ranch right now. He hoped Blue was okay. He hoped his truck was more or less in one piece. He figured that he would have probably heard about it by now if Mr. Briggs had decided to take his anger out on his errant ranch hands' possessions.

But he hadn't heard from Mr. Briggs. To his knowledge, neither had Connor. You'd think that he'd have gotten in touch, you know. He'd never been one to keep quiet when he'd been wronged, and it didn't take too much squinting to perceive him as having been wronged here. It was just...odd. You'd think he would have been one of the first people blowing Ty's phone up demanding to know where his daughter was.

Maybe Ty was gonna find out about that when he got his truck back.

Ty was a few blocks from the fleabag when his phone buzzed in his pocket. He had a text from Skip. Connor. Whatever his name was.

Get a cab to the Larkspur. I booked Room 204 for you until Friday.

268

Ty glared at the phone display. There was his pride again, telling him to put the phone away and keep on walking. Connor could go fuck himself, and Linda could go fuck herself, and Greg could go fuck himself most of all for having started this bullshit.

But there was his common sense, too, steering him back toward the bar so he could find a ride to his hotel and take a shower.

Chapter Twenty-Seven

It didn't take Connor too long to find Bonito and Blue, at least. Given the way the rest of the ranch was looking, he'd been afraid that Mr. Briggs had taken some of his rage out on his ranch hands' innocent critters.

But no, he'd just let them loose, and they'd wandered out on the front pasture where the grass was green and the ground was flat and soft. Bonito knew Connor's voice, and he whickered and raised his head when he heard Connor yelling for him.

"Yeah, buddy, it's me," Connor said, spurring Linda's horse forward and loosening one of the halters tied to his saddle horn. "Did you have a nice time out here while I was gone?"

For a second, Bonito and Blue thought about taking off and staying out here. But they were good horses, and they didn't make it too difficult at all for Connor to get them haltered without even dismounting.

From this distance, the Triple V Ranch looked like the very lap of peacefulness itself. The tops of the pasture grasses were starting to turn yellow in the heat, and the low light of evening made the fields look like someone had thrown gold netting over them.

Connor took his time riding back. It was nice to be away from the miserable, buggy humidity of Texarkana, and it was nice to have enough solitude that he could get a thought in edgewise.

Even if he did wind up thinking about Ty.

He'd never meant for it to get this far. He never should have let Ty get close to him in the first place, no matter how lonely he was or how much he wanted

Ty. He should have stuck with Greg's plan—no, Greg's plan was going to be stupid no matter what Connor did or didn't do with Ty Gibson.

But maybe, if he hadn't been such a horny idiot, he would have seen that sooner. Maybe he would have put more effort into convincing Greg that this wasn't worth it, that Linda's destructive streak was too wide and too unpredictable to handle.

Or would he? Even after all this bullshit, Connor still couldn't shake the idea of Greg giving him the ranch. His ranch, or at least it almost was. It seemed like every time Connor got determined to turn Greg off of Linda for good, he was struck by a vision of himself riding herd on cattle that he owned, or standing on the front porch of the house that finally had his name on the deed.

Maybe that was greed. Maybe that was pride. Connor would admit to both of those flaws any day of the week.

But if he wasn't doing this to win back his ranch, then what was it all for? Why had he taken on this fake identity and put himself through a job not fit for a pack mule? Why had he spent weeks kowtowing to a man so far down the path of madness that only the law could save him now?

He knew the answer. Dammit. He knew the answer full well and he didn't like it one bit.

***

Linda's mother had not been there when they came back to the ranch. She was sure there now, sitting cross-legged in front of her front door and weeping with her head in her hands. She wore a light blue bathrobe over a set of pink velour sweats; her hair had settled in an oblong halo around her head.

271

She had torn down half of the X of crime scene tape covering the shattered glass door. Judging by the keys sitting on the ground next to her, she'd made a good effort at getting inside the house.

"Morning, Mrs. Briggs," Connor said as he walked up the sidewalk.

"I guess it is morning," she said. It took her a little sniveling before she could calm herself down enough to say anything else. "They took Marshall off to jail."

"I'm sorry to hear that, Mrs..."

"He came back here and he got that damn gun of his, and I got his truck keys and I..." She put her head in her hands and rocked back and forth, bawling like a calf.

Connor winced and approached her gently. "Hey, it's gonna be okay," he said. "I..."

"It's not gonna be okay, Skip!" Mrs. Briggs said. "I was so scared once he started breaking windows, I went straight to Rachel's house and I spilled all my guts." She stifled a wail.

"Well, it's good that you had a friend there," Connor said. He sat down beside her on the stoop.

Instantly, she clung to him while she wept, burying her face in his arm. "I don't know what I'm gonna do, Skip," she said. "This ranch was my whole life, everything I ever knew, but I knew the whole time I wasn't gonna be able to run it myself..."

"Aww, Mrs. Briggs," Connor said. "You don't need to worry about that right now."

"We're long past worrying, Skip," Mrs. Briggs said. "The bank's been giving us time and giving us time and giving us time, and they're not gonna give us another day after this." She sniffed and started fishing in her pocket. "We were on thin ice before. Him going to jail..." She pulled a tissue out and blew her nose loudly.

"Look, I know it seems hopeless," Skip said. "But..."

"No, Skip," Mrs. Briggs said. "I just met with Mr. Petersen from the bank yesterday. He told me the best thing to do now is just...just go on and start bankruptcy proceedings," she said. "But Lord, I don't know how I'm gonna get Marshall to agree to that."

"I don't think he has a choice," Connor said. "I mean...once the bank takes possession..."

If there was a worse combination of words to present to Mrs. Briggs at the moment, Connor didn't want to know about it. She clung to his shoulder with a renewed ferocity, digging her chipped fake nails into his flesh like she was trying to climb him to safety.

He patted her shoulder softly. "Hey, hey, don't worry so much," he said. "The last thing you need to do right now is panic."

"I don't know what else to do!" Mrs. Briggs said. "I don't know if Linda will have enough to bail Marshall out, and if she does...oh, if she does, I don't even know if I can look at him!" Her back suddenly straightened. She stared down the walkway with her eyes clear and her jaw set. "If my daddy had lived to see him take up a gun in his house..."

"So, this is your ranch, really," Connor said.

"It was," Mrs. Briggs said.

"Oh, man," Connor said. "That's...that's a lot to go through."

Mrs. Briggs nodded as she whimpered. "My whole life growing up here, I never once thought..."

Connor's phone interrupted them. He checked the front display. "It's Linda," he said.

"Ohh." Mrs. Briggs shrank back, her eyes big and round.

"Hello?" Connor put the phone to his ear.

"Hey," Linda said. "Your brother's going to Prestley to get the cash for Dad's bail."

"He's...hang on, how much was bail?" Connor said.

"That's my problem, is how much it was," Linda said. She'd gotten used to talking to him like he was the help, hadn't she?

"Actually, I think that's a pretty important detail," Connor said. "Along with what he was charged with, when his trial is, and..."

"Look, we can deal with all of that later," Linda said. "I need you to do me a favor real quick."

"It had better be *real* quick," Connor said. "I got Gibson's horse in the trailer, and..."

"Gibson can get his own damn horse," Linda said. "This is important. Our lawyer's gonna send a guy out with you to ride the pastures and the grazing permit areas, and I need to make sure you're, uh, *familiar* with *everything* that's out there." She cleared her throat. "Before we take the lawyer out."

"I think I'm pretty fa...oh." Connor froze for a second as he realized what Linda was trying not to say out loud. "So you want me to make sure everything's on the up-and-up out there?"

"Yeah, basically," Linda said. "Just take a few days and…"

"Look, this is going to have to wait until I get Gibson his horse and truck back to him," Connor said.

"It's not going to wait another minute," Linda said. "This is going to be *extremely important* for the bankruptcy, and…"

"Linda, you are in enough legal trouble already without fucking over one of your ex-employees," Connor said. "I'm already doing damage control here, and you should be mindful of how much you're asking of people."

"Well, this is your new priority," Linda said. "You don't know the situation like I do, and…"

"And that's why I'm not going to drop everything and go off with another Linda Plan, Copyright, Trademark," Connor said. His pulse had picked up an ominous rhythm; his free hand clenched as he stood up. "Ever since I showed up here, you have been running one hare-brained scheme after another to try and get your daddy out of hot water he boiled himself, and one after another those schemes have blown up in your face."

"Skip, now is not the time…"

"Is he in the car with you?" Connor said. He flashed a snarl at nobody. "Do you wanna put him on the phone with me and maybe *he'll* tell me what he's charged with and how much his bail wound up being?"

"Skip, we can discuss this later," Linda said. "I have to go."

"Then go," Connor said. "I'll see you when I get back from Wichita."

"You're not going to fucking..."

Connor hung up the phone. He took a couple of calming breaths before he turned to Mrs. Briggs.

"Looks like your husband's out of jail," he said. "Now, I don't know if you want to see him or not, but if you don't, I suggest getting out of here pretty quick."

Mrs. Briggs stood up slowly. She was still sniffling, hiding sobs behind a tissue that had been worried into the consistency of a nimbus cloud. "Oh, Skip, I don't know," she said. "I don't...I love him, Skip. I know I'm just a stupid old broad, but..."

"Aww, Mrs. Briggs, don't talk like that," Connor said. "You've been married a dog's age. You brought a kid up together. You've got all this history."

"I know," Mrs. Briggs said. "I know, Skip. I can't just...I have a duty to stay by him," she said. "I promised at the altar. Through richer or poorer, for better or worse..."

"He ruined your family's business and, uh, threatened you with a gun..."

"Oh, the gun wasn't for me!" Mrs. Briggs said, laughing faintly and swatting at the air in front of her. "That was just him being a jackass wanting to make noise and cause a scene."

"Well, it's worrisome," Connor said. "You've got to understand that, at least."

"Oh, I know," Mrs. Briggs said. "But I'll be fine. You're right about Mr. Gibson, you know." She straightened her bathrobe around her shoulders and dabbed at one kohl-ringed eye. "It's a shame we can't keep him, but if he's gone we need to do it right."

"Well, be careful," Connor said. "I'll try to get him, his horse, and truck and make this sort of quick and painless if I can." A bitter smile creased his face. That was a pretty large "if" he was dealing with right now.

***

Wichita had never ranked particularly high on Connor's list of places to be. Accordingly, as he came in through Goddard, he couldn't for the life of him tell what was actually new development and what was older. It did seem like every time he visited some city, there was about five minutes' worth of suburbia on the edges that he didn't remember being there last time.

Ty Gibson was waiting for him at a feed store just off the highway. He was sitting on the tailgate of an old pickup with an unfamiliar cowboy, eating popcorn out of a big shiny bag that sat open between them.

When he saw Connor pull up, he took his hat off and waved it as Connor navigated his way through the parking lot. For a three-horse gooseneck, Ty's rusty old trailer was surprisingly easy to shimmy between the rows of cars.

Connor parked next to the old pickup and shut the engine off. He had to take a second to stretch his legs and get the blood flowing once his feet hit the pavement. A weird, light-headed rush came and passed.

"Well, shit," Ty said as he walked up to Connor. "I was about to put good money out that you wouldn't actually show up."

"I wouldn't do that to you." Connor tossed the keys over to Ty.

"Yeah?" Ty was looking him up and down. His features were hardened and lean, and he hesitated in front of Connor like a horse who hasn't decided if it wants to get caught or keep running around the pen.

Connor rubbed the back of his neck. "Look, I'm sorry," he said, almost under his breath.

"You all good?" The other cowboy slammed his tailgate shut with the hand that wasn't holding the popcorn gang. Connor knew he recognized him from somewhere, but couldn't quite put the face to the memory.

"Yep," Ty said. "Thanks for the ride out."

"No problemo, buddy," the other cowboy said. "Either one of you," he said, winking at Connor, "just call me if you need anything."

Ahh. That would be the guy who'd taken a shine to him at the rodeo in Texarkana. Small world they lived in, wasn't it?

"Yep." Ty nodded and beckoned to Connor. "Come on," he said. "I'm heading out to Shiprock. The Triple V isn't too far out of my way."

"You could always just take me to the airport," Connor said. "I've got enough for a ticket..."

But Ty was staring at him, just barely shaking his head as he kept his eyes locked on Connor's.

Connor sighed. "But I'll take you up," he said. "As long as we stop for lunch on the way out of here. I'm starving."

Chapter Twenty-Eight

It was going to take Ty most of three days to get back to the ranch with Connor. He had time to say what he was gonna say. Better to sit and think about it for a while, and wind up saying the right thing, than to fuck it all up because he just had to open his mouth right away.

Trouble was, the longer he spent in the truck with Connor, the more things occurred to him that he needed to say. The more things that occurred to Ty, the less time it seemed to him that he really had to say them all.

"What do you want?" he said as he pulled up to the drive thru window.

"Nine-piece tenders with signature chipotle sauce, two orders of tater tots, and a medium vanilla milkshake." Connor pulled his wallet out from his back pocket. It was made of nice Havana brown leather, carefully tooled with a floral pattern around the border. It was probably worth more than everything Ty was carrying in his own wallet right now.

"I'll buy," he said anyway.

"Nah, I got it," Connor said. "Least I can do, after everything I've...everything you've been through this week."

Ty didn't respond.

"Welcome to the Chicken Chapel," the girl on the speaker said. "What can I get started for you today?"

"Uhhh, yeah, I'll get a nine-piece tenders, a triple decker barbecue sandwich, three orders of tots, a large cherry cola, and a medium vanilla shake," Ty said. "Uh, and signature chipotle sauce."

The girl hemmed and hawed while the order appeared on the screen. "Okay, sir, that's gonna come up to be twenty-six thirty-seven at the first window."

"Thanks," Ty said.

"Here you go." Connor handed him a crisp fifty. "Don't worry about the change."

Ty snatched the bill from him as he pulled forward to the first window. "I don't need your spare change," he said.

"Suit yourself," Connor said, turning to stare out the passenger window.

Ty could feel his self-control slipping as he paid for their lunch at the drive-thru window. There were five hundred different things he wanted to scream at Connor right now, and he couldn't keep his mind still enough to rehearse a single one of them.

So he said nothing. And Connor said nothing. The two of them continued saying nothing while they got their lunch and started heading West on Highway 400, back toward the accursed place where all this bullshit had started.

***

They were sixty miles outside of Goddard when Ty lost reception on the radio station he liked. He started flipping through channels, dismayed to find a commercial or a godawful song playing on each one.

"It should be illegal to write country songs about rock songs you liked in the eighties," Connor said.

"What's wrong with country?" Ty said.

"Nothing," Connor said. "It's just, I don't know. There's just something off about some of those songs."

280

Ty shrugged. "So? If a song means something to you, why not sing about what it means to you?"

"Because they're not singing about what it means to them," Connor said. "I don't...it's hard to put my finger on it." He took his hat off and carefully set it on the pile of stuff in Ty's back seat.

"It's the same thing as the old country western singers writing songs about honky-tonk music," Ty said.

"No it ain't," Connor said. "See, when they're singing about honky-tonk, it's 'honky-tonk,' the whole genre of music. Nobody's out there writing a whole song specifically about listening to 'The Strawberry Roan' or what have you."

"The Strawberry Roan's a honky-tonk song now?" Ty said.

"You know what I mean," Connor said. "And shit, if you're at work listening to Top 40 Country all day long and you got three different songwriters reminiscing about listening to The Strawberry Roan and saying it was a honky-tonk song..."

"Which it ain't," Ty said.

"My point is, your opinion on a song isn't enough to write a song about," Connor said. "It just bugs me that it's sort of the thing to do right now."

"Well, it does seem to me like it's a little lazy," Ty said. "But not if you're just mentioning the song once or twice..."

"That's just doing a little reference," Connor said. "That's different."

"Anyway," Ty said. "There's a CD wallet back there if you want." He pointed his thumb back behind him. "Don't think I got The Strawberry Roan back there, though."

Connor laughed as he unbuckled his seatbelt and turned around to look for some tunes. He rooted around among spare equipment and emergency tools for a minute and re-emerged with one of the beat-up black zipper cases that Ty had acquired over the years without remembering how.

"See if you can't find Steven Blackburn and the Wranglers in there," Ty said. "Speaking of honky-tonk."

"Sure," Connor said. "I haven't listened to them in a dog's age."

"You know them?"

"Greg likes the throwback stuff," Connor said.

Ty could feel his face tighten at the mention of Connor's idiot brother. "Oh," he said. "Well, uh, my mom used to date their bass player."

"Which one?" Connor leaned back and squinted at Ty.

"Clem Tucker," Ty said. "He was their second one, I think."

"Yeah, he was," Connor said. "Shit, it's a small world. He used to date this gal up in my hometown, still comes around to play at her bar now and again."

"No shit?" Ty said. He realized once again that he had no idea where Connor was actually from or how he'd come to be in this situation. "What town is that?"

"Salty Fork, Montana," Connor said. "Said to be one of Theodore Roosevelt's lesser-known vacation spots as well as a possible birthplace of the legendary outlaw Dallas O'Hara."

"Do you make shit up for their tourism board, too?" Ty said.

"You know, the thought had not yet occurred to me," Connor said. "But now that you mention it, that could be a great new career."

"Huh." Ty nodded.

Connor pulled a CD from the wallet and put it in the mouth of the disc changer. The thermometer in the dash read eighty-seven degrees; Ty suspected it was a good deal hotter than that already today. To the west, a line of thunderheads was already marching across the green-yellow plains.

"I don't know, Ty," Connor said as Steven Blackburn's wail started coming through the speakers. "I just...I don't know if the ranch is worth it."

"What?" Ty said. "Linda's ranch?"

"No, it's..." Connor pinched the bridge of his nose. He looked out the window for a verse, watching the trees and the farmhouses pass by beyond his own reflection. "My mom died not too long ago," he said.

"I'm sorry to hear that," Ty said.

Connor shook his head. "It's...it's complicated," he said. "It still doesn't feel like she's really gone, if I'm being honest."

"Yeah?" Ty said. "I can't imagine losing my mom. I mean, we don't have the best relationship, but..."

"Oh yeah?" Connor said. "I thought she didn't have much of an issue with you turning out gay."

"I mean she didn't," Ty said. "But at a certain point, you know, there's basic shit you gotta have in a relationship with your mom, and she was just...I don't know. She's still a kid in a lot of ways, I guess."

"How old was she when she had you?" Connor said.

"Twenty-one," Ty said. "I think it was honestly getting married to my dad that fucked her up more than anything else. Just, living up there all isolated, and he could be a real nasty sumbitch when he was drinking."

"Nasty like Mr. Briggs?" Connor said.

"Sometimes," Ty said. "My grandma was always real good people. Tried to help mom out whenever she could, but then my grandpa died and she just broke down."

"Oh, that's horrible," Connor said. "I had an aunt and uncle who that happened to."

"Yeah, you know it's...well, I like to think they get to be together in an afterlife," Ty said. "But for the rest of us, it's not so good."

"Huh." Connor looked over at him.

"What?" Ty said. "You don't have to be all religious to believe there's something else after you die."

"I guess not," Connor said. "I bet your idea of the afterlife's a lot nicer than my mom's." He laughed, but it didn't sound like he thought anything was actually funny.

"Huh." Ty nodded. "But, I mean, it sounds like you still took care of her."

"Oh, yeah, right up until she died," Connor said. "And when she died, she made sure to thank me by writing me out of the will and leaving the whole damn ranch to my brother."

"She what?" Ty tapped the brake reflexively as he turned to stare at Connor.

"Yep," Connor said. "I get two entire dollars out of the whole estate and everything." He leaned back in his seat and shut his eyes. "That's how Greg convinced me to go along with this secret identity plan of his, you know."

"Wait, *she wrote you out* of her will?" Ty whistled and set his eyes back on the road ahead of him. "That's the coldest thing I ever heard of."

"And that ranch was my life's work, man," Connor said. "I grew up there, I learned everything there was to know about running the place, and I spent every day of my life working my hands down to the bone there." He sighed. "Man, I love Greg with all my heart, I do, but..."

"He seems like...a good guy," Ty said.

"But he'd rather party and hang out in the background," Connor said. "When Mom died, getting him running the place was just a shit show..."

"But he's still gonna hold it over your head until he gets what he wants," Ty said. "Nice."

"I wouldn't say he's holding it over my head," Connor said, but his voice was less than convincing. He looked as if he was weighing Ty's words in his mind as he spoke. "I mean...the ranch is in his name."

"Nobody's making him hang on to it," Ty said. "Whatever, though. It ain't my family."

"Shit, I hardly feel like it's my family anymore, either," Connor said. "Jesus. Just...this whole thing got out of hand..."

"It was out of hand when you decided to come up with a fucking secret identity and get a job at the Triple V Ranch," Ty said. "Did you go into this knowing how Linda treats your brother?"

"Not really," Connor said. "And that's another complication in this whole business. Do I just ditch him with—"

"Yeah, you do," Ty said. "That's pretty fucking obvious."

"But it's not that simple," Connor said. "I mean, I don't have another job lined up..."

"For fuck's sake, you have probably more than a decade of experience managing a ranch," Ty said. "There's outfits from Oklahoma to Oahu where you could make a killing! Do you have any idea how lucky you are to have that kind of work experience?"

It didn't look like he did. Connor tipped his head to one side like he was trying to do math without a pencil and paper.

"Look, I know how close you are with Greg," Ty said. "Shit, I love my mom more than anyone else in the world, and I had to leave her sitting in the dirt on her ass, because that was what she needed to finally get on her own two feet." He reached over to the cupholder for his drink. "It sucks, and you'll feel like shit, but..."

"It's not just Greg," Connor said. "You're talking about leaving my whole life here behind. My friends, my family friends, my church back home..." He turned to look at Ty. "You wouldn't leave what I have."

"I don't know if you and I have the same impression of what you have," Ty said. "But maybe you're right. I've never had a ranch, or a church, or a little town in Montana where apparently people like me."

"I thought you liked me," Connor said with a hopeful grin.

"I don't know if I like you or not," Ty said. "I knew this guy once named Skip McCoy. I liked him."

***

Among Connor's friends in his real life were an elderly saddle maker and his wife. They had a little farm a few hours north of Taos where, for a small fee, you could put your horses up in a stable and rest your own bones in a guest cabin by the river.

Ty fed Blue while Connor yapped with the place's owners. It had been a long day of driving, and he was eager to clean up and get himself to bed.

The showers were under a roof but not really in a building, if that makes any sense at all. The shower structure had a central wall that divided the gentlemen's portion from the ladies, and all the pipes were run through that wall to supply hot water to a row of showers on either side. The walls were more like privacy fences, and the floor was concrete textured with little pebbles.

Ty turned the water up as hot as he could stand it and scrubbed himself off. Despite the relative lack of privacy, he found himself spacing out perfectly effectively.

"You know, this used to be a milking parlor." Connor's voice came from outside the cubicle. "You

287

can tell from the elevated floor where the showers are."

"Is that so?" Ty said.

"Yeah, I guess they've really fixed this place up," Connor said. "It's nice."

"I hear there's more than one shower stall," Ty said.

"Only one with a good view." Connor's voice was teasing.

"I didn't take you for a tourist," Ty said. He pushed the door to the shower cubicle open and frowned at Connor.

"I'm interested to know how you would take me," Connor said. He stepped forward, reached out to touch Ty's hip.

Ty immediately thought of how open and exposed they were in this building, but he didn't push Connor away. He let Connor's tongue push his lips apart, wrapped one wet hand around Connor's waist as they tasted each other.

"We shouldn't be doing this," Ty said under his breath.

"We'll be fine," Connor said. "Unless you're still mad at me…"

"Mad at you or not, I still want you," Ty said. "It's just…"

"We're not gonna get caught." Connor smushed up against him with another wet kiss. "The owners have turned in to watch their soaps, and they're both deaf as bricks."

"And you're sure there's nobody else...here?" Ty shuddered with delight as he felt Connor's hand wrap around his cock.

"Yeah, we're good." Connor pushed Ty backward gently as he walked into the shower cubicle and closed the door behind him.

Ty pulled Connor back to him for a kiss; Connor fumbled with his shirt as he took it off. Ty's cock was already hard, and it swelled even tighter as Connor peeled off his clothes and his boots.

Connor noticed it, too. He flashed Ty a mischievous grin and got on his knees to take Ty's cock in his mouth.

"Oh, Lord..." Ty stifled his moan with one hand as Connor took his cock all the way down his throat. He could feel the subtle noises Connor made as his head bobbed up and down. "Oh, fuck..."

As Connor's mouth grew tighter on his cock, Ty's heart raced in his chest. He needed to fuck him, needed to take him up against the wall and have him completely.

"Did you bring lube?" Ty said.

Connor licked his lips as he looked up at Ty. "Yeah," he said. "It's in the pocket of my jeans."

Connor reached back to grab his jeans. Before he could reach them, Ty had grabbed him by one arm and hauled him to his feet. He briefly stooped down to grab Connor's jeans and find the lube in a front pocket.

"Get up against the wall," Ty said, leaning close to whisper in Connor's ear.

"Yes, sir," Connor said.

Ty spread lube up and down his cock with one hand and held Connor up against the wall with the other. Connor's ass was ready for him. He moaned as he yielded to Ty's cock, shutting his eyes and arching his back.

"You like that?" Ty said. "You like having my fat cock all the way in your ass?"

"I want you to cum in me," Connor said. He was grinding hard against Ty's cock, eyes half-shut and face slack with pleasure. "Fuck, I love your cock."

The more Connor moaned, the harder Ty slammed his cock into him. He grabbed Connor's hips and pulled himself deep inside him as he came, burying his face in Connor's shoulder as he spilled his load.

He heard Connor gasp, then looked down and saw that he, too, had finished and was leaning on the wall for balance.

"Hey." Ty stepped back into the hot stream of the shower, gently pulling Connor with him. "Come get cleaned up."

Connor smiled at him as he joined Ty in the hot water, gently wrapping his arms around Ty's waist and laying a line of kisses along his collarbone.

"So," Connor said. "Are you mad at me after that?"

"We'll talk about that later." Ty kissed Connor on the lips. "Right now, I just want to look at you."

Chapter Twenty-Nine

They were back on the road before the sun was up the next morning. Connor let Ty sleep in the passenger seat while he drove across the high desert. He didn't feel like playing the radio today.

And at about nine AM, the truck's check engine light came on.

Connor grunted and reached across to shove Ty in the shoulder. "Hey," he said. "Hey."

Ty did a pretty good impression of a sitting hen for a second there. "What do you want?" he said.

"Check light's on," Connor said.

"Oh, dammit." Ty sat up straight and blinked his eyes open as he looked around. "Where are we?"

"We're twenty-five miles to Hermosa and fifteen out of Teat." Connor looked in the rearview. "Think there's a shop back in Teat."

"And I know there ain't shit in Hermosa," Ty said. "Pull over and we can see what we're looking at."

Right. That was the real reason people still kept driving these relics. If you had a paperclip and a Hives Manual, and if you could count, you could generally get a pretty good idea what was wrong with your vehicle before you ever managed to get it to a shop.

"You know, on the way up I noticed it shifts a little rough out of..."

"Out of overdrive," Ty said. He was frowning at the contents of his glove box as he searched through it. "Yep. It does that."

Connor nodded. "But weirdly enough, if you're going 60 or 70 down a hill, it..."

"That's nice," Ty said. He pulled out a little section of blue wire stripped on the ends and unbuckled his seatbelt.

Connor made to do the same.

"This is gonna be a one-person task, bud," Ty said. His voice was calm and neutral, but he had a mean gleam in his eyes that made Connor nervous. "Can you check on Blue?"

"Uh, sure." Connor nodded and continued extracting himself from the truck.

Ty's horse was an easygoing little fellow, and he was perfectly content pretty much anywhere he had a net full of hay in front of his face. He'd been a dream to haul so far, raising no issues and making no noise other than the occasional shifting of his feet to keep his balance. He gave Connor a brief, curious sniff before turning his attention back to his meal.

"Good boy," Connor said. He watched Ty fiddling around under the propped-open hood of his truck. He reached into his pocket, pulled his phone out. He had signal.

"Maybe I should warn them all I'm coming back," Connor said, loud enough that Ty could hear.

"Hmm." Ty didn't look at Connor as he walked back to the driver's side and opened the door.

Connor shrugged and dialed his brother. The first call went to voicemail. Connor frowned and dialed again.

This time, Greg picked up after three rings. "Hello?" he said.

"What's up?" Connor said.

"Connor, is that you?" Greg yawned. "I'm sorry, man. I had to get a new phone."

"A new…"

"Look, man, it's a long story," Greg said, suddenly sounding much more awake. "You fuckin' owe me one, that's all I'm gonna say."

"I…" Connor's eyebrows shot up. He blinked a couple times, decided not to say anything, and made himself smile and take a deep breath. "Okay," he said. "Umm, anyway, we're about to Utah and…" No, he couldn't do this. "Greg, what did she do to your phone?"

"She didn't do shit!" Greg said. "I was trying to call the bank and her daddy grabbed it and threw it in the cow tank!"

"And *I owe* you one?" Connor said.

"It was your job to make sure those damn meth heads were off the lease before…"

"It is never my job to clear a bunch of damn criminals off of someone else's land," Connor said. "And it's not your job either!"

"Well, it doesn't matter now, because the bank found out about the meth lab and they told the cops, and now the feds are coming to investigate!" Greg's voice was thin and brittle. "I've been doing damage control this whole time…"

"We've all been doing damage control," Connor said. "That's all anybody does around the Briggses, is what I've learned!"

"I thought we had a deal," Greg said.

"We had a deal because I thought Linda would make you happy," Connor said. "The way things are turning out, it looks like she's gonna get you in more trouble than you know how to handle."

"Don't tell me what I know how to handle!" Greg said. "Just get back here and help get us out of this mess we're in, and we can all go back home and forget this ever happened."

"This is a lot of bullshit to just forget, Greg," Connor said. He walked down the roadside a little way, tightening his fist and splaying his hand out again. "Does Linda not understand that her daddy's probably going to go to jail?"

"Look, we can keep him out of jail!" Greg said. "He's got his connections, and..."

"Why do you guys keep believing this crazy motherfucker when he talks?" Connor said. "Just listen to your lawyer..."

"Their lawyer doesn't understand," Greg said. "He's not part of their church, he doesn't live in their town."

"Who cares?" Connor said. "You know what I think? I think the Briggses' good name ought to be ruined!"

"Connor..."

"No, Greg, I think a good name is something you ought to earn, and you ought to earn it by not...not this," Connor said. "Man, I know it'll hurt Linda, but maybe it's not as bad as she thinks it is."

"Hey, are you done?" Ty came around the back of the trailer. "It's an O2 sensor got fucked up or broken somehow. We'll be fine until we can get you back to the ranch."

"Okay," Connor said. "One second—hey, man, we're gonna get back on the road. We oughta be back tomorrow afternoon..."

"You can make it back sooner than that if you're not a lazy ass," Greg said.

"All right," Connor said, and before he could say anything else he hung up the phone. He glared toward the mountains and shook his head. What the hell had happened to his brother? Who the hell was that making demands of him on the phone like that?

"Are you coming or are you walking back to the ranch?" Ty had the driver's door open.

Connor put the phone in his pocket and walked back to the truck.

∗∗∗

Neither one of them was much for making conversation the rest of the morning. Ty put in a CD by one of his friends' rock-blues-country-metal outfits, and Connor did his best to nap in the passenger seat.

Around two PM, they hit a stretch of construction that cut off one lane of the road for a couple miles. Ty waited for a couple minutes and shut the engine off.

Without the sound of the radio or the engine in the background, the silence between Ty and Connor grew heavy.

"Never a good sign when the flagger's having issues staying awake." Connor straightened himself up in his seat a little.

"Mmm." Ty nodded, looked out his window.

Connor reached down and grabbed one of the iced teas he'd grabbed at the last gas station. "You thirsty?" he said.

"Not really," Ty said.

"These altitude changes take it out of me." Connor chugged most of his tea. "It'll be good to be done with this whole fiasco."

Ty snorted. "That'll be the day," he said.

"What?"

"You're never gonna be done with this fiasco," Ty said. "You know that. You've dedicated your whole life to...to not actually helping people, because when you actually help people they don't always appreciate it, and they don't praise you."

"No, they just write you out of their wills and leave you to fend for yourself," Connor said.

"Don't look too much to me like you're fending for yourself," Ty said. "Looks to me like you're wasting your whole life trying to please people. And you only seem to pick people who don't wanna be pleased."

"Like you," Connor said.

"Me, I'm easy to please," Ty said. "Problem is, I'm so easy you don't fucking bother half the time."

"So, I guess you are still mad at me," Connor said.

"I don't even know if mad is the right word." Ty kept his eyes in front of him and his hands on the steering wheel. "I just..." He looked up at the ceiling. "I have enough bullshit going on in my life, Connor," he said. "I've got my mom always needing my help, I've got my own shit to get in order. I have to take care of Blue. I have to eat." His knuckles were white

296

on the steering wheel. "You know. I try not to have too many problems, but they're my problems."

"Yeah," Connor said. He frowned into his tea bottle, trying to assign a word other than "shame" to the cloud that was forming over his head. "And they are, you know, real problems."

"It's not that you all's problems aren't, you know, real," Ty said. "It's...look, your horse is skinny, you feed it more. Your cow's loose, you put it away and you fix the fence. You got a hole in the roof, you patch it. You fix the problem." He nodded his head emphatically on the last few syllables. "And the problem goes away. And you don't have it anymore. And you have time to fix other problems, so that those other problems go away."

"Yeah," Connor said. "I mean, to give Linda some credit..."

"No, I'm not done." Ty held up one finger. He was still staring at the road ahead of them. "No, it's not just that you and Greg and Linda aren't solving the problem. I'm not solving the fucking problem either, obviously."

"You were trying," Connor said.

"I..." Ty blinked a few times rapidly, then slowly turned to face Connor. "Really?" he said.

"I mean, yeah, obviously," Connor said. "Look, I had my issues with my mom, but Jesus, she...she had a very specific issue with a very specific part of me, and that was what it was, but...Jesus. I have no idea what Linda's going through, and I guarantee you Greg has even less of a clue. You get Linda, Ty," Connor said. "You understand what it's like to grow up with her mentality. Me, I don't get it."

"Damn right you don't get it," Ty said. "I..." He threw his hands up. "Yeah. You don't. At least you understand that after all this bullshit."

"I mean I thought we had all this in common, Linda and me," Connor said. "We have our churches, we have our ranches..."

"You do have a lot in common, man," Ty said. "That's why you bought into her bullshit for so long. That's why she picked you to go along and be her damn stooge, and she kept me out of the loop. You know." He shifted in his seat and turned his body to face Connor, resting his elbow on the center console. "You know what it is."

"I don't," Connor said.

"You have a lot in common with the Linda that she wants people to see," Ty said. "She's a part of her church, she runs her ranch, she goes and plays to win at the rodeos..."

"Because a gambling problem definitely doesn't run in that family," Connor said.

"That's neither here nor there," Ty said, and he said it quickly enough that Connor knew he agreed. "No, see, what it is. What it is, is you've got all this in common with the public version of Linda. Meanwhile I've got all this stuff in common with who she *really* is. As a person."

"And she doesn't like that," Connor said. "I mean, you're a good person..."

"But I'm not the kind of person who looks good in church gossip," Ty said. "And I know that, and shit, I guess it bothers me a little. It bothers the hell out of Linda, I can tell you that."

"Yeah, that's pretty obvious right about now," Connor said.

"But you know what Linda and I really do have in common," Ty said, "is we both have our pride. And we both have that pride because it is something that we got to make for ourselves and not for someone else." He narrowed his eyes. "Do you get where I'm going with this, Skip?"

Connor shrank back in his seat. He looked out the passenger side window and drank the last of his tea.

"I'm sorry," Connor said. "I don't know how many times I can even say it, Ty. I never meant to hurt anybody, and if I had known...if I had known what you were gonna mean to me, I would never have done this."

"It was just a fucked up thing to do," Ty said. "Man, I don't know. I don't know about any of this. I don't want to leave Linda by herself to deal with her shithead dad, Connor. But..."

"I think we've gotten to the point where...well, I hate to get all clinical about it, but we're basically enablers at this point." Connor shook his head.

Ahead of them, the flagger turned his sign around and beckoned for cars to come forward. Ty started his engine and put it in gear.

"Yeah," Ty said. "I feel like we're only making things worse for her by being around to carry out her dumbass ideas."

"Like I said, it's fucked up." Connor's phone buzzed in his pocket; he pulled it out and lit up the screen. "Oh, would you speak of the damn devil."

"What's it say?" Ty said.

"Come home now," Connor said. "Linda doesn't usually text in all caps."

"Hmm." Ty sounded kind of like he was choking on plastic. "Sounds like everything's completely healthy and normal back at the ranch."

Chapter Thirty

As far as crimes in the cowboying profession went, horse theft was surprisingly uncommon. The most common thing to go to jail for, of course, was drugs, followed by theft and by kicking the shit out of people who didn't need shit-kicking. Horse theft occurred, but it typically occurred to people who were less likely than cowboys were to find and murder a horse thief.

"I'm not taking Roxie. Roxie don't watch where the hell her feet are." Connor Dougherty had shed all pretext of being a bumbling ranch hand. He was walking across the barnyard like he had already taken possession of the Triple V Ranch.

"Bingo will do, won't he?" Ty said.

"She sold Bingo." Connor's face was grim. Linda had been, well, active in the days that he'd left her unsupervised. "Bella's a fuckin' bolter...shit, I guess I'll have to take fucking Roxie."

He slammed open the steel door in the front of the horse's stall.

"You know, the cops..."

"We'll get the cops involved when I get my horse back," Connor said. "If any harm comes to that animal, then I want you to get the hell out of my way and pretend you didn't see anything."

There was something terrifying underneath Connor's voice, something Ty hadn't heard from him before.

"I'll take Bella," Ty said. "She's a sight faster than Blue, and she likes me."

"Better hope she's in a good mood," Connor said. He grabbed two halters from the rack and shoved one at Ty's chest.

Ty took it and followed Connor out to the pen. The mares that hadn't been sold off were standing in a cluster in the far corner, flicking bugs away from each other's' bodies with their tails and looking suspiciously at anything and everything that approached them.

In their absence, the Briggses had cleared out most every living creature that had once occupied the Triple V Ranch. According to Linda, the bank was serious about foreclosing on Mr. Briggs's big mortgage, and they were going to have to stay with family in Georgia. There was not a conversation about what Linda and Greg were going to do. Ty didn't care about that conversation.

But he would be damned if he let Mr. Briggs just take Connor's horse.

Ty haltered Bella and led her out of the pen. She was a jumpy little thing, seal brown with a star on her forehead and a little wisp of a tail that she switched constantly back and forth. She stood watchful at the hitching rail while Ty tied her and went in after Connor to get the saddles.

"Jesus Christ!" Ty had to stop and stare around the tack room when he walked in.

"They really are selling off everything," Connor said. "I'll be damned..."

The plywood walls were nearly empty, the metal saddle racks devoid of anything leather. A pile of old, stained saddle blankets sat in one corner with a dusty trail saddle on top of it; a single barrel saddle hung on a rack at the far end.

"Is this what you want for your brother?" Ty said as he walked toward the remaining equipment. "Because I seen people do this before, man. It doesn't just happen once."

"Yeah, I know," Connor said. "People don't change..."

"They can change," Ty said. He put his hand on the small of Connor's back. "Just, they generally don't change when people keep feeding them money and keep making excuses for their bullshit."

"Spare me the lecture, Ty," Connor said. "I just want to go and get my damn horse back."

***

They may all have been ready to kill each other over different matters, but Ty and Linda and Greg and Connor were all in agreement on one thing: if he was running north on a stolen cow horse, there was only one place Mr. Briggs could have been going.

"Do you think maybe the meth lab folks did leave some guns behind?" Ty said.

"Hard to say," Connor said. "Just because there was enough evidence to get Mr. Briggs in trouble doesn't necessarily mean there's enough free shit to get him out of trouble."

They stopped by the same ponds where they'd gotten busy last time they came out here. Today, they only had time to let their horses drink. The day had come up cloudy and stayed that way, and an early fall chill was coming down from the high peaks.

"Have you decided what you're gonna do when you catch him?" Ty said.

"I'm gonna tell him to cut the shit out and give me my horse back," Connor said. "And if that doesn't work, I'm gonna shoot him somewhere that won't kill him and then I'm gonna tell him again to cut the shit out and give me my horse back."

"That sounds fairly generous," Ty said.

"You'd be surprised what you can accomplish just yelling at people," Connor said. "Especially people who aren't used to being yelled at."

"I might not be," Ty said.

Connor gave him a sheepish smile. "Come on," he said, pulling Bella's head up from the grass. "The sooner we get this over with, the better."

Ty followed Connor up through the hills at a good clip. Just as Connor had feared, Roxy had a couple of spastic moments that were gut-wrenching to watch. Bella, on the other hand, was surprisingly sure-footed on the harsher bits of terrain.

The higher they got, the colder the wind blew. It started coming cold and shrill from the northwest, edged with raindrops that felt an awful lot like snow when they smacked against Ty's skin. It smelled good, though, like cut pine branches and ancient dark dirt left over from the Ice Age.

The first time he heard the horse whinny, he thought he was getting lost in his thoughts.

Connor stopped in front of him. "Do you hear that?" he said.

"Yeah," Ty said. "I thought it..."

"Bonito!" Connor spurred Bella forward and ran up a game trail to the north. His little black cow horse ran over to meet him, head flung high and eyes wide.

He was still wearing his saddle, though his bridle had come off and there was no rider in sight.

Later, Ty would try to blame the sinking feeling in his gut on the sun going deeper behind the rising dark storm clouds. It was just a coincidence, he would say, especially when he was working alone in the dark.

In that particular moment, though, Ty knew. And he knew that he knew.

He legged Bella forward and approached Connor and Bonito as quick as he could. Bella walked reluctantly, her pretty neck arched and her ears pointed hard forward.

"This ain't good," Connor said. He was scanning the brush around him, his face growing pale. "If he's around here hurt somewhere..."

Later, Ty would claim he noticed his horse eyeballing that particular outcropping of rock. But he would also secretly remember that Bella had been looking at the other two horses when he had gotten that tickle in the back of his mind. Or maybe his brain was just distorting the memory, editing in something more exciting than what really happened.

But what really happened was this, in one way or another: Ty walked Bella up this little rock outcropping, and behind this little outcropping he found a little gulch that ran into the larger draw they were in. And in that little gulch was Mr. Briggs.

"Oh, my God," Ty said.

"What's up?" Connor came riding up behind him. "Did you fi--oh, holy shit..."

"He's dead," Ty said.

"Yeah, no shit, he's dead," Connor said. "Living people's arms don't bend like that."

Ty's stomach made a suggestion. Ty ignored it and turned Bella right around and rode back down the outcropping. "We gotta get the hell out of here," he said. "This is over my head."

"Yeah?" Connor came riding down right behind him. "Yeah. Yeah, we..."

"Cops."

"Cops." Connor nodded. "We..."

A bolt of lightning connected with the next ridge. Their horses didn't even have time to startle before the air split in two around them.

"Jesus Christ!" Ty held on to Roxie's mane as she reared up and went skittering up a hill. Thankfully, she didn't get too far before realizing she was going to make the situation a lot harder on herself.

Ty jumped off before another bolt struck. Falling off your horse was the least of your worries in an electric storm.

"We gotta find somewhere to hide," Connor said. He had to raise his voice for Ty to hear him over the wind, which was now carrying little freezing bullets of sleet.

"It's a little far to the meth lab, isn't it?" Ty said.

"Let's go for those aspen trees down there." Connor pointed to a little island of green down the gulch from them.

It didn't take them too long to reach it, and when they did, they were well rewarded. The trees and the nearby rocks made a decent shelter from the wind, and there was a little spring fed stream running nearby that provided grass and water for the horses.

Once their horses were picketed and their saddles were off and covered with a canvas tarp, Connor and Ty wasted no time in stringing up a little tarp shelter in the trees. If there were bears or cougars out here, that was just going to have to be a problem they dealt with in the moment. The wind was getting savage, and the rain would turn into pea-sized hail and back again at a moment's notice.

Though it didn't take them long at all to strip down to their boxers, Ty had never felt less sexy. His heart was pounding in his chest, and his jaw was shaking.

"Here." Connor sat down beside him, pulled Ty down to the ground.

Ty shut his eyes and pressed his body against Connor's. "Holy shit," he said. "Holy shit..."

"We're gonna be okay," Connor said. "We're..."

"He's just sitting out there..."

"Ty, we have to leave it be," Connor said. "If there was, you know, if someone shot him, the cops have to come and get evidence."

"Yeah?" Ty liked the idea of someone else handling that body.

"Yeah," Connor said. "You and me, Ty, we're gonna be fine." He reached over and grabbed a little scratchy fleece blanket from his saddle bag and threw it over both of them, then scrunched his jeans up under his head for a pillow.

"I wish I could fuckin' trust you," Ty said. It felt good to lean into Connor, to take shelter in his big strong frame. But he had to remember how they'd come to be in this situation to start with.

"It's fair that you don't, I guess," Connor said.

"What if Linda blames me?" Ty said.

"I'll vouch for you," Connor said. "Come on. Don't worry about the...the body."

"It was just, fuckin..." Ty shuddered. "I've never seen anyone been dead before," he said.

"I know," Connor said. "Shit. This is...this is a lot."

Above them, the sky lit up as another thunderclap echoed on the rocks around them. The horses snorted, but Ty didn't hear them busting the pickets or running away.

"Dead men can't steal horses, at least," Ty said. He felt bad cracking any kind of joke with Mr. Briggs's remains just...kind of sitting there. His eyes hadn't even been closed.

"Yeah," Connor said. "They can't throw a fit about going through bankruptcy proceedings, either."

"Shit, I hadn't thought about that," Ty said. "What do you think will happen to your brother?"

"Hell if I know," Connor said. "I mean...I don't know how much Mr. Briggs owes. Owed."

Ty frowned. "If it was enough that they're gonna foreclose on the ranch..."

"Don't worry about it." Connor squeezed him tighter. "It's not like it's our business, anyway," he said.

"Are you sure about that?" Ty said. "You have a way of making these people's drama into my business."

"What if I didn't, though?" Connor said. "What if I just found a way to get my ranch back on my—"

"Is that really what you still want?" Ty said. "I mean, do you really think it's worth everything your brother is gonna put you through to get it back?"

"I mean, yeah," Connor said. "It's...you don't understand, Ty," he said.

"No," Ty said. "I guess I don't."

Outside, the rain turned to hail again. Marble-sized stones pinged off of tree trunks and rattled against the flimsy tarp shelter. Ty could hear rivulets of water running down the rock formations outside. He couldn't help but think that he was technically downstream from a dead body right now.

He shook his head and screwed his eyes shut tight. "Man, you have some fucked up priorities," he said. "That's all I can say."

"If you'd ever been there, you'd understand," Connor said. "It makes this place look like a dump."

"This place is a dump," Ty said. "I bet I can go and find work on a ranch somewhere pretty and not have to deal with any damn dead people."

"What if I get a place of my own?" Connor said.

Ty laughed and pressed himself closer against Connor's body. "If that actually happens?" he said.

"It will," Connor said.

"If you ever actually get a place of your own, you'll never get me to leave," Ty said. "But you and I both know how...what was that?"

This time, they both heard it. Something heavy, dragging across the rocks above them.

Over by the brook, a couple of horses snorted and stomped on the ground.

"Help..." The voice was unmistakably familiar. Still, Ty got a feeling like a bucket of ice getting dumped on him.

"He's alive!" Connor pushed Ty away and both of them jumped up. "Mr. Briggs!"

"Help..."

"Holy shit," Ty said. He scrambled behind Connor up toward where he'd heard the voice.

Mr. Briggs was half-standing on a low rise in the ground about twenty yards off, leaning on a rock for support. With his face pale and bruised, and his arm hanging grotesquely from his shoulder, he still looked enough like a corpse that Ty's lizard brain told him not to get any nearer.

"Come on," Connor said. "Let's get him on one of the horses so we can get him back home."

Chapter Thirty-One

On the way back to the ranch, they had to lay Mr. Briggs face down over Bonito's back like a sack of potatoes. Connor assumed that Mr. Briggs was half dead in the first place because Bonito didn't like him, but the two barrel horses seemed to like him even less. That was what he got.

As they rode down the last hill toward the ranch, Connor could see the blue and red lights of the ambulance—and of a couple of cop cars that were blocking the driveway.

He'd never seen the barnyard of the Triple V Ranch so very full of people.

"I don't like this," Ty said. "How long do you think they've been there?"

"Can't have been long," Connor said. "We only got back in cell signal an hour and a half ago."

"What the fuck do they think they're gonna need cops out here for?" Ty was scowling down at the ranch.

"Well, they know Mr. Briggs a hell of a lot better than they know us," Connor said.

"True," Ty said. "There's probably more cause than not to think we're lying."

"And that's assuming Miss Linda hasn't somehow thrown us under the bus," Connor said. He frowned. "I mean, I hope Greg wouldn't let her, but..." He shook his head. He didn't want to say out loud what he thought of Greg in this moment.

"Stings, doesn't it?" Ty said.

"Yeah." Connor nodded. "I mean, I guess it's a little naive in this world. Thinking you can always rely on your family."

"It's not naive," Ty said. "It just...sometimes people suck, Connor."

"Yeah." Connor sighed. It was hard to put words to the feeling that had hollowed out his chest since he'd called Greg and Linda.

The conversation had been normal. At least, it had been as normal as this particular conversation could be. We found your dad, he's badly hurt, call 911 and we'll have him back as quick as we can, bye. Linda had taken the news with more grace than she'd taken the hay truck rescheduling. It made Connor uneasy.

"I mean, we haven't done anything wrong," Connor said, mostly to himself. "They don't have anything to accuse us of. Shit, he stole my horse..."

"We're gonna be fine," Ty said. "Or at least I'm gonna be fine. Do you think he knows about the Skip-Connor situation?"

Connor looked behind him at the flannel-clad bulk of Mr. Briggs slung over the saddle.

"You know," he said. "I feel bad about saying this, but maybe we should have just left him where we found him."

***

The cop in charge of interviewing Connor looked like he'd just graduated high school, and that only with the help of enough caffeine to kill a bull. He kept blinking and shaking his head between questions, like he was trying hard to stay awake.

"And...and at what point were you, uh, directed to not report your sighting of the suspicious activity?" he said.

They were sitting across a card table in the Briggses' dining room. Connor didn't know whether the dignified oak table and chairs where the family had once taken meals had been bought or rented. Either way, it was long gone.

Most of the valuables in the house were gone, as a matter of fact. A few pieces of crystal or china remained on bric-a-brac shelves or countertops, and family portraits still hung on the pink-papered walls. The smiles were unsettling when you looked at the entropy around them.

"I don't recall," Connor said. "I don't recall if I was directed to do anything at all, in fact."

"And this was *after* Miss Briggs became aware of your, uh, alias." The cop nodded and typed something out on his tablet.

"Yeah," Connor said. "She said she knew it was me the whole time, man. I don't...it wasn't a great disguise."

"Okay," the cop said. "Uhh." He looked at his tablet. "So, can you describe to me, in your own words, what you saw on the federal property you were inspecting?"

"I wasn't inspecting nothing," Connor said. "Linda sent us up there to run some cattle up to pasture."

"You weren't told to check and make sure the pasture was safe?" the cop said.

"I do not recall that being part of the specific instructions I was given," Connor said. "Look, if we're

313

going to be getting into shit that happened several weeks ago..."

"I understand, Mr. Dougherty," the cop said. "But can you please describe what you saw?"

"I saw a building in the woods where there wasn't supposed to be a building," Connor said. "And I saw some dudes out front with some weapons. That's about as specific as I can get with you. I just figured it was something I had better let the authorities handle, and I thought Linda was going to let the authorities handle it."

"Okay." The cop typed out something else on his laptop. "Uhm. That's it," he said, looking Connor in the eyes and smiling weakly. "You're free to go."

***

Ty's interrogation took place separately. Connor figured it took about as long to go through his brain as it had to go through Connor's. He spent the time pacing back and forth on the back patio, watching the birds decimate the ripening crop of apples and pears.

Lord, what an awful waste of a good piece of land.

He heard Linda approaching from the side of the house, but he pretended not to notice her until she was standing on the corner of the patio. She held a bottle of beer in each hand.

"Hey," she said.

"Hey." Connor turned around.

"How'd it go?" Linda took a couple steps toward him, holding one of the beers out to Connor.

314

"I thought we were going to focus more on my stolen horse," Connor said. He took the beer and walked to the other side of the patio.

Linda laughed nervously, looking at her feet (as well she ought to do). "I'm sorry, Connor," she said. "I just...I didn't realize how far I was in over my head."

"I don't think any of us thought this through near far enough," Connor said.

"Well." Linda giggled quietly, looked at her feet. "Greg and I were talking," she said.

"Yeah?" Connor felt a chill descend over him. He turned to look at Linda through slitted eyes.

She twirled slightly on one foot, grinning childishly at him. "We set a date," she said.

"Oh." Connor took a sip of his beer and shrugged. "Congratulations."

Linda froze for a second.

"What?" Connor said.

"Oh...I..." Linda let out another sweet, delicate little giggle. "Well, shit, I just figured you might be happy to hear some good news, is all," she said.

"You figured...you figured I might be happy." Connor nodded. He took a long drink of his beer, thought about how nice it was to have something cold on his lips right now. He took a long look at the golden-green orchard spreading out in front of him, at the arc of the sky mopped clean by last night's storms.

"We're finally gonna get married!" Linda said. "I...I can bring my horses up to you guys' ranch, and I can..."

"Tell me, Linda," Connor said. "What's going to happen to your dad when they fix him up at the hospital?"

She stopped mid-sentence, her mouth hanging open.

"Does he even have health insu…"

"Of course we have health insurance!" Linda said. "I don't know what the hell you're talking…"

"Linda, let me make something really, abundantly clear to you," Connor said. "When I came down here, it was because I really thought that you and Greg had something together. Okay? It was because I love my brother, and I want him to be happy, and it seemed to me like marrying you was going to make him happy."

Linda came closer to him. "He's the best thing that's…"

"Yeah, I know," Connor said. "Greg's a good guy. He's kind. He's honest. When someone needs help, he'll drop everything he's doing and run off across the country to help them. He's always been that way, and he always will be." He nodded slowly, looking Linda in the eye. "I'm sure he is the best thing that's ever happened to you. You've been a goddamn disaster for him."

"I….what?" Linda's voice squeaked. She stepped back like she'd just been hit with a cattle prod.

"I have never seen my brother so damn broken down as he was at that rodeo," Connor said. "Watching you take all your frustration out on him, treat him like a fucking punching bag so you can play cowgirl…"

"Greg *loves* me," Linda said.

316

"That's the problem!" Connor said. His voice was too loud and too angry and he didn't care. "He loves you! He loves you more than he loves himself! And that's a goddamn gift, Linda!" He was pointing his finger at her with one hand; the other clenched his beer bottle like it was going to break.

"I know it's a gift, Connor," Linda said. "I don't need advice on my relationships from some...from some..."

"From some *what*, Linda?" Connor said. "You know, I'm getting real fucking sick and tired of you laughing behind your hands at the silly queers all running around looking after your shitty relationship."

Linda's hoot of fake indignation left her mouth hanging open. "I would never! You know I have nothing but respect for your..."

"You don't have respect for anybody, Linda," Connor said. "Respect means you actually stop and think about what that whole, entire other person is going through, Linda, and then you ask yourself, gee, am I, maybe, the one making life difficult here?"

"So now my dad's problems are *my fault*?" Linda said.

"I don't care which problems are whose fault right now, honestly," Connor said. "You have used me, and you have used Ty, and you are apparently going to keep using my brother until our family's money is gone." He put his beer to his lips and finished it before tossing the bottle out into the orchard.

He and Linda both watched silently as it arced over the lawn and fell just short of the tall grass with a soft thud. Linda was standing with her back stiff and her fists clenched, mouth drawn up in a sneer that made her look very much like her daddy.

"I don't know if I'd be calling it *your* family's money," she said, her voice quiet and deadly. "Don't underestimate what your brother is willing to do for me."

"Oh, I won't be making that mistake again, trust me," Connor said. He shook his head and walked across the lawn. He didn't have anything more to say to Linda. At least, he didn't have anything more to say that wouldn't get him in bigger trouble than he already was.

He found his brother talking with one of the other cops. Connor waved him over, and Greg grinned and waved at the cop as he hurried to join him.

"What's up, my..."

"Greg, I am going to say this now, because if I come to your wedding I can assure you I will be leaving in handcuffs." Connor took his brother by the shoulders and looked him dead in the eyeballs.

"What?" Greg said. "I don't..."

"I have been working for Linda Briggs for most of the summer," Connor said. "And I can certainly see that she's a...well, she's a hell of a woman," he said, "but I am going to tell you this, and I am going to tell you this now. Walk away from that relationship."

"Walk away?" Greg said.

"Walk away." Connor nodded. "You are a young, good-looking guy with a boatload of money, and there are better women than Linda working at every branding and every roundup in the country."

"But," Greg said, spluttering, "she's..."

"I'm only going to say this once," Connor said. "You saw what happened to her daddy?"

318

"Yeah, but he brought that on himself," Greg said.

"The man has a gambling problem," Connor said. "I mean, he's an irredeemable prick no matter what you do, but he has a problem, and Linda's solution to that was to hide the problem until Mr. Briggs was half-dead and wanted by local, state, and federal authorities."

"You're making this sound like it was all her fault," Greg said. "Look, it was my idea to have you come up with the whole..."

"And we could have stopped it, Greg. Linda knew this whole damn time that it was me," Connor said. "Did she tell you that?"

"What?" Greg stepped back like he'd been slapped. "I—well, I'm sure she had a good, uh..."

Connor heard the house's screen door slam. Ty Gibson had stepped out from his questioning with the police, and he was looking sadly around the barnyard while he shook his head.

"Like I said." Connor turned back to Greg and smiled. "I'm only going to tell you once."

"Wait," Greg said, hurrying after Connor toward the house. "Connor, come on. Linda adores you!"

"I've seen what happens to the men she adores," Connor said. "And you'd be wise to take a look yourself."

Ty was watching them now, his face gone from sad to puzzled. "Uh, what are we..."

"How'd it go in there?" Connor said.

"Well enough." Ty shrugged. "I...I guess I'd better be getting on the road." He looked from Connor to Greg and back again. "I'll call you later," he said under his breath.

"Where you headed?" Connor smiled hopefully at him.

Ty gave him a puzzled, squint-eyed look. "Don't know," he said. "Boomer said there's good feedlot work in Nevada."

"Work for how many?" Connor said.

At that, Ty looked up sharply. He motioned faintly to Greg with one hand, raised a quizzical eyebrow at Connor.

"I'll explain later," Connor said. "If you'll let me."

Chapter Thirty-Two

The girl behind the counter wore her hair in two massive pigtails, each of them striped black and pink like a barred hen on acid. She moved slowly as she scanned Ty's pocket pies and his coffee. She smelled like fruit and cheap liquor.

"Uhhh." She frowned at the till as she punched in the keys. "Five twenty-two, sir," she said.

Ty pulled out a wad of bills and extracted a ten.

The girl smiled as she took it and made change, counting twice as she weaved back and forth on her feet. She was wearing fuzzy boots that came up to her knees.

Nevada was great, so far.

"Here's four seventy-eight back," the girl said.

"Thanks."

Behind him, the doorbell jingled. Ty turned around and smiled to see Connor stumbling through the door, hat crammed down over hair that needed a cut about three weeks ago. He was still wet from the shower.

"Morning, Skip," Ty said.

"Morning." Connor grinned sleepily at him, looking Ty up and down with those brazen eyes that made him blush despite himself. "Coffee here any good?"

"I haven't tried it," Ty said.

"Are you guys the ones with that horse trailer parked in back?" The girl behind the counter stood up straight, her eyes lighting up somewhere under all that mascara.

Ty blinked. "Uhhh..."

"Yeah, the horses are fine," Connor said. "They have food and water. We do this all the..."

"Can I go out and pet them?" The girl bobbled back and forth on her fuzzy feet.

"Umm, they're both mustangs," Ty said. "They bite."

"Oh, yeah," Connor said. "Buddy o' mine lost a finger to old Blue last week at the team roping."

"Oh my God, that's so scary." The girl's mouth made an 'O' of surprise. She leaned back a little. "Wow."

Connor had already escaped the conversation to make his coffee.

Ty tipped his hat to the girl before she could say anything else, and he walked out of the store into the morning sun.

When Ty had met him, Connor had been driving a beat-up old truck he'd bought with the money he'd earned sweeping floors at the theater in high school. The rig he was currently piloting put that old beater to shame. Connor's gleaming black dually was powerful enough that even the big trailer didn't give it any trouble up mountain passes. They'd been living in style and air-conditioned comfort as they made their way south.

Ty opened up the living quarters and stepped inside. This still didn't feel real. But that was his box of books sitting on the couch, and that was his bag of clothes crammed into one of the storage cubbies on the short wall.

He put the pastries on the counter and sat on the couch, blowing on his coffee through the little square hole in the lid. He could feel the heat coming off it.

Two knocks came at the door; before Ty could respond, Connor opened it up.

"Hey, man," Connor said. "Can I pet your horse?"

"I got something else you can pet," Ty said, standing up to put his coffee on the counter.

"I bet you do." Connor had gotten a big lime-green can of something disgusting and full of caffeine. He set it down in a storage cubby and took his hat off.

Ty sidled up behind him, cupped his ass with one hand and wrapped the other around his waist. Connor shut his eyes and leaned back into his arms, making a faint contented noise somewhere deep in his chest.

He liked having time to kiss Connor. Given enough time, Ty supposed he could kiss Connor's entire body all over, from top to bottom. This morning—like most mornings so far—he started with his neck.

"Mmm." Connor wriggled against Ty.

"You like?" Ty was unbuttoning Connor's shirt. He grazed the skin of Connor's neck with his front teeth.

"Mmm-hmm-hmm." Connor shrugged out of his shirt as Ty pulled it off his shoulders. He had switched back to his old aftershave; Ty didn't like it as much as Connor did. "You're gonna wear me out."

"You're hard to wear out," Ty said.

323

"And you've made a good effort." Connor reached back to rub his hand on the front of Ty's jeans.

Ty moaned softly, muffling his voice in the crook of Connor's neck.

"Quiet, now," Connor said. "That cashier girl's probably outside listening to us."

Instead of a moan, Ty was now stifling a giggle. "Stop it," he said.

"She's got her ear cupped to the wall," Connor said, turning around to grab Ty's belt buckle.

"That's fucked up," Ty said.

"It's Nevada, baby," Connor said. He unbuckled Ty's jeans with a firm, decisive motion of his hands. "Shit gets wild out here."

Ty caught Connor's mouth with his, and they shared a long and deep kiss as they each shucked the other's jeans off. It was a different kind of rhythm now than it was when they first started fucking. They knew how they each moved; they could anticipate each other's bodies in a way that felt almost psychic.

This time, Ty was the first to drop to his knees. He could sense that Connor was getting impatient. That was okay; he was, too. He sucked Connor's cock as far down his throat as he could get it, opening himself up to the rigid mass of his shaft. Connor gasped. Ty clasped the back of his thigh with one hand as he sucked harder and brought his tongue carefully around his cock.

"Oh, fuck," Connor said. He steadied himself against the counter with one hand and leaned back, thrusting weakly into Ty's mouth.

Ty's hands were as greedy as his mouth. He ran his fingers up and down the sticky curves of Connor's torso, relishing the touch of his skin while his other hand traced the downy cleft of his ass. He heard Connor whimper slightly as his fingers teased the soft skin around his hole.

"You want me to make you cum?" Ty said.

Connor nodded. He was panting; his lips hung open ever so slightly as he gazed down at Ty.

"Get up on the mattress," Ty said. "And spread your legs."

Connor did as he was told. Ty smiled at the sight of his round ass flexing as he clambered up into the bed they shared. Connor was his, all his. His real boyfriend and everything.

He was lying on his back waiting when Ty joined him in the trailer's loft. "You figured out how to fuck me without making this whole thing shake?" he said.

"Yeah," Ty said. He knelt next to Connor and turned to straddle him, facing his feet.

"Oh, I see," Connor said. He ran a hand up Ty's thigh and took hold of his throbbing cock.

Ty relaxed his hips and shut his eyes as Connor took his cock in his mouth, gently at first and then sucking harder.

Ty returned the favor. Connor's shaft was already salty with precum, and Ty felt his own cock get harder in his mouth. They writhed against each other as they sucked and licked each other, now and then making gentle, blissful noises that were softened by the rigid flesh filling their mouths.

Ty was the first to cum. It seemed to take Connor by surprise; he had to pull back to swallow before licking the rest of Ty's load off his cock.

Ty groaned, and that seemed to be all Connor needed. His cock pulsed in Ty's mouth, and Ty's throat struggled to keep up with the stream of cum. They were both out of breath, clinging to each other tightly as they both came in each other.

They were content to lie like that for a while. The morning was quiet, and the light filtered softly through the trailer windows. Connor had filled the bed area with enough cheap down comforters that it was not unlike hanging out in a cloud.

It was Connor who pulled Ty up by the shoulders to spoon him. Ty relaxed into his chest, smiling faintly as he licked his lips.

"Where do you think we'll go today, Skip?" Ty said.

"I dunno, Gibson," Connor said. He trailed the knuckles of his right hand down from Ty's shoulder to his hips. "Guess we'll see where the road takes us."

***

They stopped at an Angus ranch outside Pagosa Springs just as the sun was setting. Connor flashed his brights and honked his horn as they made their way down the driveway. It didn't look too much different from the Triple V Ranch, truth be told. The mountains rising up behind it were a little higher, maybe.

"You sure they're expecting you?" Ty said. The lights in the big house were dark, and they stayed dark as the rig approached.

"They might not be home from church," Connor said.

"Great, more church people," Ty said.

"You know, the church thing was one of the more normal parts of Linda's family," Connor said. "It was weird that they made their employees go..."

"And illegal," Ty said.

"Yeah, the law didn't have any kind of effect on those...ahh, there they are." Connor smiled as a row of lights flicked on in the house ahead of them. "You'll love the Kowalskis. I grew up with Amy. Her husband used to ride bulls, I think."

"That's not a glowing endorsement," Ty said.

"He's a good guy!" Connor said, laughing. "Just, you know. Kind of a Labrador type personality."

Speaking of Labradors, they were greeted at the front gate by five of them and a three-legged collie. Amy Kowalski came out of the farmhouse with a trucker hat shoved over a mass of red curls, holding a baby in one arm and a beer in the other.

"Connor Dougherty!" she said as she came up to the truck. "What the hell is up with you?"

"Not doing too bad," Connor said.

"Sorry to hear about your mom," Amy said. "And the ranch." Her face was dutiful and serious, but you could definitely tell which one she was actually shocked and horrified to hear about.

"Life goes on." Connor nodded, his face grave for a moment before he turned to Ty and smiled. "This is my partner I was telling you about. Ty, this is my good friend Amy."

"It's so good to meet you!" Amy grinned. "I would shake your hand, but I'm getting drunk."

"Understandable," Ty said.

"You can join me if you want," Amy said. "Unless Connor's into collecting Baptists, too."

"You know, I was shocked, they actually drank like fish," Connor said.

"Of course they were fucking secret drunks." Amy shook her head, then turned to Ty. "Do you drink?" she said.

"Sure," Ty said. "Thanks."

"We don't have much in the way of aged whisky, but there's beer, and Greg's been running the still all weekend so we have shine if you feel like it." Amy adjusted her hold on her baby, cooing back and forth with her.

"You guys have a still?" Connor said, raising his eyebrows.

"Greg's from old Appalachian stock," Amy said. "Learned how to make moonshine from his grandpa when he was little."

"Shit, I don't think I've ever seen that done," Connor said. "Oh, I gotta tell you about the meth lab."

"The meth lab?" Amy stopped in her tracks to squint back at Connor.

"Oh, my God, and you thought it was a shit show when we went to help with sheep at the Dorrance place," Connor said. "I have got to tell you about the fucking family my brother's gonna marry himself into."

***

After they got the horses put up and some beers put down, Amy and her husband grilled them up some bratwursts. They sat on the porch and pigged out for a good couple of hours, shooting the shit and filling the Kowalskis in on the whole saga of the Briggs family.

Amy turned in for bed around ten, and her husband made to follow her shortly thereafter. He didn't make it far. Ty could hear him puttering around with something in the kitchen that had caught his attention.

"Shit, this is nice," Connor said. He was sitting in a rocking chair, looking out on the purple sky with his beer resting on his knee.

"Yeah," Ty said.

"You heard from your mom lately?" Connor tilted his head.

"She's doing good," Ty said. "I need to send her some more money here in a few weeks. Don't like the way she's been talking about her boyfriend."

"Mmm." Connor's face darkened momentarily. "You know, I can always..."

"We can talk about it later," Ty said, waving the issue away. He knew he was going to accept the money, but...whatever. "You ought to meet her," he said. "I think she'd really like you."

"Yeah?" Connor said.

"Amy reminds me of her," Ty said. "Maybe not so spacey, though."

"You gotta watch out with Amy," Connor said. "She always ran circles around me when we were growing up."

Ty laughed. "I kinda like meeting people you knew growing up," he said.

"Next, we oughta go see Luis," Connor said. "He was my dad's right-hand man, the whole time growing up. Smartest motherfucker I ever met. Could have been a nuclear physicist or whatever, the way he was with machines." Connor shook his head and sipped on his beer.

"I've heard you talk about him," Ty said.

"Yeah, he retired to Minnesota," Connor said. "Invests in start-ups, makes some money on it here and there."

"Minnesota," Ty said. "That's a long trip."

"Yeah, we'd have to stop a few times on the way." Connor rocked back and forth. "You ever see Mount Rushmore?"

"Not yet," Ty said.

"Well, I haven't run out of travelling money yet," Connor said. "I bet you and me will see plenty of shit before we give up and get jobs."

Ty smiled and reached over to grab Connor's hand. "Yeah," he said. "We got the time."